"Who are you, and what are you doing in my bathroom?" Claudia asked, inching down into the still-warm water until only the tops of her breasts peeked above the line of bubbles.

"My name is Austin Harwood, and this is my bathroom. The hotel made a mistake in sending you here." He sat down on the edge of the tub, and the light glinted on the thin gold watch he wore on his left wrist. Claudia stared at the numberless face of the lapis lazuli dial rather than at the handsome stranger who sat mere inches from her naked body.

"You appear to be a reasonable and intelligent woman," he began in his rich voice. "Not to mention a beautiful one. I think we can get this straightened out in a minute or two." He leaned across the small space that separated them and placed his index finger at the base of her throat for a long moment, then slowly, maddeningly, he ran it down her breastbone, through the cleavage between her breasts and into the water. "The water's getting cold," he said and reached out to open the drain. The water began to gurgle out rapidly. Claudia's breasts, no longer covered by bubbles, were exposed to his constant gaze....

Dear Reader,

It is our pleasure to bring you romance novels that go beyond category writing. The settings of **Harlequin American Romance** give a sense of place and culture that is uniquely American, and the characters are warm and believable. The stories are of "today" and have been chosen to give variety within the vast scope of romance fiction.

As in *Canvas of Passion*, Deirdre Mardon once again tells a sophisticated urban story set against the backdrop of Manhattan. Both Claudia and Austin are real, and I know you'll be wrapped up in Claudia's search for her biological mother.

From the early days of Harlequin, our primary concern has been to bring you novels of the highest quality. **Harlequin American Romance** is no exception. Enjoy!

Vivian Stephens

Vivian Stephens
Editorial Director
Harlequin American Romance
919 Third Avenue,
New York, N.Y. 10022

Destiny's Sweet Errand

DEIRDRE MARDON

Harlequin Books

TORONTO • NEW YORK • LONDON
AMSTERDAM • PARIS • SYDNEY • HAMBURG
STOCKHOLM • ATHENS • TOKYO • MILAN

For Allan

Published December 1983

First printing October 1983

ISBN 0-373-16033-X

Printed in Canada

Chapter One

She first saw him on the train.

He was married, of course. Few single men rode the Conrail suburban line from Connecticut, especially single men who looked as worldly and sophisticated as the one who swept onto the grimy car at Greenwich. She saw immediately that he was a powerful man—a man accustomed to exerting control. A commuter near the door stood to offer him a seat on that sultry Monday morning in August. Claudia seldom rode the train herself, but she knew instinctively that she was witness to an unusual incident. She doubted she would relinquish a hard-won seat to any person who exuded such health and affluence. She had not failed to notice the blue limousine with dark-tinted glass at the station, and the crisp cut of the chauffeur's uniform as he stood at attention next to the glowing Rolls-Royce. She had even noted, however subliminally, the orange-and-blue New York State license plates on the car.

Claudia was pleased when the stranger declined the offer of the seat, as she wanted to admire his profile. His nose was a shade too large, her artist's eye appraised, but a determined jaw balanced that minor flaw. His suit was English, very English, and had been tailored to camouflage the firm and imposing bone structure hidden beneath its drape of elegant summer wool.

His fingers were long, those of an aristocrat, but his hands were large and tanned to the color of maple-sugar candy. She fantasized that he played polo.

He wore no jewelry.

Claudia stared out of the window as the express train raced past the New York suburbs and through The Bronx. Lack of ring did not mean lack of wife. She hadn't been married to Peter long enough to forget the lessons of her single days: the thin, untanned line around the third finger, left hand; the vague excuse when phone numbers were exchanged—"I'm never home. Why don't you call me at the office?"; the aura of being married, indefinable but distinct to the discerning eye. Now that she was nearly single again, she vowed to remember those lessons. Married men were heartache to be avoided at all costs.

When the train entered the black tunnel under Park Avenue, Claudia stood with the other passengers and moved toward the door. Her white linen dress, so crisp that morning when she had slipped it on in her in-laws' Darien guest room, was now wrinkled and clung uncomfortably to her damp skin, but the tall stranger still looked as if he had just stepped from a shower. She stood near him while the train jolted to a stop at the Grand Central platform. He smelled of soap and lemon. She tried to hold on to his clean scent when the doors slid open to emit the dank air of the terminal.

She next saw him at the fine lingerie counter at Bergdorf Goodman.

Four months had passed—months during which Peter's parents stopped inviting her to Darien for "one last talk about the marriage." Eventually they realized that she and their son had been living apart for more than a year, that the divorce was final, and that no good intentions would revive the dead alliance. During those months she redecorated the apartment to her taste, landed her first assignment with the New York City affiliate of a major television network, experienced the agony of her first blind date, and wrote her own Christmas cards, signing them with her maiden name—Claudia Cleary. How strange it had seemed to write one name at the bottom of the crisp white card, but how right the words had looked.

Claudia placed the stranger immediately. She drifted to the counter and waited to be served by the lacquer-haired saleswoman who showed him a selection of peignoirs. She recalled his clean scent and drew close to inhale it once more. He actually spoke to her in the time-honored phrase of a busy husband who shopped but once a year for his wife.

"Excuse me, miss, would you mind telling me your size? You're about the same height and..." His voice was soft and deep and cultivated, as she had known it would be. She had to lean toward him to hear over the hubbub of Bergdorf's fourth floor just before Christmas. She was pleased to note that he smelled just as she remembered. His eyes were blue, the light blue of cornflowers, and tiny white lines spidered from their edges. He looked about forty and he was as sun-tanned in December as he had been in August.

"Eight. I wear a size eight," she answered.

When he bought a slate-gray gown of fine French silk, Claudia listened to the smooth tones of his voice as he gave the saleswoman instructions for sending the gift. He rounded his vowels to perfect spheres, as would an actor trained to the Shakespearean stage. The quality of his voice mesmerized Claudia's ears, and he had to repeat his words before she realized that he had been addressing her.

"Thank you for your help, miss. And Merry Christmas."

"Merry Christmas," she called to the back of his camel's hair coat. He was already nearing the elevator door by the time she found the wit to respond.

"Some hunk," said the saleswoman, shattering the image of mock cultivation she tried so hard to project.

"But married," answered Claudia. The two women bent their heads over the sales notebook and read the information written there: "Mrs. A. Remington Harwood IV, Silver Hill, New Canaan, Connecticut."

"All the best ones are," said the saleswoman, sighing.

Claudia fantasized his Connecticut estate, so large a street address was not required. She imagined walking there in the extensive woods on a winter day, leaving a trail of footprints in the soft snow that even then clogged the traffic below on Fifty-seventh Street outside of Bergdorf's chic windows.

So it really came as no surprise when she finally met A. Remington Harwood IV. Some things, after all, were meant to be.

"Claudia Cleary," she answered on the third ring. It still seemed odd to answer her home telephone with her name, but ever since she had taken the plunge and become a free-lancer, her Gramercy Square apartment was her office, or at least her central base of operations.

"Hold the line for Mr. McLaughlin," commanded a crisp voice. Claudia's imagination conjured up a mental picture of the news director of WNYZ, the New York City television station where she had worked for five years. She stared through the new shoots of a six feet ficus plant in front of the living room window overlooking the placid trees of Gramercy Square Park. Mc-

Laughlin was fat and nervous, given to chain-smoking cigarettes and chewing on Rolaids. No one with his disposition should have been in the news business, in which every day was a series of deadlines and disasters.

"Arnold, is that you?"

"The same, but I've changed my name back to Cleary. Why don't you call me Claudia? Then I'll always answer."

"Yeah." She heard him take a long pull on a cigarette. "You free for an assignment?" Without giving Claudia a chance to answer McLaughlin launched into a detailed tale of woe. She half-listened to his nervous whine, familiar with his compulsion to explain everything in a tone that implied disaster and immediacy. Claudia was free. In fact, she was slightly desperate for work, having ordered a new couch two months earlier. The final payment would probably be due within the next few weeks, when the couch was delivered.

"And so the artist is sick. She's going to have a baby, she announces, and she can't stand the long hours. She drops right out at the start of the juiciest trial in years. Can you believe it?"

Claudia clucked sympathetically, but her heart leaped with excitement. McLaughlin was asking her to fill in on short notice for the pregnant woman, who was one of the best-known courtroom artists in the country. She didn't care that WNYZ hadn't chosen her first, or that the production department had most probably called around town to find more experienced artists before selecting her name for the job. She was struck speechless with pleasure.

McLaughlin took her silence for reluctance and offered her double what he had paid for the two assignments she had done for WNYZ in the spring and early summer, plus out-of-town expenses.

"Please tell me you can handle it, Arnold."

"It's Cleary. I can do it."

"You can leave tonight and be in Montauk for the jury selection tomorrow?"

"Sure. What's the case again?"

"What's the case? You've got to be kidding! *New York* versus *Shorter*. The rich dame who's accused of shooting her husband."

"Oh, yes. Of course." Claudia had read something about the incident in the papers when it happened, but it seemed so long ago.

"She thought he was a prowler and she shot him? Is that the one?"

"Yeah, that's the one. And therefore she came into four million dollars just before he divorced her," McLaughlin said in a bored voice. McLaughlin had seen and heard it all six times, but his voice was effusive again when he returned to the details of her assignment. "Thank you, thank you. We'll take care of the hotel arrangements. The camera crew and the reporter are already out there. There's a little commuter plane that goes to Montauk tonight at six-forty-five. I'm sending you tickets, an advance and a press pass right now by messenger. Just be at La Guardia Airport before six-thirty. Got it?"

"No problem."

"And Arnold, the network is going to buy this stuff, you'll see. Your artwork will be on the national news. Have you got an agent?"

Claudia gave McLaughlin her agent's name and number. He would work out a better price for her with the network than she would dare to ask, as she had no idea how much having a drawing shown on national television was worth.

Claudia raced around the four airy rooms of the

apartment, watering the plants. Once it was hers alone, she grew to love the apartment with its high windows overlooking the tiny park, which was locked at all times. Only the residents of Gramercy Square had keys to the ornate wrought-iron gates. Title to the apartment had gone to her in the divorce settlement in lieu of alimony. Its sunny rooms were the only visible remains of five long years of marriage to Peter—six, if she counted the year of limbo during which they had been separated. Enormous plants graced every room except the bathroom. Their shiny green leaves were her passion, but actually she had purchased them for practical reasons: Peter had claimed all the furniture. At the time she hadn't cared, wanting only to be through with the marriage and with him, not thinking that she would be forced to replace everything they had acquired together. All the good pieces had been given to them by Peter's family, anyway, and Claudia was a fair person. She would never have kept anything that was not rightfully hers.

The invisible remains of the marriage were the scars in her heart. Like any woman, she had looked forward to a lifetime with her husband—helping him with his academic career, supporting him emotionally during the bad times, and rejoicing with him during the times of success. There had been only the success, and Peter wasn't so good at success.

The messenger arrived within the hour. As she was packing a gray crepe suit she stopped to check her calendar. Dinner with her sister was penciled in for that night, and a meeting of her local group of ALMA—the Adoptees' Liberty Movement Association—for the following evening. She left the half-packed suitcase and telephoned Tina's office to postpone their date.

"Jacqueline Fashions."

"Miss Cleary, please."

Breathless and impatient, Tina barked into the telephone.

"Tina, have to cancel tonight. I have a trial assignment in Montauk. I don't know when I'll be back."

"That's all right. I met the most divine young man. He asked me to have dinner with him. I was just going to call you and postpone anyway."

"*Young* man?"

"Well, I'm not certain how old he is...."

"What does he do?"

"Umm... he's a student."

"I see." Claudia tried for a neutral tone, but she knew a note of disapproval floated over the telephone line. Claudia thought Tina was fifteen years older, more or less, than she, but wasn't really positive anymore. Tina had been so long inclined to shade the truth to her own advantage that her actual age, long a taboo subject for public discussion, had grown fuzzy. Tina had a current proclivity for very young men—men who were no more than boys to Claudia's eyes. To hear Tina explain it, there was a practical reason for her new desire for younger men. All the men her age were either married or, if unclaimed, marked by some very distinctive characteristics that kept women from looking at them.

Claudia told herself for the hundredth time that Tina's love life was none of her business and that unattached men—even very young ones—were preferable to Tina's former love interests, married men.

"Have a good time," she told Tina with an enthusiasm she hoped would nullify her previously judgmental tone. "I'll call you when I get back." It came as no surprise that Tina neglected to ask her a single question about the assignment. What surprised Claudia was that her sister had found time to talk at all. Jacqueline Fashions, the firm for which she designed, was so chaotic, she seldom was able to talk on the telephone.

"Do. I have two great outfits for you. I'm dying to see how they work out. You must have got dressed right, kid."

"Got dressed right?"

"To get a good assignment." Tina turned her head away from the telephone and shouted an obscenity to someone in the workroom with her. "You know, I think Jake's into hiring the mentally handicapped now. Or this new kid is a relative. Hell, what's the difference?"

"Got dressed right?" Claudia repeated to prompt Tina.

"You know, like I always told you. Right hand, right leg first. Did you do any buttons wrong? *That* always means good luck."

"Tina, you're incredible. How can you believe all that garbage? As a matter of fact, I got dressed wrong; I put my panty hose on inside out and had to start all over again." Claudia laughed, half in exasperation, half in disbelief that someone as sophisticated and successful as Tina could be so superstitious.

"You see? That's the luckiest of all! Got to go." The line went dead.

Claudia forgot all about Tina until the two-engine commuter plane took off from La Guardia Airport later that day. As the small plane banked and turned in the clear air of the gathering September dusk, she noticed that the pilot was guiding the craft over a cemetery. Not until afterward did she realize that she had held her breath the entire time they were flying over it, just as

Tina had taught her to do when she was a small child. If you didn't, Tina used to say, the spirits of the restless dead would enter your body when you inhaled. Claudia didn't believe it, any more than she believed that spilled salt or spilled milk brought you bad luck. Just the same, she always put the salt shaker down in front of someone when she was asked to pass it; she never handed it to anyone directly.

That's ridiculous, she told herself. *I'm not at all like her—she's not really even my sister.*

The lights of The Inn shone placidly as the taxi neared, momentarily luring Claudia into thinking she might be able to luxuriate in the surroundings of a hotel known for catering to the well-to-do who desired placid, elegant weekends at the very tip of Long Island. Except for Montauk's famous surf-fishing, the village's only activity in the off-season was exploring the windswept dunes sprouting with tufts of vegetation, or perhaps picking the fruit of the beach plum bushes that grew among whispering pines. Behind The Inn a small lake shimmered, catching the winking lights of houses on its other shore. When Claudia entered the hotel's spacious lobby, her small suitcase in hand, she noted the chaos the scandalous trial had brought to the sleepy beach town.

The lobby walls were constructed of a warm beige fieldstone, and her feet, as she crossed the expanse to the registration desk, sank into a red wool carpet that muffled her footsteps. To the right a dark hall led to a bar where the hubbub of voices and music told her the press corps had made their night headquarters in its dark recesses. Claudia approached the desk, but she had to wait while the clerk took two telephone calls and while he went through a door behind the desk and ordered the switchboard operator to screen his calls more thoroughly. When Claudia finally caught his attention, the sheen of perspiration on his upper lip told her that he and The Inn were incapable of handling the excitement and furor of their present situation.

"Cleary? Cleary? I can't find your name. We're full."

"Look under WNYZ," she suggested patiently. "Then try Arnold," she added, remembering that McLaughlin wasn't used to her maiden name. Claudia wasn't worried. McLaughlin never made mistakes, even if the desk clerk might.

"Yes, yes, here it is. Arnold. Single room." He pushed back a lock of hair that had fallen over his forehead. "We *are* full. I just gave away the last single room." He nervously paged through a book Claudia could not see. "Just a minute..." The telephone at his elbow buzzed again, but he ignored it and went into the back room once more.

When he emerged, he held a key in his hand.

"All I can give you is a one-bedroom suite. Same price as a single room, since it's our mistake. You can't imagine what a mess this trial is making!" He slammed his hand down on a bell on the desk. "The bell-hop will be here in a minute to help you with your bags."

Claudia signed the registration card, using the name Cleary, and waited for the bell-hop. The clerk tapped the bell impatiently, but no one came in response.

"Look, I can find the room myself. All I have is this one bag."

"Fine. Fine. You won't have any trouble. There are only two suites on the top floor. Take the stairs behind you." He indicated the stairs with a distracted wave of his hand. The telephone at his elbow buzzed again. A trio of men, slightly unsteady on their feet, had emerged singing from the bar and then approached the desk.

Claudia picked up the canvas bag at her feet and made her way up the carpeted stairs to the third floor. Away from the lobby, the hotel was quiet, and glancing at the number on the key the clerk had given her, Claudia had no trouble finding the door to her suite.

Once inside she dropped her bag on the floor, which was covered with a thick silver-sand carpet, and removed the quilted jacket of her khaki-colored suit, throwing it on a long couch that was placed in front of a fieldstone fireplace. The clerk had been wrong. The suite contained two bedrooms. She explored the rooms, openly pleased at the turn of events that had deposited her in such unexpected luxury. Glancing quickly into the bedrooms, she chose the larger one, which held a queen-size bed, a color television, and a small refrigerator. She opened the draperies to see that a small balcony overlooked Lake Montauk behind the hotel. Opening the doors, Claudia realized that from the third floor she could barely hear the music from the lounge below and not at all when she slid the glass doors closed against the cool autumn air. The room that most captured her imagination was the enormous bathroom, with its floor and walls of brown marble and its fixtures of a scrolled gold color. Highlighting the room was an oversize whirlpool bath, big enough to contain a small if intimate dinner party.

Claudia slipped off her shoes and felt the cool, smooth marble through her stockings. She crossed the shiny floor to the double sinks, where, to her delight, sample-size packages of German bath gel, English bubble bath, and French and Swiss shampoos were placed in a Lucite tray. She calculated that even if she stayed a week and took a bath and shampooed her hair twice a day, she would be unable to try them all.

A small smile played on Claudia's lips as she returned to the living room for her bag. She carried it into a dressing room off the larger of the two bedrooms and opened it, then she removed her skirt and her blouse and hung them up neatly. In only a bra and half-slip she returned to the living room and crossed to a small, well-stocked bar where a discreet notice asked that she make note of what she consumed on a preprinted note pad. Claudia opened the door of yet another small refrigerator under the bar and picked a chilled half-bottle of Chilean white wine, dutifully noting her choice on the pad. After filling a tulip-shaped glass with wine, she carried it and the bottle to the bathroom.

While the tub was filling she took down her long auburn hair, which earlier she had pinned into a loose French twist, then she carefully laid aside the Japanese ebony comb and pin that had held the thick mass. The comb was a prized one from her extensive collection of hair ornaments. Even as a child she had considered her hair to be her best feature, as it was thick, glossy, and gently waved by the capricious gods who in other areas of her life had dealt her a handful of mixed cards. Aware that its beauty attracted attention at the most unexpected times—literal strangers had approached her on the street to stroke it—Claudia most often wore her hair up in soft, gentle, full styles reminiscent of the Gibson girls. As she brushed it while waiting for the tub to fill and inhaled the herbal, woodsy scent of the German gel she had chosen for the bath, she noticed that the soft curls covered her rounded breasts in front and reached to the center of her back.

In a single, practiced motion she pinned her hair up once more and stepped into the full tub, sinking down into the aromatic spume of the bath gel. She wiggled her toes in the warm water and took a sip of the crisp white wine, and then she reached for the control dial on the wall, slowly adjusting the whirlpool until she had tried all the possible variations of strength available and decided which appealed most to her. The pulsating jet of water played on her back, her thighs, the sole of her feet. Claudia put her fingers against the underwater outlets and felt the strong massage on the tender inner skin alongside her knuckles.

With a wet hand she reached for the wineglass and, holding its thin stem, lifted it aloft and toasted aloud. "When I finally hit the lottery, I want a whirlpool bath in every room."

Claudia sighed and lowered her body down even farther into the tub, stretching her long legs in front of her, but she was unable to reach the foot of the tub. She closed her eyes, letting the soft bubbles just touch her chin. Every so often the cool air of the bathroom caressed a protruding nipple, and she would shift her hips a fraction of an inch lower in the tub. She felt as if she were bathing in a secluded forest glen.

In the near silence, above the unobtrusive hum of the whirlpool jets, she became aware of the murmur of two voices, those of a man and a woman. The man's voice was calm and soothing, the woman's much higher and more emotional. At first Claudia assumed the voices belonged to guests on the floor below and were carried up to her through the bathroom pipes, but then, suddenly, the voices were nearby, right outside the bathroom door. She froze in the water. What were they doing in her room? They were speaking normally, not trying to hide their presence. Indeed, as she heard their private conversation, she realized that they were totally unaware that anyone was listening to them.

"...that I did. Everyone knows anyway. I might as well just admit it and get it over with," said the woman.

"As your attorney, I don't want to know any details at all," the man stated firmly. "We won't put you on the stand, and therefore no one can question you. I insist that you not tell me another word, Glenda. Believe me, the not-guilty plea is the right one."

"But, if I explained everything, then anyone would understand. They'd see I *had* to do it. I *had* to. No one would convict me. You'll see." The note of hysteria in her voice grew.

"Glenda, they won't understand. You are a young and beautiful woman. You stand to inherit a fortune. You are sexually involved with another man—*and* he's not the first lover you've had since you were married. If you admit you knew you were shooting your own husband, they'll convict you. Juries have a thing against beautiful, rich, immoral women, believe me. Look at Patty Hearst. Look what happened to Jean Harris, for that matter. Even if you had the best reasons in the world—even if I agreed that you did—the jury will not see it that way. Glenda, I've never lost a murder case and I've defended people guiltier than you are."

Claudia was as still as she could be. She wanted to turn off the whirlpool jets, but she was afraid to move, for fear the two people on the other side of the door would hear her just as she could hear their every move. She supposed the woman was wringing her hands in distress. Even though she had only seen a grainy newspaper photograph of Glenda Shorter, she pictured her on the other side of the door: blond, tan, thin, and very high-strung. The man with the soothing voice was obviously her lawyer. Claudia held her breath, awaiting the woman's reply.

"Guiltier than me? How could anyone be guiltier

than I am? I'd wanted to kill him for a long time. I only half-thought he was an intruder, and I'm not sorry. I hated—"

"Not another word! Don't you understand yet? You can't tell me these things if I am to defend you. Lie down on the bed. I'm calling for a doctor to give you a shot to calm you down." They moved away from the door.

"No, I'm all right. Call my driver. I want to go home now." Their voices drifted away from the bathroom as Claudia heard a door open and then close, leaving the room silent.

All thoughts of the strangers in her room fled from Claudia's head as the import of what she had heard sank in. So—she shot him on purpose, and her attorney knew! Not an accident. Not a prowler, as the story in the newspapers had quoted Glenda Shorter. Claudia then remembered the story. "I was alone in the house with my babies and I heard what sounded like a prowler. I tried to telephone the servants' cottage, but the line was dead. I called out, and when no one answered, I took the gun that my husband gave me to protect myself and I shot blindly when the man came through the door. It wasn't until I turned on the light that I realized I had killed my own husband."

Claudia stood up in the tub. She didn't know what to do with the information she had just heard. She had to call McLaughlin. Claudia was no reporter, but she had worked as a graphic artist in the newsroom of WNYZ for five years and she recognized news when she heard it. The bubbles clung like tulle to her full breasts and her long thighs. She was standing to reach for the faucet with one hand and the control of the shower with the other when the door from the bathroom opened and a man walked in.

Their eyes met in the half-steamy mirror. Claudia gasped and tried to cover herself with her hands. The man spun around and stared at her with his mouth open.

As one, each said,

"What are you doing in *my* bathroom?" And then, as if in chorus, "What do you mean *your* bathroom!"

Claudia didn't know whether to laugh or to scream. Both reactions choked in her throat as they stood staring at one other. She read shock and horror on the man's face as the pupils in his cornflower-blue eyes grew larger. In a millisecond she saw anger replace surprise. The blue eyes narrowed, closing the fine spidered sun wrinkles that flanked them.

He took one menacing step toward her and said in a low, clear voice, "Answer me!"

She took a step backward, trying vainly to cover herself from his piercing gaze. Despite his visible anger and her own shocked surprise, Claudia had never felt a man look at her as he did, in a way that made her so totally aware of her womanhood. The skin on her back and her hips hit the cold marble wall behind her, and she lost her footing and fell into the enormous tub, splashing up a tidal wave of herbal-scented water and bubbles that sprayed all over the man's oxford cloth shirt and pin-striped trousers.

"Oh, my God!" he uttered.

Claudia regained her composure immediately, realizing that she was totally covered by the sudsy water, and she lowered herself into the opaque depth of the bubbles. The man was sopping up the water that had soaked through his clothes with a fluffy white terry cloth towel he had taken from a stack of similar towels on the gleaming brown marble beside the double sinks. He was tieless and the sleeves of his white shirt were rolled up to reveal strong and muscular forearms that glistened with blond hairs against the tan of his skin. From the smooth tone of his voice she realized that he was the lawyer she had overheard, and then she recognized him. He was the man she had seen on the commuter train and then in Bergdorf's so long ago. What red-blooded woman could have forgotten? But he did not know who Claudia was, and she intended to keep her secret.

"Who are you, and what are you doing in *my* bathroom?" she began, inching down into the still-warm water until only the tops of her breasts peeked above the line of bubbles. Even as she talked, Claudia saw another expression cross the man's sun-bronzed face.

"My name is Austin Harwood. This is my bathroom, and I was about to ask you the same question, young lady." He looked at her quizzically. "You'll think this is an awful line, but don't I know you from somewhere? Have we met?"

"It could be, Mr. Harwood. We've seen each other before, but have never been formally introduced. However, don't you think we could have this discussion another time? It's a bit inconvenient for me, you might have noticed."

"Not until you answer some questions for me."

He took a fresh towel and wiped off the side of the tub. She watched him warily, not believing what her brain told her he was about to do. He sat down on the edge of the tub, and the light glinted on the supremely thin gold watch he wore on his left wrist. Claudia stared at the numberless face of its lapis lazuli dial rather than at the handsome stranger who sat mere inches from her naked body.

"You appear to be a reasonable and intelligent woman," he began in his rich voice. "Not to mention a beautiful one. I think we can get everything straightened out in just a moment or two.

"I like to think I *am* intelligent, Mr. Harwood. But right now I have to ask myself if an intelligent woman would entertain a stranger in her bathroom. Would you mind leaving? I'll put on some clothes, and if you care to ask me some questions, as you put it, we could talk like civilized people over a drink in a more neutral setting." She was actually enjoying herself and she wiggled her toes in pleasure.

Knowing who he was had removed any vestige of fear from their encounter. Of course, she had heard his name before. Who hadn't? He was a renowned trial attorney, a younger Melvin Belli, but thinner, more handsome, and certainly more imbued with the quiet good taste that comes of fine breeding. She eyed him sideways as he sat staring down at her. His initials were embroidered discreetly above one pocket of the white shirt in white thread, nearly invisible. His sun-streaked brown hair fell over his tanned forehead engagingly, softening the angular line of his face, giving him the endearing look of a mischievous young boy. The only flaw on his handsome features was a nearly two-inch vertical scar that ran alongside his right eye, an intriguing scar reminiscent of the dueling scars of Heidelberg. Surprisingly she wanted to touch the line in his skin, wanted to ask him where the scar came from. She asked herself if she was crazy and searched quickly for another flaw in his features. His aquiline nose was just a shade too large, she decided.

He was gazing into the water around her breasts. Without hurry Claudia pushed a few bubbles toward her throat to assure herself that she was covered. She didn't mind being stared at by an attractive man, but it was a situation that could get sticky, and she realized that the man, whose clean lemon scent seductively filled her nostrils, had a way of staring at her that was causing an unaccustomed tingle in her abdomen and in the tips of her toes.

"How long have you been here in the bathtub?"

Ah, he wanted to know how much she had heard; that's why he was acting in such a suggestive manner. The sweet tingle disappeared, only to be replaced by a feeling of disappointment and irritation.

"Either long enough or too long, depending on which side of the battle you're fighting on," she answered acidly.

"So you *are* a reporter, as I thought. Is that why you're in my suite?" His expression was unreadable.

"I believe this is my suite, and you're the one in the wrong room. It appears you've been given the wrong key. And, no I am not a reporter. If I were spying on you, would I actually be taking a bath in what you claim is your room? Come on, Mr. Harwood, use *your* intelligence! I'm just a guest here. I'm in my own bathroom minding my own business and I'd thank you to leave— the sooner the better."

"Let's stop playing around. What did you hear?" His patience had worn thin and his voice had lost the bantering tone of a moment before.

"I heard your client confess to premeditated murder."

"And what are you going to do about it?"

"I haven't decided."

"Please do. Right now."

"Why should I?" Claudia's tone was belligerent.

"What's your name? Who are you working for?"

"That's none of your business. I can't help it if your client murdered her husband and has a loose tongue. I was simply taking a bath in my own bathroom. I didn't come here to spy on you or Mrs. Shorter—"

"Look, Miss..." He waited for her to supply her name.

"Yes?" answered Claudia.

"If you don't cooperate with me, I'm going to have to call the desk and have you evicted from here."

"Go ahead and do so, Mr. Harwood. You're going to be extremely embarrassed, believe me. Extremely."

His face was still calm. She knew he was angry, yet nothing on his face or in the tone of his voice betrayed his anger. But then, weren't all good trial attorneys superb actors? she thought.

"Please feel free to do what you have to."

Their eyes locked, his light blue eyes with her green ones. Claudia felt her legs grow so rubbery that she knew she could not have stood up at that moment even if she wanted to. She tried to drop her gaze, but suddenly she was unable to break the invisible current that seemed to hold her to him. A shudder went through her. Not fear...something else. Something the French called the *coup de foudre*, the thunderbolt. She recognized it immediately.

"You're a good poker player," Austin Harwood said at last in a quiet voice.

"So are you." She returned the compliment, finally able to turn her eyes away from his, but the words were unsteady.

As he leaned across the small space that separated them the scent of lemon came with him. He placed his index finger on the pulse at the base of her throat for a long moment, then slowly, maddeningly, he ran it down her breastbone, through the cleavage between her breasts, and into the water. She felt the smooth edge of his nail as his finger trailed across her skin, leaving an invisible line of flame in its wake.

"And I play a good game of hardball, too. The

water's getting cold. You shouldn't sit in cold water. You'll make yourself ill."

Harwood reached out and opened the drain, and the water began to gurgle out rapidly. He then stood up and crossed the bathroom in one step, picking up the telephone on the wall to dial two numbers for the front desk.

"Throw me a towel," Claudia said in a panic, but he ignored her. She scooted to the foot of the tub to close the drain before her body was uncovered. Harwood leaned across in front of her and closed his strong hand over the latch. The water drained noisily and rapidly. Claudia's breasts, no longer covered with bubbles, were exposed to his gaze. Never taking his eyes from her, he spoke into the telephone, but she was not listening to his words. She knew she would have to leave the tub to grab a towel on the other side of the room and that there was no way to stand without exposing herself totally to his incisive blue eyes. Claudia clenched her teeth and leaped out of the tub, making for the pile of dry towels at Harwood's side. He stared at her placidly. At last an expression of amusement crossed his face.

"Telephone for you, Miss Cleary," he said calmly.

Claudia's hands fumbled as she wrapped the fluffy bath sheet around herself. Her fingers trembled in anger and refused to obey her silent commands. Finally satisfied that she was covered, she took a deep breath to regain her composure and extended her hand for the telephone receiver.

"Thank you, Mr. Harwood." She answered as if it were the most normal thing in the world to be taking the telephone from him under those circumstances. Inside she was seething. He would see how mistaken he had been! She couldn't wait to hear the arrogant man's apology.

"Miss Cleary," said the desk clerk in an unctious tone. "Oh, Miss Cleary. I'm terribly sorry. I can't tell you how embarrassed I am. Such a crowd and all. I gave you the wrong key. You are in Mr. Harwood's suite. Yours is the *one*-bedroom suite next door."

Her eyes locked again with Harwood's as the clerk explained that her belongings would be moved immediately. She hung up the receiver in silence.

"I'll see you in the bar in twenty minutes," ordered Harwood. "Be there." He gave her one last glance— half amused, half victorious—and went out of the door, closing it firmly behind him.

Chapter Two

Claudia locked the door behind Harwood. She dressed rapidly in the gray crepe suit and a shell-pink silk blouse that enhanced the red highlights in her hair. As she applied her eye makeup automatically she fought to keep down the feeling of outrage she was experiencing in the pit of her stomach. How *dare* Harwood be right! It wasn't her fault that the desk clerk had given her the wrong key. Anyone could see the man was an imbecile, totally incapable of handling the excitement the trial had brought to his sleepy little village. Harwood must have known she wouldn't have been so cool under the circumstances if she had actually sneaked into his suite—into his bathtub—to eavesdrop. She supposed some women, some reporters, might try such a stunt, but she wouldn't. Claudia was usually shy and withdrawn with new people and, actually, her reaction to Harwood had been quite out of character.

A small smile played across her lips as Claudia thought back on the scene—she naked in the bathtub, he seated mere inches away. She tried to keep her upper lip still and concentrated on drawing a straight line of mocha color across its width with a fine sable lipstick brush. It was no use. She tissued the color off and began again. Her right hand still trembled slightly when she thought of how his finger had traced a path down between her breasts. She closed her eyes at the thrill the memory gave her.

Crazy! She was crazy! He was obviously a pretty arrogant man—and she hadn't missed the implied threat in his order to meet him in the bar in twenty minutes. Be there. Be there or what? Harwood couldn't do anything to her. She really had not done anything wrong. What was he so upset about? What would happen if she did make public what she had heard? Could what Harwood said be true: Would the Shorter woman automatically be convicted? Hadn't she killed her husband, anyway? Claudia supposed it was only justice that she take her punishment, but she wasn't certain she wanted the responsibility of making such a decision alone. She hurried to apply the rest of her makeup so that she could call McLaughlin before she went down to the lobby.

McLaughlin was out to dinner when she reached the WNYZ switchboard in New York City. Without leaving a message she hung up and sat on the edge of the queen-size bed, tapping an unpolished fingernail on the bedside table. She knew her former boss's routine well. He'd be back by nine thirty and would work through the eleven o'clock news show. She had to talk to him first, before Harwood used his no-doubt superlative forensic skills, not to mention his very real sex appeal, on her. Claudia would simply have to avoid Harwood until she had an opportunity to reach McLaughlin. She repacked her bag and left it on the bed for the tardy bell-hop to move to the other suite.

If anything, the noise from the bar on the first floor was greater when Claudia descended the stairs to the lobby. It crossed her mind to tell off the desk clerk, but the sight of his overworked face behind the registration desk stabbed her with compassion. She forgot him and went directly into the dining room, purposefully not glancing at the hall that led to the lounge, where she assumed that Austin Harwood awaited her.

The dining room was dark and quiet. Most people had finished dinner by the time she arrived, if they had eaten at all. She imagined the hotel would make most of its profits that night in the bar if, as seemed probable, the bulk of the guests in the hotel were newspeople.

"Claudia, is that you? Over here. Claudia."

She peered nearsightedly into the gloom. It was too much trouble to dig into her purse for her glasses, although she would be using them at the trial the following day.

"Is that you, Alex?" She recognized the voice of Alejandro Gómez-García, a Latin-American reporter who worked for WNYZ, before she actually saw his face.

"Yes, come and join me. You don't want to eat alone, do you?" His English was letter-perfect, without a trace of the exotic accent he feigned for his adoring audience in New York City.

"What are *you* doing here—and alone? The great Latin lover without a dinner date?" Claudia said, laughing, and joined him, carefully taking the chair opposite his, rather than the empty chair at his side. She welcomed a companion for dinner, but not one for the entire night, and she had no desire to get into a prolonged discussion about the subject.

"I just arrived and needed to gather my strength to work the happy hunting ground down the hall. Besides, my expense account will not cover dinner for anyone but myself. You're on your own account, aren't you?" he asked quickly.

"Yes, Alex. Don't worry."

"And how is your famous husband?"

"He's more famous than ever and no longer my husband."

Alex stood and moved to the chair at her side. "The light was shining in my eyes," he explained with a quick smile from his perfectly capped teeth. Claudia's back stiffened slightly. "Tell me what happened," he said in a smooth and ingratiating voice.

"I'll tell the world that your real name is Adelberto Schwartz-Puig and that your mother works in a deli in Far Rockaway if you don't get your hot hand off my knee," she promised with a steady, dazzling smile.

Alex sat up straight.

"Nothing has changed between you and me, Alex. Pass the menu, please."

They ordered dinner and established an uneasy truce. Their entrées had just arrived when Harwood walked into the dining room, his gaze sweeping the few occupied tables then resting on Claudia's auburn hair. He crossed with a purposeful stride to where she and Alex sat.

"I believe you and I had a date, Miss Cleary," he began immediately.

Claudia looked up at his glowering face, then down to the breast of chicken on her plate. She cut a small piece of skin off the chicken and set it to one side. Then she looked up at Harwood again.

"It must have slipped my mind," she said sweetly. "Would you care to join us? Do you know Alejandro Gómez-García? Alex, this is—"

"No, I don't care to join you. I want to talk to you alone," said Harwood, obviously making an effort to control his temper and bereft of all the composure he had exercised an hour before when he had knowingly held her captive in his own territory.

"Well, as you can see, Mr. Harwood, I already have

a companion, but I thank you for your flattering display of interest." She returned her attention to the entrée cooling on her plate. Claudia had no idea where the newfound nerve was coming from, but the darkness of the room assured her that Harwood was unaware of the blush creeping up her cheeks. From the corner of her eye she could see his left hand clenching and unclenching and the gleam of a heavy gold signet ring on his small finger. She was also aware that Alex had withdrawn a small notebook from the breast pocket of his suit. She wanted to giggle. Alex was no reporter, although he liked to pretend he was. He was merely a very seductive reader of the news whom McLaughlin often assigned to sensational stories to enhance WNYZ's position in the twice-nightly war for local news ratings.

"No notes, Gómez," said Harwood. "This is totally off the record. And if she has told you anything already and you broadcast it, I'll sue."

"I haven't told him anything. Leave him alone. For that matter, leave *me* alone," said Claudia emphatically. "You have no right to bully me, Harwood."

At last Alex stood up, his fractional drop of Latin blood kicking in to provide him with delayed gallantry.

"My colleague does not care to talk to you, Harwood."

"Your colleague! So you *are* a reporter, after all." He looked back at Claudia. For once Harwood seemed to be speechless. A muscle on the left side of his jaw worked and an opaque hood came down like a shade over his ice-blue eyes.

Claudia felt the tension of the moment like a hot and angry rivet in her stomach. She gave up any pretense of eating and with a slight grimace of disgust pushed her plate an inch toward the candle in the center of the table. All she had wanted was to buy a little time before she talked to McLaughlin, yet the entire situation threatened to reel out of control. She dabbed at her lips with the napkin.

"Mr. Harwood." She drew out the syllables of the word *mister*. "This man can be a crazy animal when aroused." She inclined her head toward Alex without actually looking at him. "I wouldn't take a chance if I were you. As well known as you are, he has guaranteed access to the airwaves. The hotel is filled with reporters—fellow reporters. His brethren, if you will. Imagine the headlines: 'Defense Lawyer Takes Swing at TV Reporter.' Imagine the scandal. I have not said a word to him, or to anyone. I don't intend to do so until you and I have our talk. But *I* will decide when that will be, Mr. Harwood. Do you understand?"

Claudia was relishing her power. That would show him for pushing his weight around. Once she had a witness, she knew Harwood was in no position to do anything to her.

She tilted her head up to Alex, who was looking at her agape.

"Sit down, Alex. Don't you think we should order coffee?" She graced him with another dazzling smile, totally ignoring Austin Harwood.

However, Claudia hadn't counted on her opponent. Harwood placed his tanned hands flat upon the table and leaned down until his face was a mere two inches from hers. Then, in the voice he obviously used to address the back row of the jury, he said, "You certainly look different with your clothes on, Miss Cleary."

His voice echoed through the silent room. Claudia was painfully aware that the diners scattered throughout the room had stopped eating and were staring at their corner table in curiosity and amusement. Her mind was stunned to blankness, and not a single clever rejoinder came to her lips. In any case, it was too late. Harwood was already leaving the room, his broad shoulders erect as he strolled out the door, his head held high.

At last she turned to Alex.

"On second thought I'll skip the coffee," She had to clear her throat and repeat the words; she seemed to have lost her voice. "It keeps me awake."

"*Caramba*!" said Alex, audibly exhaling. "I wouldn't want him for *prosecuting* attorney!"

"I don't want to hear another word," she answered.

Claudia picked up her handbag and left the table, keeping her eyes averted from the other diners. A roar filled her ears. She knew her cheeks were aflame.

"The flu? He's not there? McLaughlin is never sick."

"He's not in and he's not expected, ma'am."

Claudia knew it was hopeless, but she tried. "Can you give me his home telephone number? It's really important."

"You know I can't do that, but perhaps there's someone else who can help you."

"No, I need to talk to him. What time do you expect him tomorrow?"

"If he comes in, he starts at three o'clock."

"I'll try then. Thank you."

Claudia had trouble getting to sleep. As she lay at one side of the queen-size bed in the second, smaller suite assigned to her, the vision of Austin Harwood sitting on the edge of the bathtub continued to haunt her. She pictured those long, thin, tanned fingers splayed on the white tablecloth while the attorney made his embarrassing announcement to every diner—especially to Alex, who would carry the spicy gossip back to the

WNYZ newsroom. No doubt Alex had already amused all the drinkers in the bar off the lobby by repeating Harwood's comment. She closed her eyes in chagrin. If Harwood said one word to her the next day, she'd— she'd— She didn't know what she'd do. She could tell Alex then, that night. Claudia was angry enough to spill her secret, but why should she give that conceited skirt-chaser a scoop? She could call the newsroom directly. She glanced at the neon hands of her traveling alarm clock. It was already too late to make the eleven o'clock news, and she had promised Harwood that she would discuss it with him first. A promise was a promise, despite his shocking announcement.

After half an hour of wrestling with the problem, she decided to go on as before, avoiding him until she had a chance to discuss what she had overheard with McLaughlin. One more day would not make any difference, would it? At last she was able to turn onto her right side and fall asleep.

The next day dawned cold and overcast, and Claudia ordered a light breakfast sent to her room in order to avoid Alex, Austin Harwood, and the eyes of anyone else who might have witnessed or heard about what happened in the dining room the evening before. She distractedly pulled on a jade-green silk dress that Tina had designed, oblivious to the way its shimmering color deepened the green of her eyes to the color of a tropical lagoon. She brushed her auburn hair until it glowed, thinking all the while of the supplies she would need for the day in court, and she pinned up the long tresses with a pair of Victorian mother-of-pearl combs she and Peter had found in the Portobello Road antique market on a trip they had made to London shortly after his first book was published.

Claudia hadn't seen Peter for the past ten months

and, as she thought fleetingly of that long-ago trip during which they had spent every penny of the modest advance for his ' ok, she remembered that at the time they had had no idea how popular and famous he was destined to be. If one of the fortune-tellers whom Tina loved to visit had gazed into a crystal ball and told them that Peter's self-help volume, begun as a joke, as a glib parody of the self-help movement, would be taken seriously from coast-to-coast, would climb to the top of the trade paper back list in three short weeks, would make him rich and independent of his job as an associate professor of psychology at New York University, they would have laughed in her face. Well, not laughed exactly, but they would have exchanged that secret little smile of amusement and understanding that they had communicated with since the night they had met. A twitchy little smirk would have played around Peter's lips. Claudia used to think of Peter's smirk as a sign of his superior intelligence. Presently she considered it a visible reminder of his arrogance and meanness of spirit. Sometimes she watched him talk about his books on Merv Griffin's and Phil Donahue's shows. Once he had even been on Johnny Carson's show. As Peter spoke seriously about his work, Claudia would see the smile hovering around his thin lips and wonder if she was the only person who knew what was on his mind. Sometimes she felt crazy when she thought that way. How could she be the only one who knew the truth? How could thousands of people pay good money for ridiculous dictates about their married lives and their parenting from a man who was neither a husband nor a father?

Peter's latest book was about how to use psychology to achieve success as a single person—sexual success, Claudia assumed, although she did not intend to read the book. At least in that book he would have some expertise: He had lived like a single person for the last year or two of their marriage, and Claudia had been the only person unaware of it, as she worked the night shift at WNYZ. Peter now lived in a luxurious contemporary house on the beach at Malibu, and she had heard that he was about to buy a second place in New York City. Claudia hoped it would be far from Gramercy Park.

In the hotel lobby she met two cameramen from WNYZ and obtained a ride in their van to the old courthouse. The men, whom she knew from her days at the station, treated her normally, and she began to think that perhaps Alex had not spread the word. Claudia took a seat in the press section of the courtroom and noted that despite the coolness of the air outside, the room was already hot and stuffy from the number of people overflowing every available seat in the spectator section. An expectant hum vibrated through the high-ceilinged room.

Claudia withdrew her sketch pad from the flat leather envelope in which she carried her paper and colored pencils. She began to sketch Glenda Shorter where the woman sat at the defense table, ten feet ahead and to the left. The principals had to be sketched first. No matter what drama happened in the courtroom, the station would want a picture of the defendant, the woman who had everything—money, beauty, sex appeal—and stood to lose it all if the jury found her guilty.

She sketched quickly. Glenda Shorter was an attractive woman with long, curling eyelashes and a determined chin. Her nervous agitation detracted from her loveliness, but who would not be nervous under similar circumstances? Her eyebrows were dark, but her hair was very blond. Obviously colored, Claudia mused. She wore a conservative dress of thin black wool softened at the throat by an ecru lace collar that gave her the incongruous appearance of a nun caught without her headdress. Claudia knew the virginal look was a studied one and she could imagine Austin Harwood giving orders as to the clothes to be worn to the trial. She envisioned him going through Mrs. Shorter's closets to choose the correct attire. A small stab of— was it jealousy?—shot through her at the thought of the lawyer visiting Mrs. Shorter's boudoir. Claudia shook her head slightly in disbelief. She returned her concentration to the sketch in her lap. Conservative clothing notwithstanding, Glenda Shorter could not hide her sensuality from the onlooker. Subtly Claudia enlarged the strokes on the pouty lower lip to achieve a certain look on the defendant's face.

At the defendant's side sat a well-dressed man with thinning hair. From time to time he consulted a yellow legal pad that lay before him on the scarred oak table. Glenda Shorter inclined her head to him and whispered in his ear. He shook his head silently and turned his eyes away.

Claudia finished the quick sketch and turned the page of the pad, looking up once more at the defense table and straight into the electric blue eyes of Austin Harwood. For a moment their eyes locked across the ten feet that divided them, then he dropped his gaze to her breasts and slightly to the right, where her identification badge was pinned below her shoulder, then to the sketch pad in her hands. So finally he knew who she was and why she was there. She continued turning the page and tore her eyes away from his mesmerizing gaze, willing herself to look as calm as he appeared to be. Only a small muscle twitched at the side of his firm jaw. He too leaned across to the man with the thinning hair and said a few quiet words. The man turned in his seat and stared openly at Claudia. She bent her head in self-conscious confusion and began to sketch Austin Harwood, attempting to be oblivious of everything that was going on around her in the crowded courtroom, only raising her head at the entrance of the judge and the resultant noise as all stood and listened to the instructions of the bailiff.

Harwood immediately requested permission to approach the bench. He and the prosecuting attorney, a stout man whose trousers hung down to the floor and covered his heels, stood with their backs to the courtroom in quiet conference with the silver-haired judge. Claudia admired the cut of Harwood's gray pin-striped suit, the line of his hair on the back of his strong neck just above the snow-white collar of his shirt, and the width of his athletic shoulders, not quite disguised by the fine cut of his suit. She was lost in the sudden memory of the touch of his finger between her breasts when the judge announced that the trial would recess until the following Monday morning. An audible groan of disappointment went up from the crowd, and the judge left the courtroom. Harwood was back at the defense table with Glenda Shorter, replacing papers in his briefcase. Claudia put away her sketch pad, grateful for the foresight that had impelled her to do a picture of Mrs. Shorter right away. Trials were still a mystery to her. The two she had worked on recently had reminded her of an extremely stylized Japanese dance in which only the dancers—the judge and the two attorneys—knew the steps. Everyone else, including the defendant, comprised the audience.

"Miss Cleary, a moment of your time." She turned at the gentle touch on her elbow. "My name is William Lindhurst. I am Mr. Harwood's associate." Lindhurst removed his glasses and began to polish them with a white handkerchief. Claudia looked directly into his seemingly unfocused gray eyes since he was approximately her height.

"Yes?"

"Mr. Harwood would like to talk with you. Step this way, if you please."

She looked across at Harwood and Mrs. Shorter, who were surrounded by half a dozen reporters all attempting to question them at one time. Harwood looked hot and harassed and wasn't looking her way.

"He'll have to find me first, Mr. Lindhurst."

"Miss Cleary—"

Claudia left the courtroom by the side door and made her way out to the street, where, among others, the WNYZ cameramen were poised, ready to film the participants of the trial as they emerged from the yellow stone building.

"Going back to the city? Can I have a ride?"

"Sure. Wait in the van. We'll be done here in ten minutes."

Claudia jumped in the back of the WNYZ van before Harwood, Lindhurst, and Mrs. Shorter emerged from the courthouse, pushing against the throng of shouting reporters who blocked their path. She watched from within as they made their way to the dark blue Rolls-Royce that awaited them, the car she had seen before, long ago. A smile of satisfaction played across Claudia's face. She was safe from him until Monday, and by then it would not matter, because she was certain she would find McLaughlin before Austin Harwood found her.

They stopped at The Inn to check out and then rode back to the city in near silence. Claudia worked on the sketch of Glenda Shorter, enhancing a detail here and and a shadow there. Once in a while she glanced at the quick lines of her beginning sketch of Harwood, knowing she had not captured the essence of the man in her drawing but aware that another observer would not see the lack. It was obvious only to her artist's eye, already colored by an unexpectedly emotional involvement with the man. She closed the sketch pad and stared out the window at the potato fields and the stands of scrub oak on either side of the Montauk Highway.

The sketch appeared during a quick story on the six o'clock news, which Claudia did not see. She was at Tina's apartment for a light dinner before her monthly meeting of the Adoptees' Liberty Movement Association.

"Why don't you come with me, Tina? You'll find it interesting. And I know you don't have anything else planned." How often they had been through that discussion. Tina certainly would find an excuse not to attend, as usual.

"I have to do my hair. The roots are showing."

"The only roots that show are the color of the rest of your hair. Come on, Tina. How can you be so close-minded?"

"What makes you think I want to spend a free evening in the company of a bunch of neurotic adoptees who don't know how to leave well enough alone? What would Mother say if she knew what you were doing? Don't you think she'd be terribly hurt?" Tina's hand closed around the bottle of wine they were sharing and drew it closer to her. She poured another glass after silently offering Claudia a refill. Claudia shook her head slightly. The neck of the bottle chattered against the wineglass, and a few drops spilled on the magenta tablecloth, spreading slowly as they blotted into the fabric.

"No, I don't think she'd be hurt and, actually, I plan

to tell her very soon. I'm certain she'll understand." Their mother—Tina's mother and Claudia's adoptive mother—had been felled by a stroke and lived mutely in a nursing home in Cincinnati, where the two women had been raised.

"What you don't realize is that I am not looking for a mother to take Mom's place. It's just a—a—I don't know, a deep biological curiosity to know who gave birth to me. I really can't expect you to understand, Tina. You've never had to wonder about yourself. Like where does my red hair come from? How come I have artistic talent? Why are my eyes green? You already know all those answers about yourself. You take it all for granted—those things and your relatives and their histories. I may even have sisters and brothers I don't know anything about. Did you ever think of that? Half sisters and brothers, anyway."

Tina was skeptical. "I don't know. I'd be afraid of what I might discover. You were probably illegitimate, you know."

"I take that for granted."

"You do?"

"Of course."

"But maybe it's worse...."

"You mean like insanity or incest?"

"Yes." Tina looked away from Claudia.

"I can take it. I've thought about all that already. It's worth it to me to know. Anything is better than the uncertainty. and if you were the product of incest, you'd want to know that before you had children, wouldn't you?"

"But you're not even married!"

"But I may marry again someday and want to have children. What about diabetes? Tay-Sachs disease? Sickle-cell anemia?"

"Claudia, you're getting carried away. There's no way you could be a carrier for Tay-Sachs disease or sickle-cell anemia. Really!"

Claudia got up from the small round table and walked to the window overlooking the turbulent East River. An aerial tram had just begun the journey from Manhattan to Roosevelt Island across the water. She watched its progress for a silent moment, having always admired the view from Tina's place since the times when, as a young child, she had made infrequent trips to New York to visit her sister, who had been living in the same rent-controlled apartment for as long as Claudia could remember. She imagined Tina's monthly rent was less than half of what she paid in maintenance alone on her much smaller Gramercy Park place, but they never discussed money.

"I know that, Tina," she said, sighing. "But that's not the point. There are members of ALMA who are worried about those very diseases. I think—no, I *know*—we have a right to know about our biological heritage."

"What have you discovered so far?"

"Virtually nothing. The one lead I had led nowhere. I've been registered on ALMA's computer ever since I joined the organization, but that won't do any good unless my birth mother registered, too. Then ALMA would be able to match up the data we both supply for the birth time and place. I don't have a time and place, not really. All I have is my amended birth certificate and I can't be positive that the information was correct to start with. Some girls give false data, you know."

"No, I didn't know," said Tina from behind her.

"The only lead I have is the foundling home I lived in. My case is a little unusual in that I wasn't adopted until I was almost three years old and I lived in the home until then. When I went back to the home to ask, they told me that my birth mother came to see me every weekend, but that later she put me up for adoption, although the files indicated she had been trying to get her life together to keep me."

"That's all they would tell you? What about the father? What about where the woman lives now?"

"That's all, Tina."

"Why do you have to tell Mother you're looking?"

"Imagine if someone else told her. Imagine if Aunt Geraldine heard about it!" The room was silent as the two women conjured up personal visions of their formidable aunt Geraldine, the family's judgmental busybody.

"Geraldine's crazy. Nobody listens to her, anyway."

"Mother has no choice. She's paralyzed."

"I see your point," said Tina, sighing audibly.

Claudia whirled around to face her sister. Her eyes were ablaze. "Imagine some bureaucrat sitting across from you, just two feet away, with everything you'd die to know written on a paper in front of her. And she won't tell you!" She shook with remembered anger.

Tina came over to Claudia at the window and put her arms around her. The top of her head just reached Claudia's nose. "It's all right, sweetie, it'll work out," she said soothingly. "I'm certain it's only a matter of time. Come into the bedroom. There are some dresses for you to try on."

"I have only twenty minutes if I'm going to make the meeting on time. Won't you come with me tonight?"

"No, really, I don't want to. That's something you have to do for yourself. But, Claudia, don't get so wound up. It's not good for you, believe me. You may not like what you find if you do track down this woman."

"Don't worry about me," said Claudia. How could she expect Tina, or anyone else, to understand? She had no desire to hurt their ailing mother. Even if she was fortunate enough to discover who her birth mother was, she might not even make contact with her, let alone attempt to establish a relationship. She only wanted to know, no matter what.

Claudia followed Tina into a large and messy bedroom to try on some of her sister's latest creations. Tina often gave her dresses and suits she had designed for the next season's line in exchange for Claudia's promise to give her practical criticism of their construction and to pass on comments made by others about her designs.

Forty-five minutes later she sat on a folding chair at the monthly ALMA meeting, a cup of black coffee in one hand. To her left sat a serious-looking middle-aged man, one of the few men in their group, which in all other ways represented a true cross section of New Yorkers. The members were young, old, black, white, married, single, rich or not well off at all, the only common trait among them being their curiosity about their heritage. They were the people with whom Claudia felt entirely comfortable. No one else in her life, past or present, could understand her all-burning desire to know where she came from. She had virtually stopped discussing the search with anyone. Peter had never understood, Tina was gently opposed, and her adoptive mother did not know.

The man at her side greeted her warmly. She knew he had been searching for almost forty years and that he was beginning to despair that it was too late to find his birth mother alive. His was one of the most difficult cases: He had been a foundling, abandoned literally on the steps of a Brooklyn orphanage half a century before. Claudia knew his chances of tracing his mother were practically nil, but she admired his courage in persevering.

To her right sat a woman about her own age who had already found her birth mother, but who stayed on as an active member of their ALMA chapter to give support, both moral and practical, to the other members. She had the experience necessary to teach the still-searching adoptees how to find their way through the labyrinthine red tape and stuffiness of the bureaucracy in charge of birth, marriage, and death records. The woman stood up and moved to a small podium at the front of the room. She would speak that night; afterward the group would divide into small clusters or seminars in which they would exchange hard information, words of encouragement, and offers of mutual help.

"I'm here tonight to teach you how to lie and steal," she began. "We have to use any methods we can to ferret out information that is virtually free for the asking to. the nonadopted. It's frustrating and it's time-consuming, but you can be successful. I'm going to tell you how I found my birth mother; perhaps my story will help you find yours."

A familiar sense of outrage filled Claudia. She had heard the lecture before. The fact that adoptees had to employ subterfuge, flirtation, even private detectives to get information that others could simply request for a two-dollar fee never ceased to overwhelm her with indignation. At one time she had been so fired with righteousness that she had seriously considered quitting her job at WNYZ and volunteering her services to

ALMA's ongoing legal fight to make adoptees' birth records public, but the looming divorce from Peter had made her more practical.

"I'm going to get another cup of coffee," she whispered to the man at her side. "Can I bring you one?"

"No, but thanks, anyway." Claudia left the row as quietly as possible. The lecture was for the benefit of the newer members, who were easily identified by their rapt expressions they wore as they listened to the speaker's fighting words.

Claudia made her way to the back of the room and refilled her Styrofoam cup from the coffee urn. She chose a shortbread cookie from an assortment of sweets on a paper plate.

"Careful, those cookies could be dangerous to your lovely measurements," said a low voice at her side. She looked up into the eyes of Austin Harwood.

"*You!* What are you doing here?" His eyes were truly beautiful, she thought with a start, and they seemed to be looking right through the peach cable-knit sweater she wore. He was gazing at her in frank admiration.

"Don't you ever wear your hair down?" he asked her.

Unconsciously Claudia touched the back of her head where the pearl combs held her hair in place.

"Sometimes. Never in public."

"Why not? It must be very beautiful. I'd like to see it sometime."

An unexpected thrill went through her at the intimacy his words subtly suggested. His voice was very soft.

"People touch it. Strangers. Strangers on the street," she said slowly.

"Yes, I can see why they would. The Met has that

problem with their statues. That's why they have those velvet barriers—the hands wear away the marble."

"Well, not *that* many people." She laughed, forcing herself to break the spell his smooth voice seemed to cast over her. She couldn't imagine that he was an adoptee in search of his lineage, not Austin Remington Harwood IV. But how did that name come to mind? How did she know his whole name and that there was a number following its euphonious syllables? She was astonished that such a specific piece of data popped out of her subconscious mind. She was certain he could trace himself back to the Mayflower and beyond and she said as much. His eyes never left hers, his gaze very disconcerting.

"No, I'm in search of a child, not a mother."

"There are no children here. You have to be eighteen to even join. Or if you're looking for a child, the child has to be eighteen, and you don't look old enough to have an eighteen-year-old child."

"*You're* somebody's child, aren't you?"

"Aren't we all?" she said forlornly, gazing around the room filled with fellow searchers.

"Well, I'm looking for you."

"Me? How did you know I would be here?"

"You come to this meeting monthly, don't you?"

"Yes, I do," she answered, bewildered. "But how do you know that?"

Harwood smiled enigmatically. The white lines where the sun had not tanned the skin next to his eyes disappeared as the smile creased his features.

"What else do you know about me?"

"You're twenty-nine, you live at Sixteen Gramercy Square, you're an artist, you just had dinner on East Sixty-first Street, and—"

"Just a minute! I don't care for this one bit—"

"And, of course, you look terrific naked. I like that little mole on your backside," he said in a stage whisper. Someone in the back row turned around and shushed them.

Claudia looked around frantically. She grabbed Harwood's arm through the gray pin-striped wool and pulled him out of the room and into the vestibule.

"Don't start that again! I will not be manipulated by your theatrics, Mr. Harwood." Claudia's eyes sparked with anger. "What do you want?"

"I want you to have dinner with me," he said.

"I've already had dinner. You told me so yourself. I don't want to see you at all. Get out of here! You have no right to be here."

"This meeting is open to visitors, is it not?"

"Interested visitors."

"I'm interested."

"Not in what interests us."

"How do you know?"

"You're only interested in whether I'm going to tell your little secret. That's what I know."

"Are you going to have dinner with me or not?" he asked calmly. He was still smiling, but Claudia was not. Her face was flushed with anger and with the effort to keep her voice to a whisper.

"Not on a bet. I told you we'd talk when I am ready, not before. There must be a law against harassing people like this. Why don't you check your law books?" She stepped back a foot, up against the wall of the corridor. Harwood was standing so close to her, she could smell his refreshing lemon scent with every breath she took.

He placed one arm on either side of her head and trapped her against the wall as he leaned forward, continuing to smile in a manner that brought her to new heights of controlled fury. "Shall I go inside and tell them about your little mole?" he whispered close to her ear. "It might help you in the identification process."

"You wouldn't!"

"You *know* I would."

She did.

Claudia thought for a long moment, then she said, "I resent this. I resent your manipulation. I resent your levity about this meeting. ALMA is extremely important to me. This organization is involved in very serious matters—matters of life and death, if you will. I resent *you.*"

"And they say lawyers talk a lot,' he replied dryly. "May I assume that your answer is yes?"

"Do I have a choice?"

"Not really, I suppose." His eyes were laughing.

"My answer is yes, but—" Her teeth were clenched. "I swear I won't bring up the trial."

"You won't bring up the trial?" she repeated, confused.

"No. I simply want to have dinner with you."

Chapter Three

"I have already eaten," she reminded him, gazing around at the French provincial decor of La Columbe d'Or. They sat in a banquette upholstered in printed chintz sprayed with tiny rustic flowers. Above their heads on the roughly plastered wall hung a fair repro- duction of a Léger painting. Claudia had passed La Columbe d'Or often, as the restaurant was not far from her apartment, but she had never been inside.

"Aren't you at all hungry? It's almost ten o'clock."

"Perhaps a bit." It wasn't as difficult as she had imagined it would be to act civilly toward Austin, as he had told her to call him. He was proper and charming during the taxi ride to the restaurant, which he had sug- gested. Claudia was surprised to find him so familiar with her neighborhood. Not too many people were, es- pecially with the restaurants, except for Joanna, which was the superchic place of the moment.

"If you care for something light, let me recommend the raspberry soup," he suggested.

"Fruit soup? I've never heard of such a thing."

"Would you like to try it?"

"It sounds enchanting."

He ordered the raspberry soup for Claudia and some- thing called Pates Fraîche Printanière for himself.

She had no idea what the dish was, but she knew at least that it was not red meat, because she recognized the name of the white wine Harwood finally settled on after a discussion with the wine steward. Claudia never ate red meat, finding it distasteful, and she did not enjoy watching others do so.

"Do you come here often? Do you like French food?" she asked searching for a subject as far removed from the trial as possible. What could she say to Austin, whose life was so entirely different from hers? A Rolls-Royce...an estate in Connecticut... Had he mentioned Connecticut in the taxi? He must have. How else would she know? she asked herself.

"I like some French food," Austin answered, breaking a piece of crusty homemade bread in half. Claudia watched his long fingers and imagined his warm hand on her skin once more, mentally shaking her head in awe at the conflicting emotions raging within her. Although she was angry with him for forcing her to acquiesce to his will, Claudia was secretly, delightedly pleased that he left her no other choice. She was stunned at the turn of events that found her seated across the small wooden table from him, able to look into his hypnotic eyes, able to listen to the mesmerizing tones of his melodious voice. In a moment she would insist that he tell her how he had found her, but then she simply wanted to sit across from him and bask in the warmth of his body near hers. For although they were not touching, she was acutely aware of him there, almost as if he were surrounded by an invisible aura that raised the temperature of the air around him—an aura Claudia knew only she of all the diners in the half-full restaurant sensed and reacted to. Once his knee brushed against hers under the table. Austin drew his leg away slowly, and not before Claudia felt a thrill snake up her thigh at his fleeting touch.

"Some of it is too fussy, but I do like the food from Provence. It's hearty. I like Spanish and Middle Eastern food for the same reason. What about you?"

"Mexican food," she answered. "Thai, Indian."

"Hot and spicy—like your temper." He grinned.

"I don't have a bad temper usually," she said and smiled. "You just got off on the wrong foot with me."

"Will you give me another chance?" He lowered his fingers over one of her hands, which rested on the table. Claudia looked down at his hand. She reminded herself that Harwood wanted something from her, that most probably he would do anything to get his way. He had merely changed his battle tactics from outright blackmail to attempted seduction. She willed herself to withdraw her hand, but an invisible electric current held her to him, almost as if his skin were magnetized. His hand was so warm, and he had beautifully shaped fingernails as well.

Claudia looked up into his eyes and, despite the warning her brain was sending her in frantic Morse code, she felt a quick charge in her breast as her heart turned over. She opened her mouth to reply, but before she was able to answer, the waiter arrived with their entrées. Gratefully she pulled her hand away as if from a flame, and momentarily the spell was broken.

The waiter placed a bowl of polished red liquid studded with whole raspberries before her. Harwood had ordered homemade noodles in a cream sauce, sprinkled with toasted pine nuts. Chunks of vegetables were visible through the cream, and Claudia could smell the dish's pungent garlic even from her side of the table. The waiter ground fresh pepper over the noodles and offered her a dollop of unsweetened whipped cream for the jewel-colored soup.

Claudia tried the ruby liquid. It was unexpectedly cold, which came as a pleasant surprise, and tasted both tart and sweet at the same time. She held a raspberry on the back of her tongue to savor its contrasting flavors, then exhaled slowly through her nose in an attempt to divine the ingredients of the mysterious concoction.

"Well, what do you think?" he asked.

She swallowed the berry and answered, "Another fruit. There's another fruit in it." She took a second small spoonful and rested a berry on her tongue, repeating the tantalizing experience. She tasted brandy and a fortified wine—Madeira, perhaps—and the elusive second fruit. "What is it? I'll go crazy until I know."

Austin sat back in his chair, watching her with a pleased expression on his face. He had not yet picked up his fork.

"I don't know. They'll never tell you. The chef here is known for his bad humor."

"Here, taste it." She took the coffee spoon from her place setting and dipped it into the cool soup, inclining across the table toward him. She feared the liquid would spill if she handed him the spoon, so she offered it directly to his mouth, realizing too late how intimate a gesture feeding a man was. Harwood touched her hand lightly to steady the spoon and his penetrating eyes never left hers. Just like two lovers, she thought. And suddenly she had a premonition that they would be lovers—soon—that very night, perhaps.

Claudia dropped the spoon in confusion at the heady vision of lying naked in his arms. The silver clattered noisily on the bare wood of the small table. Doubts and hesitations nagged at her—something she knew about him, some piece of damning information just out of reach at the edge of her subconscious. She willed the knowledge to surface.

"You're married," she announced finally, sitting back.

"Peaches," he said simultaneously.

"That's a new excuse. What does it mean?"

"It means the other fruit is peaches. Even Freud said 'Sometimes a cigar is just a cigar.'"

"Oh, yes," she answered, flustered that she had forgotten the entire pantomime had taken place in search of an elusive soup ingredient and even more embarrassed at the sexual reference to Freud's famous comment. It was almost as if he had read the images in her mind.

"No, I'm not married. Are you?"

"You mean you didn't find that out about me? I thought you knew all there was to know about me already."

"Well, my sources aren't perfect and they didn't have much time." He did not elaborate.

Claudia had a choice. She could follow up on how he obtained his detailed information or she could follow up on his civil state, which was suddenly, inexplicably much more important to her. She chose the latter. To buy time she took another spoonful of the raspberry soup, but her tongue did not taste the savory liquid. Her mind worked frantically to nudge her subconscious for a wispy memory. She knew that something important lurked in its recesses.

At last she remembered. Bergdorf's. Christmas. Mrs. A. Remington Harwood IV.

"You're married and you live in Connecticut," she stated firmly. "You are A. Remington Harwood the Fourth, are you not?"

"I am the fourth and only. All the others are long

dead. But there is no Mrs. Harwood, and I live in the city. Always have, except when I was in school." He began to eat his noodles. "Would you care for a taste?" he asked her, holding up a forkful of the cream-covered pasta.

"No, thank you." She bit her lower lip in earnestness. "I don't go out with married men. They just invite heartache."

"You know that firsthand, I take it. Or is that simply a piece of folk wisdom the ladies exchange?"

"Don't play lawyer with me. I don't have to know it firsthand; the evidence is everywhere." She thought of Tina and her long affair with Jake, the proprietor of Jacqueline Fashions, and after Jake, another; and after him...

"I swear I'm not married." He raised his right hand in mock solemnity.

"You have seen me before, Austin. You asked me at Christmas what size I wore when you were shopping for your wife at Bergdorf's. For *Mrs*. Harwood."

"Yes, I remembered. After I saw you dressed, of course." His eyes twinkled in amusement, no doubt at the memory of seeing her undressed.

"Please. Don't bring that up again," she snapped.

"I have no wife," he said blandly.

"Is that the truth?"

"Yes. I have no wife." His tone expressed irritation.

"All right, I'm sorry." But Claudia persisted. "That's really true?"

"Look, I haven't asked you to do anything that even a married man could not ethically ask an attractive woman who is not his wife to do. So why such a big fuss? I told you that I'm not married. I really don't want to discuss it anymore."

"Yes, I can see that."

They looked into each other's eyes for a long electric moment. The question, unspoken, but crackling and alive, lay vibrantly in the air between them. Claudia knew she stood at a fork in the road that could alter the course of the evening, the week, perhaps even her life. She swallowed hard. Did she dare? *Oh, well,* she thought, *In for a penny, in for a pound.*

"But perhaps... just perhaps I was going to ask *you.*" She wondered what Peter's book on the single life would say about that. She could not believe that she had actually given words to her thoughts, words that formed an open invitation that obviously he heard and understood clearly.

Harwood put down his fork and wiped his mouth with his napkin. He took a sip of his wine. The silence roared in Claudia's ears. The certainty that he would say something cutting overwhelmed her. She put her suddenly cold hands into her lap for fear he would see them trembling. Why had she said those fateful words? They had fallen from her lips as if someone else had uttered them, but she knew they were hers and hers alone. She had never felt such overwhelming desire for a man, and her feelings had made her careless, daring, even wanton. She squeezed her eyes shut. How could she have been so mistaken? God, what a fool...

Mere seconds had passed when Austin said quietly, "But I *was* going to ask you something."

"What?"

"Will you take down your hair for me?"

"Yes," she whispered, opening her eyes and looking into his.

At the top of the stairs she turned her back to him and inserted a key in the upper lock of the door to her apartment. Claudia felt the light touch of his hand on the back of her head, then his lips on her nape, and his breath was warm on her skin. Austin's arms slid around her waist from behind and drew her to him, burying his head in her neck. Her knees went weak with desire for him. His clean scent was in her nostrils, and she inhaled deeply and slowly turned around to face him, leaving the silver key ring to clink and dangle in the lock. She imagined how he would make love to her, how he would gently undress her, removing each garment deliberately with his beautiful tanned hands... how he would kiss the space between her breasts along the line his finger had traced... how he would kiss the little mole he had mentioned before... how they would soon lie in the darkness under a Ficus tree, making love long into the night.

Austin drew her to him and put his mouth on hers, lightly touching her lips until her mouth responded. She inhaled deeply, wanting more of his citrus bouquet, more of his warmth on her, more of the hardness of his firm body all over her. Gently he touched the tip of her tongue with his, testing her reactions. Claudia's mouth opened fully to admit him and she slipped her arms up around his neck, pulling his head to her, caressing the back of his neck where the hair was clipped shortest, and its ends pleasantly scratched her palms. They kept their mouths together, their tongues touching. He was very tender with her, kissing her with passion but not urgency, stretching the moment to savor every drop of its dizzying pleasure. At last he drew his face away and looked deeply into her eyes. His blue eyes glittered with desire.

"Will you let me take down your hair?" Austin whispered.

"Yes. Oh, yes," she responded. Her own voice was a hoarse whisper. Claudia buried her face in his chest against his red-and-blue silk tie, inclining into his hard, lean body. Her legs were weak, threatening to buckle beneath her, and she held onto his strength to keep her balance.

Austin placed his hands on either side of her head and slid his long fingers under the loosely knotted hair. She heard him exhale slowly and unsteadily.

"Let's go inside," she whispered.

With one arm still firmly grasping Claudia by the waist, Austin reached behind her back with the other and removed the key, inserting it in the lower lock, turning it easily. The door opened, and they entered the apartment together.

Claudia stopped just within the living room.

"I didn't leave all these lights on," she whispered urgently. From her bedroom drifted the muted mechanical sounds of television voices. "Or the television. Someone's here!" She tugged at Austin's sleeve, attempting to pull him back through the door into the hall.

"No, wait. Let me go and look. You stay here," he ordered her calmly.

"Austin, that could be dangerous," she said to his broad back as he walked confidently toward the darkened bedroom door from which the chiaroscuro reflection of the television screen flickered.

Harwood returned in seconds.

"There's someone in the shower. A man. He's singing," he said without expression on his face.

"A man? Singing? In my shower?" she echoed foolishly.

Claudia brushed by him and strode into the bedroom, all traces of fear gone. An open suitcase lay on the floor. The bed had been turned back and someone had been lying on it. The periwinkle-blue quilt she usually slept under was pushed to the foot of the bed and had slipped halfway to the floor.

She pounded on the closed bathroom door.

"Come out of there!" she shouted. She turned to Harwood and said in a bewildered tone, "There must be some mistake. I can't imagine—"

The door to the bathroom opened to emit a cloud of steam. A man's blond head appeared at the door.

"Peter! What are you doing here? I thought you were in Los Angeles."

Peter looked at her stunned face and then at Harwood's. A small smirk played on his lips.

"Obviously you weren't expecting me—again," he gloated. "Oh, how history repeats itself!"

Claudia knew immediately to what he referred. Those had been her exact words the second time she came home unexpectedly from work and found Peter in bed—*her* bed—with a comely graduate student from the psychology department.

"Peter, I want an explanation!"

"I think I had better be going."

"Let me just slip into something."

All three spoke at the same moment in distinctly varied tones of outrage, civility, and banter. The bathroom door closed and reopened at once. Peter strolled out, wrapped only in a bath towel, the thick blond hair on his arms and legs shining with droplets of water. Calmly he walked to the bed and sat on its edge. He extracted a cigarette from a pack on the table, lit it, and leaned back against the headboard, lazily extending his legs out on the bed in front of him. The smirk Claudia knew so well played across his thin lips.

She stood speechlessly staring at him..

Harwood, without saying a word, returned to the living room. Claudia turned and followed him.

"Austin, I can explain—"

"Go ahead." He looked at her steadily, an unreadable expression in his steely blue eyes.

"I—I guess I can't explain. I don't know what he's doing here. I thought he was in Los Angeles. I'm shocked to see him!"

"That's obvious." He was already at the door that lead to the hall.

"Going so soon?" Peter stood at the door of the bedroom in a black silk Japanese kimono. "I thought we might have a little drink together. Very modern and civilized, don't you think?"

"I'm leaving," said Harwood. "I was simply seeing Miss Cleary home." The actor's mask had fallen over his eyes and he had paled under his warm tan so that the scar beside his eye stood out in the light of a nearby lamp. His resonant voice roared in Claudia's ears, although he spoke in normal tones.

"Ah, you must mean Mrs. Arnold. These liberated women, you know. Always trying to stick to their maiden names. I believe I neglected to introduce myself and my wife seems to have lost her tongue. I'm Peter Arnold and you are...?" He paused and smiled engagingly, awaiting Harwood's reply, which was not forthcoming.

"Peter, stop this farce! Who do you think you are, Noel Coward?" Claudia's fists were clenched and she took two steps toward her former husband. "I want you out of here right this minute! You have no right—"

The door that led to the hall clicked shut behind her. Claudia turned to see that Harwood had gone and moved to follow him, but Peter grabbed her by one shoulder and dug his strong fingers into her flesh.

"No hello kiss? My, my, you seem to have forgotten all your manners, Claudia."

"Let me go, you worm!" She pulled free from his grasp and ran to the door. The hall was empty.

Claudia stood silently at the door, gathering her wits. She longed to chase after Austin, but what could she tell him? She could not explain Peter's presence in her apartment and she knew that she appeared to be the faithless wife caught in a tawdry extramarital tryst, thanks to Peter's malevolent remarks. Even if she ran after Austin and explained that Peter and she were long divorced, that she had not seen him in more than ten months, the evening was already ruined. Her breast ached with disappointment and frustration and her stomach burned from the searing acid of anger that bubbled there, threatening to spill over at any second.

She knew Peter would love to see her explode. If she gave in to her inclination to rave and rant, he would become cooler, more logical, and unbelievably infuriating. He would speak to her in the slow, patronizing tones of a superior psychologist dealing with a totally unreasonable neurotic. During their marriage she had been the unwilling victim of his cat-and-mouse game more often than she cared to remember. She refused to play the game again. With an enormous effort she vowed to keep her wits about her. Under no circumstances would she allow Peter to see how angry and disappointed she was. Nor would she tell him who Austin was or why he had been in her apartment.

Claudia returned to the living room. Peter still lounged insolently against the doorframe.

"You owe me an explanation, Peter," she said through clenched teeth.

"My dear, you make me seem so unwelcome here. I bought this apartment, don't you forget. I needed a place to stay and I naturally assumed that—"

"You assumed wrong."

"—that you would be willing to allow me to stay here. After all, you are always welcome at my place in Malibu."

"If I ever decided to do such an incredibly unlikely thing, I would have the common courtesy to call first. For God's sake, Peter, even when we were married I called first to make sure the decks were clear before I came home from work. You forced me to degrade myself like that." She heard her voice go up half an octave and she realized she had already said too much.

"But I *did* call. I left a message on your answering machine." He shifted his eyes to the machine, and hers followed. Truly, the red button indicating that messages waited on the tape glowed brightly.

"That matters not one bit. I would *never* have let you stay here. Peter, it's over. We're divorced. Through. Finished. I don't even want to be your friend. Can't you understand? I've made a new life, and you are not part of it. I am no longer Mrs. Arnold. And even if you did buy this apartment, it's not yours now, and I have the papers to prove it. You were happy enough with the settlement when you signed. I'm certain your attorneys told you that you got away with murder, since I didn't ask you for alimony or for one single penny from your books. What about that, Peter? A deal's a deal." She stood with her feet apart, her arms crossed over her breasts.

"Claudia, you're so bitter. You must learn to deal with that burden of anger within you or you'll build up a slush fund that can make you ill and then—"

"Spare me!" she shouted. She pulled herself together and lowered her voice. "Spare me your pop psychology," she said more quietly.

"Do you know anything about the International Brotherhood of Laborers—the IBL?" he asked.

"Don't change the subject, Peter."

"I'm not changing the subject. The IBL is the largest trade union in the United States, perhaps even in the world."

"So?" she asked warily. Peter had always been tricky, and she wondered where the new tack was leading. "What does that have to do with your unwelcome presence here?"

"Everything. The IBL is holding its annual convention in New York City this very moment, and all the hotels are full.

"Surely not all the hotels, Peter. Surely one little room exists somewhere for a famous television celebrity such as Dr. Peter Arnold, Ph.D. S.E."

"S.E.?"

"Schmuck *extraordinaire*."

"Claudia, you're worse that I thought. My poor dear." He came toward her. As he approached she noticed for the first time that he wore a heavy gold chain around his neck. A gold disk with a carved unicorn nestled on the thick mat of blond hairs on his chest. She gave him a look of clear contempt when he tried to slip his arms around her waist, and she stepped back. He followed and wrapped his arms tightly around her. She stood as still as a marble statue, her back erect, every muscle tensed.

"A former colleague of mine at the university has opened his own private practice. He's very good. I know he's booked up solid, but I may be able to talk him into taking one more patient as a favor to me. You have a lot of things to work out, you know—the adoption, your birth mother's denial of you. That kind of influence on the early life of a child should not be underestimated. Feelings of abandonment—real or imagined—color the entire life of the psyche." His voice was calm and infuriatingly patronizing.

"Horsecrap, Peter."

"And that vulgarity. You never talked like that when you were my wife. What kind of people are you seeing now, Claudia?"

"None of your business."

"And you're so defensive, so stiff and unyielding," he said, his voice dripping with concern. He dropped his arms and walked into the bedroom, where she followed him. Peter was back on the bed, lighting another cigarette, perfectly at home with his legs stretched out in front of him.

"Tell me, my dear, do you do a lot of drugs?"

"I don't need drugs; I get high on the thought of you being out of my life. Peter, get dressed and get out of here!"

"I have no place to go, I told you."

"Call your little friend, the graduate student."

"She's married and has a baby."

"Go to Maxwell's Plum and pick up a stewardess."

"It's too late."

"There's no room for you here. I don't even have a couch for you to sleep on."

"I thought we could sleep together in our connubial bed."

"You took our connubial bed to Malibu."

"So I did. But I sold it and bought a water bed. You should try a water bed, Claudia. They're fantastic."

"Out! Out!"

The exhaled smoke from Peter's cigarette formed perfect rings in the still air of the bedroom. Claudia spun on her heels and returned to the living room. She grabbed her handbag and marched back through the bedroom and into the bathroom, where she tore open the medicine chest and pulled out her makeup, shoving it into her purse carelessly. She dropped a toothbrush on top and snapped the bag shut.

"Where are you going?" he asked.

"*I* have friends, at least."

"That man? Who is he?"

Claudia did not answer. She grabbed a blazer from her closet and raced through the living room and out of the front door, slamming it loudly behind her.

"Tina, this is Claudia." she stood at a pay phone on the corner of her street.

"My God, what's wrong? It's after midnight."

"I need a place to stay. May I come over?"

Tina hesitated. "Of course," she replied at last. "But give me forty-five minutes. Is that all right?"

"I'm sorry to interrupt anything, Tina. I wouldn't ask unless it was a real emergency."

"I know. I'd do anything for you, you know that."

"That's why I called you."

"Make it half an hour."

"That jerk. You should never have married him. And you'll have to change the locks now," said Tina, chewing on small bites of whole wheat toast. "Expensive."

"I know. I suppose I should have in the first place, but who would have thought he'd practically break in like that?" They sat eating breakfast at the small round table next to a window that looked out on the East River. Tina's visitor of the previous Friday night was gone by the time Claudia arrived at one in the morning. She had gratefully accepted sleeping space on the couch.

"Are you kidding? Perfectly in character."

"He wasn't always like that, Tina. He was quite nice when he was young and when he was still teaching. He changed after those books made him famous."

"No, he didn't. *You* changed. He was always the

same slimy egotist he is now; you simply couldn't see it. When did you wake up and start to see him the way he really is?''

"The second time I caught him in bed with that woman from his department. The first time—actually, it was a different one the first time—I forgave him. I felt guilty. I was working nights, as the late news was the only television job I could get, and I thought that if I had been there when he came home from school, if I'd just had more time to spend with him, it never would have happened.''

"No, it would have happened anyway. You would have caught him another time. People don't get caught unless they want to be.''

"You really think so?''

"Positively. I know a million guys like Peter. I can even tell you the line he used on the girl to convince her it was safe to go to your apartment.''

Claudia laughed. "I bet you could!''

Tina looked at her sheepishly. "I can't help myself. I love men.''

"I know. I didn't say anything.''

"You didn't have to.'' But at least Tina's eyes were smiling.

"I really do have to dye my hair this afternoon. Maybe you'll help me. Now I really feel like I'm getting old and that every year is showing. Just look at that gray!''

"I'd love to help. We hardly ever get to spend time together.'' Tina was usually busy. She often worked late and she had an unbelievably active social life.

"But right now I have to get dressed,'' said Tina. "I have an appointment with a fortune-teller. You want to come?''

"I don't believe—''

"You don't *have* to believe. Come on; it'll be my treat. I was going to invite you anyway, and here you are."

Tina took her to a building on Ninth Avenue in the West Forties. Claudia expected to find an old gypsy staring into a crystal ball in a shabby storefront, but she was mistaken. The taxi stopped in the middle of the block in front of a modern apartment building, a city-funded victory over urban decay. The fortune-teller was neither old nor a gypsy. She was in her mid-twenties and had fair skin and bright red hair, which was tied back in a pony tail. She greeted them at the door of her clean and sparsely furnished fifth-floor studio apartment. One of her eyes was blue and the other was brown. Other than the disconcerting appearance her eyes lent her face, she was an attractive young woman and perfectly ordinary.

A curtain divided the room in half. The woman asked them to sit on two rattan chairs while she changed her clothes, and then she went behind the curtain.

"What do I ask her?" whispered Claudia.

"Nothing. Don't lead her. Let her tell you," whispered Tina in return. "People who do this for a living are very attuned to picking up hints. Don't give her any, or she'll tell you what she thinks you want to hear."

The fortune-teller emerged from behind the curtain, wearing a black caftan. Her wiry red hair hung loose and framed her face with an aura of mystery. The change was dramatic.

"Who's going to start?"

Tina volunteered. Claudia was pleased, as she wanted to watch the procedure first. The woman set up a card table in front of them, on which she placed an ordinary cigar box that she pushed in front of Tina.

"Open the box, please."

Tina opened the box to reveal a pile of thin plastic rods of the type children use to play Pick Up Sticks.

"Throw the sticks."

Tina removed all the sticks, and the woman put the box on the floor at her feet. Tina tossed the sticks onto the table.

"Pick up five. Any color."

Tina chose five yellow sticks, not bothering when the ones she chose disturbed the jumble of sticks on the table. She held them in a bunch. The woman closed her hand over the sticks and bent them toward her until they made a straight line between her and Tina.

"You have had many men in your life, but you have loved only one. It is long past time to put all thought of him away. You will find another man to love and you will at last be happy. Watch for him, for he will come into your life very soon. Next."

It was all over so quickly that Claudia hoped Tina was not paying the woman too much for the reading. She looked at Tina for some sign of disappointment, but Tina seemed pleased. She was smiling impishly and a dimple showed on her full face. Her sister couldn't really believe that stuff! Heavens, Tina had loved everybody, simply everybody.

"Next."

Claudia gathered the sticks and threw them onto the table as she had seen Tina do. She picked up five of assorted colors. The woman eyed the sticks for a moment before touching them, then she grasped them and bent them toward her. After a pause she asked Claudia to place her hand on the table. She put her own hand on the table, spreading and curving her fingers so that their tips just covered the tips of Claudia's. Irreverently Claudia noticed that the woman bit her nails. The red-haired fortune-teller sat with her eyes closed. There was a long silence during which the only sound was the traffic below on Ninth Avenue. Claudia shifted slightly, but she was careful not to move her fingers.

At last the woman began to speak.

"You are thinking about three people, looking for them, perhaps." She hesitated. "Isn't that right?"

Claudia knew she wasn't supposed to lead the fortune-teller on, so she looked at Tina for direction, but her sister was staring at the colored sticks.

"No, one person." She thought of her natural father. Somehow she had never been as interested in finding him. "Well, perhaps two. I'm definitely not looking for three," she answered.

"Not looking for three . . . but wondering about three. Well, that is not important. Three separate people is what I feel. Are you certain you want me to go on?" The blue eye and the brown eye looked directly into Claudia's.

A slight shiver ran up Claudia's spine and made the skin on her scalp contract. Her fingertips were cold under the dry freckled hand with the ragged fingernails.

I don't believe you, anyway, you charlatan, she thought.

"Of course," she answered lightly.

"You will find *one*," she said with finality.

"Which one?" Tina whispered shakily, after a pause.

Again the woman did not speak for a long minute. "Two are dead," she said at last. "You must believe them when they tell you."

"Who? Who?"

"Whoever tells you. I don't know." She withdrew her hand and dropped her end of the sticks.

"No, who is dead?" Claudia's voice reflected the cold alarm she felt in her breast.

"The woman is dead. Not long ago."

"Oh, my God," Claudia said in a low voice.

Suddenly she pulled her hand away and looked at Tina. Her sister's face was ashen and the happy smile was gone.

"Tina, you don't believe this! Tina!"

"Yes, I believe it," Tina whispered weakly.

"Well, *I* don't!" Claudia stood up and dropped the bundle of ridiculous plastic sticks on the card table. Her legs felt rubbery when she went to the door and waited while Tina paid the woman. She leaned her forehead against the jamb, which felt ice-cold and unreal to her touch. All the searching...the futile trip to Cincinnati...the years of ALMA meetings. *She can't be dead,* she thought. *This is claptrap, superstition, garbage. Tina is the only person I know who believes in this junk.* Nevertheless her legs were still weak when they silently descended to the street level in the elevator.

"How would she know?" asked Claudia.

"It's just a gift certain people have," answered Tina.

"I won't believe it." Those were the only words they spoke during the cab ride back to Tina's apartment.

Claudia called her own place from Tina's to see if Peter had left, but he answered the telephone. However, he told her he would be gone by late afternoon, having at last obtained a hotel room.

"A man has telephoned twice. He wouldn't leave his name."

How strange, she thought, to have Peter answer the telephone when a man called her. She hoped it was Austin Harwood. On second thought she hoped it was *not* Austin. Heaven only knew what Peter had said to the caller.

"If he calls again, give him Tina's number." She hung up the telephone without saying good-bye.

"Peter's still there," she told Tina as she began to apply dark brown dye to the roots of her sister's wet hair. "You *are* getting gray. And your hair seems lighter, almost reddish. Did I tell you Peter's gone totally Hollywood? He wears a big gold chain and he sleeps in a water bed."

"And I bet he starts buttoning his shirts in the vicinity of his navel." Tina laughed.

The telephone rang, and Tina went to the bedroom, out of Claudia's earshot, to answer it. She returned to the bathroom.

"A man for you." Claudia started toward the door. "No, he's coming over. He wants to talk to you."

"Who is it?"

"I forget his name. A lawyer from Harwood and Harwood, I think he said."

Claudia told Tina about meeting Austin and overhearing Glenda Shorter's damning admission. Self-consciously she left out the fact that everything had taken place in a bathroom.

"You're blushing, Claudia. Is there something between you two?"

"There was—until Peter told him that we were married, that is. But I can explain all that when I see him."

"He's not married, then?"

"As if you care, Tina."

"Of course I care. For you. For me, too. You heard what the woman said. I'll find a man soon. From now on no more married men for me. No more students. I need someone steady and reliable.

"And naturally you believed her."

"You didn't answer me, Claudia."

"No, he's not married. At least he told me he wasn't married."

When the doorbell rang, Claudia had finished rinsing the last of the brown dye from Tina's silky hair. Her sister sat on the edge of the tub, dressed in faded blue jeans and an old purple T-shirt blotched with dye stains, while Claudia checked her own hair in the bathroom mirror and pinched her cheeks to make them glow. She rushed to the door to meet Austin Harwood, a growing warmth of excitement within her.

Chapter Four

"Miss Cleary? I'm William Lindhurst. I believe we met in Montauk." Claudia could not hide the crestfallen look on her face from the small balding man.

"I telephoned. You *were* informed I was coming?"

"Oh, yes, Mr. Lindhurst. Come in." She stepped back so he could enter. "I was expecting Mr. Harwood."

"He sent me in his place. He said to tell you that under the circumstances it is better if he does not see you again."

"What?"

"He said when someone is married, it just brings a person heartache." He recited the obviously memorized message. "He said you'd know what he meant."

"I certainly do," she said. "But he's mistaken. Tell him for me that I would like to see him again to explain the confusion. He misunderstood everything. Perhaps you'd let me have his telephone number. I'd like to call him."

"Call the office on Monday; he'll be certain to get the message. But we'll be seeing you in Montauk at the trial on Monday, won't we? You could speak to him then."

"I meant his home telephone number."

"Oh, I couldn't do that, Miss Cleary."

"And you know why!" said Tina pointedly from the door to the bedroom, behind Claudia. "Are *you* married?" she asked Lindhurst directly.

"No," he answered. "No, I am not." He blinked startled eyes behind his glasses.

"Good." She left the room.

"That was my sister," explained Claudia in distraction. Her mind worked frantically. So Harwood *was* married! Thank God nothing had happened, then. But she knew that even if Austin Harwood had told her the truth the previous night, even if he'd said he had seven lovely children, they had passed a point of no return, a point where it was too late to change things between them. She had known from the moment he looked into her eyes in the bathtub, from the moment she felt that electric stab, that thunderbolt, that magic.

"Miss Cleary, I spoke to your husband—"

"My former—" Why explain then? For once she was grateful for Peter's unexpected presence, which had inadvertently saved her from heartache she had seen Tina suffer so often. But Claudia was in charge of her destiny, and it was not too late to change its course.

"Sit down, Mr. Lindhurst. You spoke to my husband?"

"And he told me I could find you here."

"Yes, that's correct. I told him to give you the message. And you want to talk about Glenda Shorter."

"My, you two certainly get to the point quickly." Lindhurst swallowed nervously and looked up as Tina reentered the room. She wore a modest and seductively simple white caftan that demurely covered her from neck to toe. A matching white turban hid her still-damp hair. She sat on the couch next to William Lindhurst and smiled openly at him.

"I wanted to talk to you privately, Miss Cleary," he said, turning to Claudia.

"Tina already knows. You can say anything you want in front of her. But as long as we're speaking frankly, tell me about Mr. Harwood's wife in Connecticut," said Claudia levelly, a flame of anger quite visible in her green eyes to anyone who knew her well.

"You know about his wife? About Connecticut?" He took off his glasses and began to polish them with jerky, rapid movements. Claudia felt sorry for him; he was so obviously nervous. He hadn't seemed nervous when he spoke to her in Montauk, so she assumed that he was unused to being in the presence of women.

"That's all I know. I was hoping you would tell me more."

"I could not do that, Miss Cleary. That's a very sensitive subject. Mr. Harwood would not—"

"Of course not," interrupted Tina. "Can I get you something to drink? May I call you Bill?"

"Most people call me William," he said, nonplussed.

"I'm going to call you Willy." Tina smiled shyly at him. "You look like a Willy to me."

Claudia put her hand over her mouth to stifle a giggle. In spite of all the anger and disappointment, she was afraid she might laugh out loud. Poor Mr. Lindhurst was about to be led to slaughter. Willy the Lamb. Tina would leave him for dead. Tina shot her a warning look replete with daggers while Lindhurst replaced the sparkling glasses on the bridge of his nose. He *was* kind of cute, she thought as she turned her head away to compose herself. Cute, but definitely not Tina's type. Tina went off to a small bar to pour three Dubonnets, for that was what Lindhurst had requested.

"So, Miss Cleary—"

"Something from you first. How did Mr. Harwood find me? He learned a tremendous amount about me in a very short time. I don't like that. I'm a very private person."

"We are an outstanding firm in the field of criminal law. Sometimes we require background information on people in the pursuit of our cases. Usually I take care of that aspect for Mr. Harwood. I don't do the actual legwork, of course; I merely coordinate our data with that which we contract from specialists.'

"I think Willy means a private detective," called Tina from the bar.

"Ah, yes. Yes, that is exactly what I mean." He had the grace to look quite embarrassed.

"He had a private detective spying on me? A private detective!" Claudia stood up, livid.

"Nothing nefarious, I assure you, Miss Cleary."

"Nothing nefarious? Is that what you call it? Nefarious? I call it smarmy and deceitful and—and very, very underhanded! I can't believe he'd do such a thing to me! To anyone! How dare he! How dare *you*!"

"But it's standard when one needs information quickly, Miss Cleary."

"Maybe for criminals... adulterers in divorce cases... things like that. Surely not for ordinary people."

"On the contrary," he said calmly. "We use them for lots of things. Legacies, paternity cases, many absolutely ordinary investigations."

"And are they effective?" she asked in a more normal voice.

"Quite." Mr. Lindhurst relaxed visibly, aware that the storm had mysteriously passed. He sat back on the couch and actually smiled shyly at Tina as she approached them with a tray of drinks balanced in her hands.

"And they always find what they're looking for?"

"I can't recall a single failure."

"All right, Mr. Lindhurst. You want me to keep everything that I overheard, everything Glenda Shorter said, to myself. Is that correct?"

"That's the general idea."

"You've convinced me. I promise to do it."

"I have? But I haven't said anything that would convince you, Miss Cleary."

"I know. But you will. I want you—I want your specialists—to find my mother. Do that, and I'll be quiet."

Tina dropped the tray right in Lindhurst's lap.

She ran to the kitchen and returned with a handful of paper towels, and Claudia watched as Tina began to blot at Lindhurst's suit with rapid dabbing motions. He looked embarrassed and pleased all at once. Claudia figured the little gleam that shone in his eyes signaled sure triumph at having achieved what he was there for, not to mention pleasure at Tina's ministrations.

"So you agree? You'll do it?"

"Leave him alone, Claudia. Sit down, Willy. I'll get you another drink."

"No, really. I have to be getting back to the office."

"But it's Saturday," objected Tina.

"I know. We're still doing briefs for the Shorter trial, so most probably I'll have to work the rest of the day on the case. But perhaps later this evening you'll let me take *you* out for a drink, Miss Cleary."

Claudia rolled her eyes skyward. "What about me? What about my proposition?"

"You are invited as well, Miss Cleary, of course." His voice told her clearly that she was not.

"I don't want to go out with you. I want to know if you accept my conditions, Mr. Lindhurst."

"Certainly I accept your conditions. Come to the office tomorrow." He reached into a pocket of his jacket and extracted a maroon leather card case, handing her his card and needlessly handing one to Tina as well. "I'll be working all day."

"Poor Willy, you work too hard," Tina interjected. He smiled and blushed.

"You bring with you all the data you have. Is your mother lost? My goodness, has she run away?"

"No, Claudia's adopted. She has this crazy idea of finding her natural mother. I've told her she's liable to stir up a lot of trouble, that a lot of things are better left undone, but she won't listen to anyone."

"Then you aren't really sisters? There's a slight resemblance."

"Not by birth," Claudia answered, "but, yes, we're sisters in all other ways."

"We were raised together," Tina said quickly, giving Claudia the warning look again.

Claudia did not bother to explain that Tina had left home not too many years after Claudia had arrived from the orphanage; left to go to New York to set the designing world on its ear. It was obvious that Tina had trained her sights on William Lindhurst, and Claudia imagined her sister did not want the considerable difference in their ages pointed out.

"She has barely any information," Tina said doubtfully. "Just an amended birth certificate and the name of a foundling home."

"That should be no problem," he said. Lindhurst stood and shook hands with each of them. "It's been a pleasure, ladies." Tina walked him to the door.

"You are shameless, shameless, shameless," Claudia admonished Tina upon her return to the living room.

"I know. Isn't he adorable?"

"Of course he isn't. Now I know how fortune-telling works: You listen to the future and then you make it come true. What do you think will happen now?"

"I'm going to marry him."

"Tina, really. I mean the detectives. Will they really find my natural mother?"

"You heard what the woman said, Claudia."

"I refuse to believe that she's dead. I just know inside me, deep inside, that she's alive and that she thinks about me, too."

"If she is alive, I'm sure she does. Who wouldn't? How could a woman give away her child and not think about her all the time? Only someone totally heartless could do that. What shall I wear tonight? Something serious for little Willy. I want to look like I went to Vassar."

"Little Willie doesn't have a chance! Too bad his boss turned out to be married. Tina, you don't *have* any serious clothes." Claudia laughed gaily. She could live without Harwood. She was going to find her mother! She felt it deep within her heart.

The offices of Harwood and Harwood were located in one of the enormous anonymous all-glass buildings on Park Avenue. Claudia's heels echoed mournfully in the empty lobby. A uniformed guard sat at a podium near the elevators with his head buried in the comic strips of the Sunday News. He made her sign a book and then directed her to the elevator that went to the twenty-ninth floor.

The reception desk was empty, and so she went through the double plate glass doors, passed the desk, and wandered down a hall thickly carpeted in gray wool. Door after door stood open to reveal empty offices with books and papers stacked neatly on vacant desks. As she passed each one she read the discreet brass plates beside the doors, searching vainly for William Lindhurst's name. She arrived at the end of the hall. The total silence was eerie.

"Looking for me?" A voice—a deep, melodious voice—came from the corner office.

Claudia stopped in the doorway. He sat with his feet upon papers that were scattered over an enormous desk. He wore blue jeans and a casual taupe-colored pullover sweater. He jumped to his feet.

"No, Mr. Harwood," she said coldly. "I'm looking for Mr. Lindhurst. I have an appointment with him."

"I know. He isn't here, but I can take care of everything for you." Austin crossed the wide office and walked toward her. Two walls were sheer glass, revealing a stunning panorama of the Manhattan skyline to the south and the west. The late afternoon fall sun slanted across the gray carpet.

"I'd rather wait for him, if it's all the same to you." Why was he so attractive? Why was he already married? *"All the best ones are."* The words of the saleswoman in Bergdorf's came back to her. Too bad she hadn't remembered that conversation when she had propositioned him two days earlier. His sweater was cashmere, she could tell as he approached. The wool had that special glow that only cashmere had. She wondered if his wife bought his clothes for him. If so, her taste was magnificent, for even in blue jeans, Harwood was clearly an aristocrat. She would just say farewell and go. Claudia stepped into the office to meet him; suddenly her feet seemed to have a will of their own.

"You'll have a long wait. He actually took the day off. I couldn't believe it! He never takes time off." He was at her side. She smelled the scent of lemon and soap, the distinctive odor that had attracted her originally on the train. Somewhere she'd read that the olfactory attraction was primeval, specific; that the recognition only existed between certain people and that only if it existed did nature make a match. Well, nature made mistakes, didn't she?

Austin laid a hand on her arm. She felt his warmth even through the layers of the fabric of her coat and of her blouse. "Come in and sit down. Let me take your coat." He lifted the raincoat from her shoulders. She thought he left his hands on her a fraction of a second longer than was necessary, but perhaps it was a sort of afterburn. She still felt the glow where his arm had touched hers. How could he be so cool? He must know she had found out about his wife by then.

Austin led her to a long couch against the wall. Claudia sat down and was surprised to find herself sinking into goose-down pillows. He crossed to the desk and found a yellow legal pad among the scattered papers and returned, extracting a pair of horn-rimmed glasses from a shirt pocket as he crossed the room toward her. He settled into the pillow at her side, very close to her—so close, she felt the warmth of his nearness. Claudia stared at the sun-bleached hairs on one wrist, mesmerized by the way they grew. She was crazy to be there, so close to Austin. She would tell him to forget it—forget the search, forget the promise, forget that she had ever overheard Glenda Shorter. She had to get out of there. She was having trouble breathing.

Claudia formed the words on her tongue. "Do you sleep here on this couch?" Had she really said that? There was someone else inside of her pulling the strings, trying to make her do things she did not want to do.

"Sometimes I take short naps in the afternoons. It's very comfortable." She imagined his lean body stretched out on the couch, his eyes closed. She saw herself lean over him, kiss his lips slowly and tenderly to awaken him. Her nipples hardened at the image, and she looked down at them under her silk blouse. He was staring at her breasts beneath the thin fabric. She turned her eyes away. A thrill went through her, and she shivered involuntarily.

"You're cold," Austin said in a low voice. He put one arm around her, and at his touch the dam broke. She turned to him at the exact moment he lowered his lips to hers. He kissed her as if he were drinking in her whole soul through his mouth, and she responded as if she were a person who had wandered for days through a desert, insane for the liquid of his breath. His tongue met hers, and they pushed their mouths together as if in a cosmic game of strength and hunger. Claudia heard the hiss of silk in the silent office when he pulled her blouse free from the waistband of her skirt. Then his long fingers were on her back, caressing the flesh, covering her with his warmth. He pulled one hand free and began to unbutton the tiny pearl buttons of the blouse, slowly and surely. The blouse fell open, and he slipped his tanned hand inside and pushed aside the silk in an unhurried, dreamlike motion. Her breasts were free to his gaze. She felt a flush creep up from her chest to suffuse her neck and her cheeks, and she imagined that his eyes saw the rosy glow against the milky whiteness of the rest of her skin. Claudia looked down as he lowered his mouth to one pointed breast and slowly kissed it, tracing his tongue around and around in a circle until the nipple rose to a greater hardness than she thought possible. The slanting evening sun glinted off the gossamer hairs on her skin, changing them into a fine down of spun gold. Claudia watched his wide mouth cover the tracery of veins and the dusky tip. Someone moaned, and she heard her own voice echo in the still room. Austin switched his avid mouth to the other breast, and she moaned again.

He removed her thin silk blouse lingeringly, deliberately, as she knew he would, and she watched his long fingers while he set it on the floor next to the couch. Then he placed his open palms on her breasts and rotated them slowly against Claudia's nipples, never taking his eyes from her face. His mouth was half opened and his usually clear blue eyes were opaque, the eyes of a willing subject cast into a trance by a hypnotist. The ends of his lashes were bleached to near invisibility by the same sun that had tanned his angular features, except for the lines of white around his eyes. She ran the tip of her index finger down the distinctive scar at the edge of his right eye, wondering again at its origin. Someday, perhaps, she would ask him. He seemed to awaken when she touched the deep indentation, and pulled off his sweater in one quick gesture and threw it on the floor. Gently he pushed her until she lay back with her head on the armrest of the goose-down sofa. He buried his head in the sensitive area of her midriff and flicked his tongue over her skin in short sweeps. The air cooled the moist path he delineated as his warm tongue moved surely back over her rib cage and up toward her breasts. His touch was like a searing flame on her already fevered skin.

"Not here, not now," Claudia moaned, looking around frantically at the open door and then through the transparent walls that looked out onto the steel-and-glass canyon of Park Avenue.

Harwood stood and on silent feet crossed the wide office to the door, which he closed and then locked behind him. He leaned against the door and looked across the room to where she lay. His eyes came slowly into focus.

"You got my message and you came, anyway." His voice was rough with emotion.

"I—I came to see Lindhurst. When I saw you, I couldn't help myself. This is wrong. This is crazy. I should have left as soon as I saw you here. I don't know what got into me, but I don't want to leave. I—"

"You're right. It is wrong and it is crazy. Heartache, isn't that what you called it?" He came back to her side and knelt. He took one hand where it dangled to the floor and ran his fingers lightly up the skin of her inner arm until his hand reached her bare shoulder. He grasped her firmly, yet painlessly and looked searchingly into her eyes. "But these things happen. He'll never have to know. You can trust me."

At first she did not understand. Then she realized he meant Peter. Peter would never have to know.

"But Peter's not my husband anymore. We're divorced. He was playing a sick game with me. You simply got in the middle, that's all. He practically broke into my apartment and he's gone now. I'm free to do as I like, Austin."

He smiled and kissed the palm of her hand.

"Then come back to my place. No one will disturb us there. You're right about here. I don't want to make love here like"—he hesitated—"like two furtive people involved in a cheap office romance."

"But—"

"But, what? Don't you want to come with me?"

"Oh, yes, but—"

"And I want to see your hair. You promised me, you know," he reminded her in a voice so low, it was nearly a whisper.

"Yes, but what about your wife?"

He looked into her eyes. "Claudia, I told you I don't have a wife. Is that why you said it was wrong and crazy?" She nodded. "Why won't you believe me?"

"I *do* believe you. That is, I *did* believe you, but Willy said—"

"Who the hell is Willy?" Irritation colored Austin's quick question.

"Lindhurst, William Lindhurst."

"Willy! You've got to be kidding!" He laughed aloud at the nickname. "Willy." His tone had definitely changed. "And what did Willy say, for God's sake?" Claudia was afraid of the mercurial note of harshness she heard.

"Nothing. He said nothing, really. I simply got the impression you had a wife, that's all. If you aren't married, how could I have misunderstood? Can you explain that to me?"

"I don't have a wife." He enunciated each syllable clearly, as a teacher would speak to a slow-witted child. "You may believe or not believe, that's your choice. That's all I will say on the subject—ever. Those are my terms. Do you accept them?" His eyes were hard, darkened almost to the color of polished steel.

A heavily charged moment passed. Claudia longed to believe him. She longed to lie beside him while he made love to her. Beside him...beneath him...above him. Vivid images flitted through her imagination. Her legs trembled with denied desire; her breathing was still erratic from the moments that had preceded the unwelcome interlude to their feverish caresses. He awaited her answer. Did she believe him? She tried to be as honest with herself as possible. She searched her conscience for direction, weighing the evidence—Bergdorf's, Lindhurst's hesitation, Austin's strange responses. No, she didn't believe him. She knew better. With all the instincts of a woman on her own, she knew he was married. And yet . . . and yet . . .

"Yes." She exhaled audibly. That person spoke again, that other Claudia deep within her.

"I never lie." He grinned like a young, mischievous boy and his teeth were very white against his sun-bronzed skin.

"Not even in the courtroom?" She traced the scar with the tip of her finger. She knew she was going to be very sorry.

"Sometimes I shade the truth a little," he admitted.

"Don't we all," she said quietly.

Austin's car was in the parking garage beneath the building. She had expected the Rolls-Royce, but she was mistaken. He drove a thirty-year-old MG, a shining classic.

"This is not an antique," he corrected her with a grin when she used the word. "This is my very first car. I bought it with my own money when I was a student at Yale—it wasn't new then—and I have had it ever since. The only trouble is, it's getting old and the top won't go up anymore. Hope you don't mind the wind too much." The racing-green car roared up the steep driveway to the street. He turned left onto Park, and then went uptown, sailing through five green lights in a row. The sensation of riding so close to the ground was strange to Claudia, yet after a few minutes she decided it was pleasant to feel every bump and seam in the avenue. The wind whipped the loose wisps of her hair.

"And the Rolls?" she shouted above the wind and the rumble of the engine.

"That belongs to the firm," he explained. "Part of

the image. People like their doctors, their lawyers, and their accountants to look rich. Gives them a sense of security."

"I never thought of that." She realized that what he said was probably true. Even a thirty-year-old sports car seemed luxurious to Claudia. Her mother had driven either a basic-model Ford or a Dodge all the years she was growing up. They had not been poor people, but their lives were on the austere side, and she knew that that was one of the reasons Tina had left their home in Cincinnati. Tina liked the finer things in life. She had worked hard to achieve her more than modest success as a sought-after designer and she deserved to enjoy the fruits of her labor. Tina had told her that their mother actually had an untapped streak of frivolity and gaiety in her soul, a revelation Claudia found hard to believe. Cynthia Cleary had been somber and serious for as long as Claudia could remember, yet Claudia knew her adoptive mother loved her very much.

Tina always said that her spirit had been broken by her husband, a mean and petty man who had made Tina's and her mother's lives miserable. Claudia did not remember him, as he had died just before or just after she had been adopted into the family. They had always been vague, so very vague about all the details, as if a shameful secret surrounded her birth.

"What are you thinking about?" He laid his hand on her knee, causing the warmth she had grown to welcome to burn there anew.

"My family. My mother."

"Which one?"

"My adoptive mother. I think I should go to see her. I owe it to her to explain about my search, to tell her that I love her and that nothing will ever change that. Perhaps she'd be hurt if she found out that I was looking for my natural mother, especially if someone else told her."

"When will you go?" Austin turned right onto East Seventy-fourth Street and drove more slowly.

"After the trial is over."

He pulled the car up onto the sidewalk in the middle of a tree-shaded block, jumping out and unlocking the door of a garage on the first floor of a private house. On the door the international symbol for "No Parking" was painted in black and white and red. He reentered the car and pulled it into the small garage.

"I am truly impressed. Your own garage!"

Austin flushed happily. Then he turned to her with a serious look on his angular features.

"You know what Lindhurst told you about the private investigators?" Claudia nodded. "You're going to find your mother very soon. Are you certain you're ready? Absolutely certain?"

His concern touched her deeply.

"I'm absolutely certain."

Austin walked around to the passenger side of the small car and opened the door for Claudia. He extended a hand and helped her out of the low car, then he kissed her tenderly and led the way into the house.

"Are you hungry? I have some smoked salmon." They entered from the garage directly into the kitchen. The walls were of exposed brick. Burnished copper pans hung like stalactites from the ceiling. Twilight filtered through the high windows, and Claudia realized the kitchen must have been at the half-basement level.

"Yes. No. I don't know. I'm a little shy, Austin. I'm not used to the single life, I guess."

"Neither am I," he confessed. "We'll learn together."

She was tempted to pursue the mysterious comment, but she remembered his admonition. His terms, he had said.

"Have you lived here long?"

"Forever. I was born in this house. No, not really. I was born at Flower and Fifth Avenue Hospital, just a few blocks from here, but I have lived here all my life."

"And your parents?"

"My father—he was the other Harwood in Harwood and Harwood—he's dead. My mother lives in Jamaica."

"Queens?"

"No, British West Indies. She hates the New York weather. She comes up in the fall only to shop. She'll be here in a few weeks. I'm not hungry. Come upstairs with me. I want to shower." She followed him through the kitchen into a long, narrow dining room that overlooked Seventy-fourth Street. A burnished walnut table gleamed in the fading light. Heavy Georgian candelabra sat every few feet on its polished expanse.

They went up six steps and turned at a landing. On the other side of the staircase she caught a glimpse of the living room, a fleeting impression of red Oriental rugs, Chippendale furniture, and a marble fireplace. Claudia had never been in a private house in Manhattan, only in similar buildings that had been converted years ago into so-called railroad flats—long, narrow, claustrophobic walk-ups. No feeling of claustrophobia existed in Austin's home. The rooms were long and narrow, but the overall feeling was spacious and graceful.

The house was divided into half stories, and its architecture confused Claudia. After they went up to another landing, Claudia noted that a door was open to reveal a library, bookshelves, and another fireplace—a very masculine room.

"Who decorated this house? It's beautiful."

"Lots of people. My wi—my mother, her mother— all sorts of people had a hand in the stew." She watched his broad back on the stairs in front of her. She had heard him almost say the word. It was not yet too late to back out. All she had to do was stop then and demand an explanation.

"You mean your grandmother lived here, too?" What was wrong with her? She shook her head in amazement in the gloom. Chance after chance was slipping by, and she was not attempting to extricate herself. She was falling down the tunnel into—what?

"Yes, the house was a wedding gift to her from my grandfather. He made a lot of money in shipping."

"I'm envious."

"Don't be. They weren't happy people. None of us has been. It's true what the old saw says, that money doesn't buy happiness."

"I wasn't thinking of the money," she answered. "You know who your family is—grandparents, aunts, uncles. I don't know anything about mine."

He turned at the top of the stairs and waited for her.

"I never thought of that." He kissed the top of her head as she reached his level.

"This is my room," he said, pulling her by the hand into a room that was wider than all the others because it extended across the entire back of the house. She walked with him to the window that overlooked a small enclosed garden. The back windows of a similar house behind a high garden wall faced it. The leaves of a large maple tree were beginning to turn red and gold and already some had fallen onto the cast-iron garden furniture three stories below.

"I used to camp out down there when I was a boy." Austin stood behind Claudia and slipped his arm around her waist.

"A regular urban guerrilla." She smiled.

"You made me a promise, remember?"

"I've made you a lot of promises in the last few days." She stared out the window at lights beginning to go on in the apartments across the way.

"You said you'd let me take your hair down. Will you? Now?" He whispered gently into her ear. She felt his sweet breath on her neck.

LAST EXIT BEFORE FREEWAY. Incongruously the words of a sign she'd seen once in Los Angeles flashed before her eyes. *LAST EXIT.*

"What did you say?" he asked her quietly. She must have spoken out loud.

"The little pin. Just pull out the little pin that holds the comb."

Austin undid the button and the zipper that closed her skirt, and the garment fell to the floor at her feet. He reached in front of her, and she watched his long fingers fumble with the buttons of her silk blouse; he was unaccustomed to the angle at which a woman's shirt closes. At last the blouse was open and he raised his hands up to her breasts and held them. His hands were warm and covered their fullness. She sighed with desire for him. He slipped her blouse off and laid it on a chair next to the window, never moving from his position behind her. She helped him with her panty hose, rolling them down over her waist and hips, her back still to him in the quickly darkening room. She stepped out of the hose and dropped them onto the floor.

"Someone will see us," she whispered.

"No, no one will see. It's already dark."

At last his hands touched her head. First he held them there for a long moment, then he removed the pin with his right hand and the comb with his left. Her auburn hair tumbled down to her shoulders and past the middle of her back. She heard him sigh as he lifted her silken tresses in one hand.

"Your hair is very beautiful."

Claudia was silent and her knees trembled.

Austin dropped the heavy hair and stepped away. She did not hear him move, because the rug on the floor was thick and its depth muffled the sound of his footsteps, but she missed his warm aura immediately and she knew he was standing several feet behind her.

"Turn around," he said in a low voice.

She closed her eyes and turned slowly to face him.

"Oh, you're so beautiful," Austin said at last with a long and audible sigh. "Words escape me. You're so beautiful."

When Claudia opened her eyes she saw his face in the glow from the city lights that filtered through the windows behind her. The shadow of the muntins crossed his forehead and his broad chest. She lifted her arms and reached behind her head to pull her hair forward so that the tresses hung in front, fanning out to cover her white shoulders and the rise of her rounded breasts. His eyes were alive with desire, his lips half-parted as his breath came more quickly.

"Come to me, then."

Austin obeyed immediately. He yanked off the taupe pullover and tossed it on the floor. Claudia opened his shirt and buried her face in the hairs of his chest, deeply inhaling his scent, then she opened the cold brass buckle of his leather belt and the zipper of his blue jeans and pushed them down as he had done with her skirt. The jeans fell to the rug with the muted clunk of brass. Austin removed what remained of his clothing and went to her, embracing her tightly against his naked desire.

He lifted her easily and carried her to the bed, placing her gently on the rough spread that covered it. Then he lay beside her, half on top of her body, anchoring her legs with his, his elbow propped on the pillow next to the one on which her head rested. With his free hand he gathered a thick length of her hair and arranged it on her breast so that it covered one pointed nipple. He did the same with a length from the other side of her head, then he buried his face in the hair that splayed across her breasts, resting his head near her heart. She knew he heard the beat of her blood as it coursed erratically through her veins. Her heart pounded in her own ears. She caressed the back of his neck slowly, moving her hand back and forth in unhurried rhythm as she ran her other hand through his close-cropped hair, soothing, easing.

"Are you afraid?" he mumbled into her auburn hair.

"A little," she admitted softly, continuing the smooth motion of her hand on his skin.

"Don't be. I won't hurt you, I promise."

Promises, promises. "I never lie." "I won't hurt you." The last exit is long gone.

"I know what I'm doing," she whispered unevenly. "Come whatever."

Austin unveiled one nipple and began to kiss it gently, trailing the fingers of his left hand down her midriff to her abdomen and beyond until her legs began to twitch and tremble with increasing desire for him—a rising hunger like nothing she had ever known. Her nipple hardened, and he moved his mouth to her other breast after she had pulled the long auburn hair away to give him access to her skin. His fingers teased her thighs as he ran them lightly up and down their lengths, slowly nearing the muscles that arched to his touch, muscles that suddenly had a life of their own, out of Claudia's control.

Shivering with need, she wrapped her arms firmly around his neck and pulled him to her. She smelled the lemons and was lost in a cloud of his clean, fresh scent, which was subtly, delightfully changed by his desire. He covered her body with his hard, lean frame, and she was stunned to feel the same trembling within him. He held her head firmly between his wide hands and looked deeply into her eyes.

"Yes, come whatever," he whispered to her. Austin lowered his mouth to Claudia's and entered her at the same moment.

Chapter Five

"Claudia, are you awake?" Austin called from somewhere far away. She opened her eyes slowly and peered
around the softly lighted room. Beige draperies had
been pulled across the windows overlooking the
garden. Their clothing lay abandoned on a pale Kirman
rug patterned with graceful scrolls and leafy arabesques
in muted shades of rose and mint ivory.

"Have I been asleep for long?" Claudia had drifted
into a hypnotic daze that had led to a light sleep after
they made love. The sudden recall of his touches and
caresses on her body sent a violent thrill coursing
through her. She sat up on the bed and pushed her long
hair back from her face. A soft blanket covered her. "Is
it late?"

"No." Austin glanced at a small gold carriage clock
that rested on a mahogany table at the side of the bed.
"Barely nine o'clock. We have the entire evening
ahead of us." He smiled happily and approached the
bed to sit at her side. He arranged the blanket around
her, tucking it under her legs and smoothing it over her
breasts. "I thought you might feel cold," he said, indicating the coverlet.

"Thank you." She smiled shyly at him. What could
she say then? Perhaps she should buy a copy of Peter's

book on sexual etiquette for the single person, as she had never been in the situation before. She wanted to tell him that he had led her down paths of erotic ecstasy she had only read about, but had never experienced; that he had tapped reserves of sensuality within her that she never dreamed existed; that her only other experiences—those with Peter—had often left her feeling frustrated and used. She wondered if Austin had felt the same shaking pleasure surge through his limbs when he made love to her. There was no way to ask. She would bite off her tongue before she mouthed the old cliché so often satirized: "How was it for you?"

Instead she took his tanned right hand between both of hers and raised it to her lips. She kissed the palm. The silk robe he wore gaped open, revealing his chest. She slipped her arm between the lapels and laid a hand on his ribs just below his heart. He leaned across and kissed her tenderly on the lips.

"You must be hungry."

"I am. I'll put my clothes on—"

"No, stay where you are. I'll be right back." But he sat at her side for a moment longer, his blue eyes drinking in the auburn hair that covered her shoulders and breasts and still sprayed halfway across the other pillow as well. He stood and left the room. Claudia looked around at the bedroom and said silently, *This is the room of a man, a man alone.* Chocolate-brown flannel covered the walls. The floor was carpeted in beige, and the dusky Kirman was placed in the center of the room, creating an island of warmth and color in the sea of its otherwise austere elegance. Against one brown wall stood a large eighteenth-century desk, its hinged lid open to reveal an overflow of books and papers.

There hadn't been time for him to descend to the kitchen and back, yet when Austin returned he was carrying a rattan bed tray covered with a white damask napkin. Moving to where Claudia reclined on the double bed, he placed the tray over her legs, adjusting its feet until they rested on the cover at either side of her thighs. He turned on a black-shaded brass candlestick lamp on the bedside table.

While uncovering the dish on the tray Austin said, "We'll have to share the salmon. I wasn't expecting company for dinner." Pale pink slices of the delicate fish rested on an almost translucent gold-rimmed plate. A slight aroma of woodsmoke rose to Claudia's nostrils. He cut off a small piece and offered it to her, extending a heavy sterling fork to her lips. She leaned forward. Afterward he took a piece for himself, using the same fork. Their eyes meshed, and her body went as boneless as a cat with the memory of their dinner at La Colombe d'Or, the memory of his velvet lips on the hardened nipples of her breasts, the memory of her face buried in his lemon-scented hair. She exhaled unevenly.

"Delicious."

He offered her another morsel and took one for himself. "I caught it myself last spring in Scotland. I always fish there in April. This was the last of the batch, and I'm glad you're here to share it with me."

"How do you smoke them?"

"The gillie—the guide—smokes them and then ships them to me. Do you like to fish? Perhaps you could come with me next time."

Next time...Scotland...a future with Austin...plans for April, and it was not yet October. Claudia's heart turned over in her breast. "I've never fished. Would you show me how?"

"I'd like to show you many things. You probably have many things to show me."

"Oh, I don't think so...." What did she know to show Austin, who had everything? No doubt he had already visited every destination of interest in the vast world that awaited the tourist. No doubt he dined often with the well known and the well connected. No doubt he was third-generation Yale at least, and he boasted a pedigree as long as her bare arm—a lineage inscribed somewhere in the echoing halls of the New York Genealogical Society.

"How do you know? You don't know everything that interests me yet," he said softly. No, all she knew was how his hard, lean body felt when he crushed her beneath him on the rough spread that covered the bed, how his gentle fingers touched her as they sought out the secret hidden pleasure centers of her body, how those same long fingers looked in the soft light as they closed around the stem of the paper-thin wineglass on the tray, how...

Austin held the wineglass to Claudia's lips. She drank the dry, ice-cold wine, tasting the rolling green velvet hills of Viña del Mar on her tongue.

"Chilean?"

"Yes." He seemed pleased that she recognized the wine. Then, to her surprise, he gently lowered the soft blanket and poured a few drops of the amber liquid between her breasts and without a word he licked them from her skin, making strong motions with his tongue. Deep down Claudia had always held the belief that a woman could easily control her desire, that a woman was meant only to respond to the wants of a man, but a new glow, a strange and mysterious languor, sprang to life within her at his unexpected touch, and she cared about nothing, absolutely nothing but following the call of her flesh. Her body opened to him, and she buried her face in his hair and held his head tightly against her.

"You make me a little crazy," Austin explained with a sheepish grin, sitting up. Claudia put one hand under his chin and held his face so that she could look into his intense blue eyes, and she felt as if she were drowning in their deep pools.

"It must be contagious, then." And she knew she *was* crazy to do what she had done. But she was not sorry. Her heart told her that she would do it again. And again. And again.

Austin led her down the turning stairs to the kitchen. Claudia was wrapped in a robe he had lent her—not of fine silk like the one he wore but of a dark red Viyella that rubbed her skin pleasantly. The black-and-white checked marble floor of the kitchen was cool on the soles of Claudia's bare feet. She sat on a stool at a butcher block counter in the center of the large kitchen and watched his broad back and strong calves as he dished up two portions of watermelon sherbet. He sat at right angles to her, and their bare knees touched while they ate the refreshing ice.

"I'd like it very much if you would spend the night here," he said. She realized from his choice of words that Austin was as shy about the situation as she. Evidently there was a lot to learn about the man, who had been so supremely confident when seated at the side of her bathtub. How things had changed in the past few days! But hadn't she known it would happen from their first stormy encounter?

"Tomorrow Lindhurst and I plan to leave for Montauk at six. We figured that going against the traffic, that would give us plenty of time—"

"Montauk! I'd forgotten all about it. Tomorrow is Monday. I'm not packed. I have to go home." Had she only known him since Thursday? Truly there was a new Claudia emerging from the ashes of her old life, a new Claudia who had allowed herself to be swept away by the handsome, virile man whose knee brushed hers and made her skin tingle. She laid the cold spoon against her tongue.

"We'll leave earlier. We'll stop on the way so you can pack. Lindhurst won't mind waiting, and that's what the chauffeur gets paid for, anyway."

"Oh, no. I couldn't do that! He'd know we'd been together all night and he'd tell my sister. I don't feel like sharing—" Claudia hesitated. "I don't want to share what we've had between us with anyone."

"What we *have* between us," Austin corrected her, covering her hand with his. The same thrill she felt when he had mentioned fishing in April went through her. "Your sister? How does he know your sister?"

"He's taking her out, I think." She smiled at the memory of shy Mr. Lindhurst—Willy the Lamb—in Tina's clutches. "I'll bet if you ask, you'll find he was with her today and that's why he didn't go in to the office."

"No kidding! As far as I know he hasn't been out with a woman since his wife died. It must be ten years at least. Is it serious?"

"Well, they just met, but, yes, I think it's serious. However, he doesn't know it yet." She laughed. "I didn't realize he had been married; he seemed like the perennial bachelor to me. What was his wife like? How did she die?"

"She was like him, very serious and quiet. She was a historian. They never had any children, and she died from pneumonia, of all things. You never think of young people dying from illnesses. Usually it's accidents."

"How sad. It must have been extremely painful to

lose his wife in the prime of her life like that. Poor Willy."

"Yes, it was sad for Lindhurst, but it's not always the worst thing that could happen. Sometimes it's a blessing."

"What do you mean?"

Austin did not answer. "Your sister will probably be good for him. He needs someone to love him."

"Believe me, she's not at all like his wife was. History! She could write her autobiography, and it would be a best-seller." She laughed and picked up the empty bowls and carried them to the sink, where she ran warm water into them.

"That's what a man needs—a total change. It's a disaster to make the same mistake twice. Just leave the dishes. The cook will take care of them in the morning."

Claudia followed him back to the bedroom and began to dress. Austin asked her again if she would stay, but she insisted that their privacy was important to them both. At last he agreed, after she promised to be ready at six so that the Rolls-Royce could be available for her for the long drive to the tip of Long Island.

"I want to see you early in the morning. It's not the same as having you asleep at my side, but I'll take it—for now."

Austin drove her downtown in the MG and Claudia let her auburn hair trail behind her in the cold night air.

"Don't try to come to the door with me," she suggested. In any case, there was nowhere on Gramercy Park Square to park the dark green sports car, so he pulled it into a restricted zone in front of The Players, the elegant and venerable actors' social club, and turned off the engine.

"I'll call you early so you'll be ready by six." He put

an arm around her shoulder and drew her closer despite the stick shift, which separated them. "I—I don't know what to say. I get tongue-tied around you. I'd be a disaster in the courtroom if you were my adversary."

"Don't say anything, then." Claudia laid two fingers on Austin's lips. Touching him was heady enough, and thinking about his lips, his mouth on her fevered skin made a thrill shoot down her limbs. Her knees began to tremble again, and they embraced awkwardly in the small English car.

Austin leaned across her and opened the door on the passenger side of the car, and she climbed out, momentarily dizzy. Looking down into his blue eyes, Claudia was reluctant to leave him. She knew she was becoming addicted to him, was perhaps already addicted, and was planning to increase the dose.

Claudia turned and ran into the building where she lived.

Later she packed for a week in Montauk: a gray suit, a tan suit, a silk dress that coordinated with the gray jacket, complementary blouses, cosmetics, and cologne. She added slacks and an Irish knit sweater, as they wouldn't be in the courtroom all the time. Claudia chose two silk nightgowns Tina had given her after Jake bought a small lingerie factory in Hong Kong, and she ran her hands over the embroidered bodice of one gown dreamily. While packing mechanically one small part of her mind was on the needs for the trial, the rest on Austin Harwood, but Claudia remembered to put sketch pads, pencils, and colored charcoal in her leather envelope.

When the suitcase and the envelope were ready, she carried them to the barely furnished living room and laid them on the floor. Claudia chose a mauve mohair cape from the hall closet, thinking that there was no need for a coat on the car trip to Montauk, yet she had no idea what the capricious autumn weather had in store for the week. After she was finished, Claudia wandered around the apartment at loose ends, her psyche charged with a newfound energy that she seemed unable to expel. Although she wasn't hungry, she looked unseeingly into the refrigerator twice, and although her body was tired, she did not care to sleep. At last she bathed and climbed into bed, snuggling down under the quilt, and closed her eyes. Claudia knew she would never sleep: there remained unfinished business.

The telephone at the side of the bed rang, and Austin's melodious voice came over the wire.

"Are you in bed?"

"Yes." Claudia smoothed her knee-length nightshirt down her long thigh, smoothed it over and over as she listened.

"So am I. I wish you were here with me."

"Yes. So do I."

"Good night, my little orphan."

She smiled at his choice of endearment. "Good night, my sweet."

Only then did she fall into a deep and dream-studded sleep, in which his long fingers were twined in her hair, his face was buried in her curls, and his hands removed the comb and loosened her long auburn tresses. A dream in which his arms were around her was so vivid, she felt his breath on her neck, felt his warmth on her limbs, felt the mat of hair on his chest, felt the cold and heavy chain around his neck—

Claudia sat up in bed and flicked on the light, closing her eyes in pain at its intrusion and opening them just as quickly.

"Peter, you lowlife, get out of my bed!" she shouted.

"Come on, Claudia, I've missed you so much. Don't tell me you haven't missed me, too." Peter put his hands on her waist, but she pushed his bare arms away. "I haven't missed you, I don't want to see you, and I want you out of my bed this minute! How dare you come back here again! How dare you!" The locksmith wasn't going to be there until Tuesday. She had already made arrangements with the superintendent to let him in, had already written out his shocking fee on a check that was pinned to the message pad next to the telephone in the kitchen.

"I don't believe you. I know you feel the same way I do. We had something beautiful together. Why should we let the divorce spoil what we had? We could start again together—not get married again," he quickly clarified, "but you and I could have a very nice relationship."

"The divorce didn't spoil what we had, Peter. The divorce validated what our marriage was—a total sham! Are you getting out of here, or do I have to call the police?" Claudia jumped from the bed and backed up against the wall. Her fists were clenched and her hands shook with smoldering fury.

"Calm down," Peter said in a patronizing voice. "The police won't come, anyway. They never interfere in domestic squabbles, you know that. In any case, I'd simply tell them that you are my wife, that you had a little too much to drink, and that we were having a lovers' tiff."

Claudia knew that what he had said was the truth. The police would not help. If by accident or by reason of unwonted compassion they did respond to her telephone call, Peter would say all those things, all those things and more, and the police would believe him—a television celebrity, a household name in pop psy-

chology—just as the public believed the claptrap he
espoused in his best-selling books. And it was much
too late at night to call Tina and beg her hospitality
again, so Claudia resigned herself to Peter's odious
presence.

"Your presence here is totally unwelcome. You—
you naked in my bed, in my home—are obscene!" She
pulled a pillow off the bed with one hand and the quilt
with another and she marched to the door that led to
the living room, turning to face him as he lay in *her*
bed, on *her* flowered sheets. She couldn't wait to
change the sheets. No, she'd throw them in the trash.
"I never want to see you again, Peter. I want you out of
here in the morning. Out forever. I'm having the locks
changed, so don't try to come back. I'm going to speak
to my lawyer about getting an injunction against this
harassment and I don't care what kind of scandal I
cause, because I have nothing to lose. You have already
made a fool of me publicly, God knows how often, so
what's the difference?"

She reached into the room and grabbed the door-
knob and she slammed the door behind her and stood
listening to the sound of plaster crumbling between the
walls of the soundly built old apartment house.

Lord almighty, he was an egotist! The thought of his
hand on her waist gave her nausea. She crossed to the
area rug in the center of the living room, dropping the
pillow and quilt there, and continued on to the kitchen,
all hope of sleep gone. Her stomach quivered with rage.
She looked at her hands as she filled a blue enamel tea
kettle; they were still shaking. She turned on the radio
to check the time and found it was only two thirty. She
had to sleep—she'd never make it through the long day
in court unless she did. Also, she knew a sleepless
night would leave her skin sallow, her eyes circled with

dark smudges, and she didn't want Austin to see her in that condition. After she turned off the stove, Claudia returned to the living room, lay on the rug, and rolled herself up in the blue quilt on the floor.

Peter was undeserving of the emotional energy he was costing her, and she forced him from her thoughts. She made her mind picture the red-haired fortune-teller and her ludicrous jumble of colored plastic sticks on the torn plastic top of a cheap card table. Claudia had chosen two blue sticks, one red, and two yellow. What possible significance could the colors have? None. Superstition, pure and fanciful, primitive and ultimately...ultimately unbelievable. And yet she wanted to believe that some people possessed the gift to part the clouds of the future and peer with comprehension into their wispy secrets. She wanted to believe it all, for Tina's sake, if Tina found comfort in prophesy, but for herself she held back, because Claudia denied what that woman claimed to see. She refused to accept that she would arrive at the culmination of her exhaustive search only to find the long-sought-for quarry already dead. And the end was so close. Indeed, already she had taken the final, fateful step like a pilgrim casting off from his homeland in search of the New World, aware of the day on which the water in the stores exactly equaled the water already consumed on the voyage—the last chance to turn around—what airline pilots called the moment of abort past which remained no choice but to lift the plane into the air and soar all alone—on an orphan voyage.

Claudia drifted off to sleep at last.

The telephone and the clock radio in the bedroom exploded at the exact minute. Claudia opened her eyes at their dual sounds and for a few seconds wondered what she was doing on the living room floor. Then she remembered Peter asleep behind the bedroom door and she unwrapped herself frantically from the quilt and raced to the kitchen telephone, knowing that Peter most definitely had the gall to pick up the phone on the bedside table.

"Did you sleep well?" There was no need for him to identify himself; she would have known his beguiling voice anywhere. The music from the clock radio became silent behind the bedroom door.

"I had a lot of dreams of you. And one nightmare," she added, thinking of Peter.

"Not of me, I hope."

"Oh, no, never. I couldn't imagine—"

"I've missed you. I can't stop thinking about you. I wished you had stayed with me last night—"

"So do I."

"Perhaps tonight?" he said softly.

"Yes. Yes, tonight."

"We'll be there in twenty-five minutes." He hung up, but she kept the receiver to her ear and heard the telltale click.

"You swine," she said in Peter's direction as she sailed through the bedroom and into the bathroom, locking the door behind her. She did her toilet in record time and raced over to the closet, averting her eyes from the bed while she yanked at a Wedgwood-blue corduroy dress with a high Victorian collar.

"Who was that on the phone?" Peter lay back, smoking a cigarette, one arm casually behind his head.

Claudia didn't respond. The hangers were tangled, and she tugged to free the dress, swearing under her breath.

"You're sleeping with him, aren't you?" The curve of his lips was lewd. "The experience will do you good,

Claudia. You always had outmoded ideas about monogamy, you know that? About sex in general."

"You bet. All I ever had was you for a teacher. I need a graduate course, instruction from someone who knows what he's doing for a change."

The dress came free, and she stamped out of the room. In the kitchen she made a cup of instant coffee and dressed in the dark. She knew she should eat breakfast, but her stomach was too upset to contemplate the idea of food, so she sat at the small table, drinking the coffee and anticipating the response from Peter, who could never tolerate not having the last word. When she finished the coffee she washed and dried the cup and put it away in a glass-fronted cabinet. She decided to wait downstairs in the vestibule and take no chance that Austin would see Peter in her apartment again.

The bedroom door opened just as she picked up the cape, the suitcase, her leather envelope, and her handbag and was on her way out. Peter stood there with a bath towel wrapped around his torso.

"You're a bitch," he said. "You'll be sorry."

Claudia left the apartment without a word, letting the heavy door slam closed behind her.

The engine of a Rolls-Royce really does purr, she thought happily as she watched the car enter Gramercy Park Square, its mirror finish shining under the streetlights. When the car stopped, the chauffeur ran up the steps and took her suitcase, her envelope, and her cape and laid them in the trunk. Austin opened a rear door and got out and took her hand as she approached the car. He smiled down at her. Even in the gloom his eyes were a crisp, Nordic blue.

"With an enormous effort of will I won't kiss you, because Willy is in the backseat," he whispered into her ear, giving her hand a squeeze. "But he's a Willy I hardly know. Your sister must be some woman!"

She squeezed his hand back. "She is. I want you to meet her as soon as possible."

"Willy already has plans for a meeting. You'll hear all about it. Get in, it's cold out here."

"I'm not cold now that you're here," she said.

Involuntarily Claudia glanced up at the windows of her apartment. Peter was standing in a lighted window, watching them on the street below. He signaled her with a half salute that she chose to interpret as an evil promise of trouble to come. She looked away to find that Austin was watching her closely.

"Something wrong?"

"No. No, just checking to see that I turned out the lights."

"And?"

"And nothing," she said defensively. She was a terrible liar, always had been. Tina had told her so a hundred times. Tina, of course, was a brilliant liar; she had to be in order to keep her social life flowing smoothly.

"And did you turn out the lights?"

"Yes. Yes, they're all out."

He looked up at the windows silently. "I'll sit in the middle. I'm sorry, but Willy and I will have to do some business on the way. You don't mind, do you?"

"Of course not."

He looked up at the windows again and entered the car without another word. She got in beside him, and the chauffeur closed the door.

Lindhurst greeted her warmly, as if they were already kin by marriage. Could Tina have infused him so quickly with her almost excessive vitality? The change in him was incredible. He made little jokes, he hummed, and once Austin had to ask him to stop whistling. Lindhurst told them that he and Tina—but he called her Cristina, her given name—had attended a concert of chamber music at the Cloisters, for which she had season tickets.

"She does?" The surprised words slipped out of Claudia's mouth before she had a chance to think. "Oh, of course, Tina *loves* chamber music." She smiled to herself. Tina's idea of truly enjoyable music was the Rolling Stones, Queen, and Joe Cocker, as she liked to feel the beat. Austin took Claudia's hand in the dark and made a small circle on her palm with his thumb. Claudia moved an inch closer to Austin, who smelled of lemons and soap. The Rolls smelled of leather and polished wood, and Claudia sighed contentedly.

"Is Cristina as beautiful as her sister?" Austin asked.

"Yes, in a different way," Lindhurst mused. "More mature, more—ahem—baroque, if you will." *When you're not in love, that means ten pounds overweight,* thought Claudia with amusement. Tina was usually on a short-lived diet.

"Is she much older than you, Miss Cleary?" Lindhurst asked.

Perceiving the lawyer's trap, Claudia declined to be tricked into giving away any of Tina's secrets. Lord knows what age her sister had told the besotted man she was.

"She used to baby-sit for me when I was young, so she is a *few* years older...." That was as vague as she could get.

"Yes, she said you were a beautiful baby."

"And now she's a beautiful woman," Austin said quietly. "Men have killed for less." After that strange comment he dropped her hand and turned on a pinpoint reading light. Then he and Lindhurst placed almost identical leather briefcases on their laps and opened them at the same moment the Rolls emerged from the Midtown Tunnel into the gloom of an overcast, smog-shrouded dawn.

Claudia realized they felt free to discuss the Shorter case in front of her because of her promise of silence. Didn't Austin know she would never betray him now? Even if the two suddenly businesslike men at her side didn't have the ability to discover the name she had sought for so long, she was long past striking deals with A. Remington Harwood IV. She gazed at the horn-rimmed glasses he wore as he paged through the list of potential members of the jury. He was a distinguished, intelligent, and serious attorney, yet Claudia knew what a sensuous man lurked beneath his Dunhill-suited exterior. She blushed at the memory.

Austin and Lindhurst argued amiably. Willy wanted the jury stacked with men who would respond to Glenda Shorter's obvious charms. Austin feared the prosecuting attorney had cards up his sleeve—information more damaging than already intimated in the pre-trial hearing. He thought Glenda Shorter was unstable, that she might damn herself on the stand. They both decided that she would not be permitted to testify, so that the prosecutor would be unable to cross-examine her, but Austin wanted women on the jury to swing the vote in case the trial went against his client. He wanted to reserve the right to paint the truth about the late Mr. Shorter, although the defendant had begged her lawyers to let the past be the past. Glenda Shorter had not been the big-time sinner in the family, no matter how the press had canonized her deceased husband. The women on the jury would drip sympathy if they only knew.

As the men conferred Claudia stared unseeingly

through the window, lost in a fantasy recreation of the previous night. Their thighs touched in the quiet car, only a snippet of blue corduroy, a sliver of pin-striped wool, separating her skin from Austin's. She was grateful for the opportunity to unpack the treasures of her memory in peace.

"A message for you from your husband, ma'am," said the young desk clerk to Claudia when, two hours later, she, Harwood, and Lindhurst stood before the reception desk at The Inn at Montauk.

"I don't have a husband," said Claudia decisively. "There must be some mistake." She shifted her eyes to Austin's profile, but he did not seem to be listening. His head was bent as he filled out the registration card.

"Claudia Cleary, WNYZ?" persisted the clerk.

"Yes, but I don't want the message."

"I'll leave it in your box. Perhaps you'll care to read it later," said the perplexed clerk.

"And don't put through any calls from him, either." So Peter had found out where she was and had initiated his campaign to harass her. She thought of calling the attorney who had handled her divorce, as she had threatened the night before, but legal advice and legal action cost money, which she did not have to spend at that moment. She decided to ignore Peter, hoping that eventually he would tire of the game and return to Malibu Beach and his lithe young groupies. Baiting someone was no fun if you didn't get a reaction, she reasoned, but it was unfortunate that Austin had overheard the desk clerk. She glanced his way again to see that he was regarding her with an unreadable expression on his tanned face. He smiled and took her leather envelope from her hands.

"Let me carry this. I'll see you to your room, but

then I'll have to run to be at the courthouse by ten. What's inside here?" They climbed the carpeted stairs side by side. On the second floor he took her hand.

"Supplies for my drawings," she answered, remembering that she and he had journeyed to Montauk for a trial. Somehow when Austin was around all else fell away and she thought only of him. "Austin, I think it's better if you and I aren't seen together. After all, I'm a member of the impartial press, so to speak. People make assumptions that might be bad for your firm, bad for your case."

"Perhaps you're right, but have dinner with Lindhurst and me tonight. We'll eat in our suite. We'll have all the privacy we need, and you can give Willy the information you have about your birth records then. It seems I forgot all about talking business last night. I wonder why that happened?" He smiled again.

They stood before the door to her second-floor room. At nine in the morning the corridor was empty. He slipped his arms around her waist and buried his face in her neck. "When I'm with you, I forget everything," he said into her hair. "I'll lose my practice if I don't pay more attention. Just pretending that you were merely an acquaintance in the car this morning—" He kissed her slightly parted lips, which opened fully at the gentle pressure of his. She sighed and her arms went up around his neck, and they stood in a long embrace that made her ache with desire for him.

Claudia sat with William Lindhurst at a table in the lawyers' suite. Dinner was over, and their empty coffee cups rested on the white linen tablecloth. Claudia had cleared their dishes and stacked them on the serving cart a waiter had left for their convenience in the expansive living room. Austin sat at one corner of the spacious sofa, reviewing a stack of papers he had taken from his briefcase, which lay open on the coffee table before him. Every so often he removed his glasses and looked toward Claudia, catching her eye as she talked with Lindhurst, whose back was to his colleague. Another person would have been aware of the electricity that crackled between Claudia's eyes and Austin's, but Lindhurst seemed oblivious to their silent glances. Unconsciously Willy concentrated on turning the conversation to talk of Tina at every opportunity.

"What is your full name?" Lindhurst asked, pencil poised above an ubiquitous yellow legal pad.

"Claudia Nicole Cleary."

"A lovely name. What is Cristina's middle name, may I ask?"

Claudia rolled her eyes at Austin over Willy's bent head. "Natalie. All the women in our family have the same initials. My mother's name is Cynthia Noreen. It's a family tradition of sorts." *Of their family*, she thought to herself, feeling, as was her custom, somewhat of an interloper among the Cleary women.

"How lovely—Cristina Natalie," he mused. "Do you know your legal name at birth?"

"No."

"Do you know where you were born?"

"There's the address on my amended birth certificate." She handed the photostat to Willy. "The address is a private house that was torn down years ago to make room for a public housing project. I wasn't able to trace anything. It's just been a dead end." She thought of all the futile research on long, hot summer afternoons in the public records and real estate departments of the Cincinnati City Hall.

"We'll see, we'll see. This certificate is dated three

years after your birth. Where were you in the interim?"

"In a foundling home near Dayton." She gave him the address. "But they won't tell you anything, either."

"We'll see." He copied the information. "So you were adopted by Mrs. Cynthia Cleary. Single parent adoptions were unusual in those days. What about her husband?"

"He was deceased by the time the adoption was finalized. I've always assumed that they petitioned for adoption together. But when he died, Tina came back, so my mother had two children at home and no husband."

"Came back? Where was she?" he asked, removing his glasses and polishing them with his handkerchief.

"I don't know that, either. They were always vague about those years. As I piece it together, Tina and her father never got along. He was extremely strict and oppressive. She moved out when she was in her teens and she didn't return until after he died." Claudia put her hand to her lips, thinking that perhaps, inadvertently, she had said too much. Would Lindhurst be able to approximate Tina's age from her remarks? She went on rapidly to cover the slip. "Anyway, she and my mother got along fine. I feel they were in league against him while he was alive. Apparently, he was a tyrant—a religious bigot, a real right-winger." And no wonder Tina, brought up in such a restrictive atmosphere, had sprung the other way, she mused.

"Why didn't your mother divorce him?" Austin asked from the other side of the room.

Claudia looked up at him. "Religious scruples? Loyalty? I don't know. She's always had the attitude that you stick to your commitments. And besides, that was thirty years ago."

"Some people still feel the same way these days," he replied. "On the other hand, if life is so bad, perhaps it's better to cut the strings rather than live a nightmare. Otherwise you'll regret the waste of all the years that you'll never have again."

Lindhurst turned around in his chair to look at Harwood.

"Oh, but they didn't believe in divorce," answered Claudia, missing the look the men exchanged. "No one in the family ever divorced before I did. And when I divorced Peter, they said, 'But then, of course, *she's* not one of us.'"

"Cristina said that!" Willy sputtered, whipping around to stare at her in disbelief. "She'd never—"

"No, not Tina, but our aunts and uncles. Her father's side of the family. They all thought I took divorce lightly, but I didn't. The whole process was agonizing."

"I'm certain it was," said Austin with feeling, bending his head over the papers once more.

"Anyway, Willy, I'm convinced Tina never married because her parents were so unhappy together. She was afraid to take a chance."

"And speaking of your mother," said Lindhurst, "Cristina has mentioned to me that she is worried about the effect of your search on her, due to the fragile nature of her health. Your sister asked me to implore you to reconsider before you finalize the arrangements with me."

"Willy, I've considered and I've reconsidered. Tina doesn't understand how important finding my birth mother is to me." Claudia jumped up from the table and paced around the room. "I don't expect her to understand, but I do expect some semblance of support from her. Really, Willy, asking you to intervene like this is too much! I've considered my mother's feelings. But how about *my* feelings? No one ever thinks about the rights of the adopted. Tina doesn't think of my rights.''

Lindhurst looked at her kindly. "Your sister is primarily concerned about you. She worries about what potentially adverse news will do to you. She feels that since even the state of your adoptive mother's health won't preclude you from looking, you may be, shall we say, obsessed with this search. Frankly, she's concerned for your mental stability.''

"*My* mental stability! Tina's a fine one to talk! She sounds like my ex-husband. Why is everyone always accusing *me* of being unstable? *I* think I'm perfectly normal. She and Peter—" The two men stared at her. She stopped, realizing how she must sound to their ears. Accusing Tina and Peter of being the neurotics definitely could be construed as paranoid.

"I'm strong, Willy. Tell Tina not to worry about me. No matter what you discover, I can take it.''

Chapter Six

Two full days sped by while the jury was selected. Claudia drew a portrait of each juror the prosecution and the defense agreed to choose. There was no real need for her to be present all day in the courtroom, and had the trial taken place in a jurisdiction closer to Manhattan, she would have left for home after checking in and making a few quick sketches for the nightly news. However, sitting all day in the crowded room was one way she was able to stare openly at Austin Harwood and admire his aquiline nose and his broad shoulders and remember the feel of his skin on hers. She imagined she smelled his faintly citrus cologne from ten feet away, and it seemed to her as though she were pursuing the echo of a song that flitted endlessly through her mind, ever out of reach in the formal quarters of the courtroom.

She left her seat in the press section at two o'clock daily to entrust new sketches of the trial participants to the WNYZ delivery man, who drove a van to New York City each afternoon. Her agent called to tell her not to miss the seven o'clock news on Tuesday evening, because one of the national networks had purchased rights to her sketches and had scheduled them for broadcast. Although nothing newsworthy had yet happened at the trial, all the stations wished to keep the sensational story in front of the public eye. McLaughlin, when necessary, communicated with Claudia through the cameramen, who had a telephone in their equipment truck. She neglected to pick up the steadily growing stack of telephone messages in her box at the reception desk, assuming the calls came from Peter.

Tina arrived on Wednesday by small plane in time for dinner and to spend the night. Claudia had been quite surprised to hear from Lindhurst that Tina planned to take a day off from work on Thursday to attend the trial. She was unable to recall a single instance when Tina had played hooky from work—and certainly never to be with a man. Not that Jake refused to give his best designer all the time off she might want, but her sister liked to work hard, to play hard, to live hard—and no aspect of her life had ever overlapped before. Claudia speculated that Tina's pursuit of Willy was indeed a serious campaign and she said as much when Tina arrived at her room before dinner.

"Except for trips to Cincinnati to see Mother, you haven't had a vacation in two years. You were always too busy. What are you doing here in the middle of the week?"

"Because I plan to strike while the iron's hot! It isn't often that a man like Willy comes along," said Tina, touching up her makeup in the bathroom mirror. She was wearing a demure plum-colored georgette dress with shirred shoulders. On the capelet collar she wore a simple bar pin with a single rosy-white pearl set in gold.

"You look like an affluent member of the Daughters of the American Revolution," Claudia said laughingly.

"That's the general idea. Willy's rather on the straight side, in case you hadn't noticed. Look at this," Tina said, opening a coordinating silk evening bag and extracting a black felt pouch.

"What is it?" she asked, watching as Tina pulled a small glass vial from the felt.

"It's a love potion! With this my future with Willy is assured."

"Tina, you're out of your mind! You don't need a love potion with Willy. He's already crazy about you. Why, you should hear his voice when he says your name. Anyone can hear how he feels about you."

"I don't want anything to go wrong."

"Nothing will go wrong, Tina. Where did you get a love potion? What's in it?"

"It's ground up. You don't want to know. I bought it from a voodoo priest in Brooklyn. He guaranteed its efficacy."

"And you told Willy that you're worried about *my* mental health?! I was angry when I heard that, Tina, but it's impossible to stay angry with you. You're too delightfully crazy. What do you plan to do with your love potion? Slip it in Willy's drink when he's not looking?"

"Yes. And you're going to help me by distracting him."

"Oh, no. No, I'm not!"

"Please, Claudia. You don't know how much Willy means to me."

"I'm beginning to understand. But that—that stuff—may be dangerous. How do we know it won't hurt him?"

"It's organic."

"Tina, I doubt the voodoo factory was accepted by the health department."

"What does it matter? If it makes him love me, what's a little tummy ache?"

"Is it liable to give him a stomach ache?"

"That's how you know whether the potion's working."

Claudia grabbed the glass vial from her sister's hand and pulled out the stopper. She emptied the gray powder into the sink, where it turned a putrid dark brown as it absorbed drops of water resting on the porcelain.

"What are you doing? I paid twenty-five dollars for that powder!"

"You can afford it. But you can't afford to get caught dumping arsenic or worse into a lawyer's cocktail. Tina, are you out of your mind?"

"Maybe a little. I'm so afraid he'll find out about me. You know, my past is—"

"Colorful?" Claudia suggested.

"Yes, colorful. Willy would never understand how I am—how I used to be, I mean. He would probably never speak to me again."

"Are you ashamed of your past? Who did you ever hurt besides yourself?" Claudia put her arms around Tina.

"Yes. No. Yes—some of the things I've done have been wrong, I know that now. But people change, don't they? If Willy and I get together, I swear I'll be different."

"Why don't you trust him, Tina? If he loves you, he loves you. Love isn't rational. Love isn't based on intellectually weighing a person's every action. Love just is."

"Do you think so?" Tina asked in a small voice, for all the world sounding like an adolescent girl. How their roles were reversed, thought Claudia. Her first childhood memories were of Tina teaching her to stand on her head in one corner of the bedroom they shared in a small frame house in Cincinnati. And later, when Claudia was four or five years old, she remembered standing at that bedroom window and watching for her older sister, whom she adored, to come home at night from her job as an apprentice dressmaker in a downtown shop that catered to wealthy ladies.

"Of course. Would I lie to you? Try it. If you lie to Willy in the beginning, you'll live with that lie all your life. The truth will always hang over your head like a vengeful ghost. When you walk down the street with him, you'll worry that you'll meet an old lover. You'll never be able to live with a lie."

"I know you're right," Tina said. "But I'm afraid." Her voice was torn with anguish.

"Cheer up. You don't have to tell him tonight. Let's join the men. We're already late, and I'm anxious for you to meet Austin Harwood."

The Rolls-Royce glided the two couples to a well-known seafood restaurant located on the dock of an inlet within the village of Montauk. The maître d' led them to a table overlooking the water. The fresh smell of salt air filled the room, although sliding glass doors were closed against the chill of the autumn night. The lights of houses sparkled from the opposite shore of the narrow inlet.

Tina dominated the conversation during the first part of dinner, wittily recounting anecdotes of famous people she had known during her years in New York City. Claudia noticed that her sister drank only one cocktail and that she barely touched the glass of dry white wine that sat in front of the seafood Newburg she had ordered. Then, subtly and skillfully, Tina turned the attention to

Lindhurst by questioning him until he was comfortably discussing his own past, focusing his stories on the years before his marriage, but not reluctant to mention the name of his late wife when necessary.

Austin was quiet throughout the meal. From time to time Claudia glanced at his profile, but she often found him gazing politely at whoever was speaking, or, more often, staring silently at Tina. He took Claudia's hand under the table and looked down at her slender fingers grasped within his. His gaze met hers when he looked up again. After a moment he smiled at her.

"I understand you're planning to visit your mother, Claudia," Willy said.

"One of us goes each month to see her," explained Tina. "This time it's Claudia's turn."

"Yes, but this time I plan to tell her about my search. You'll see, Tina. She'll be more supportive than you think."

"When will you go?" Austin asked.

"I planned to go after the trial, but now I think I had better go sooner. I feel a responsibility to tell her before Willy's contacts make their discoveries. Perhaps this weekend?"

"I'm going with you," Austin announced. "I'd like to meet your mother."

Tina looked startled, but she was quiet. Claudia looked at Tina and smiled impishly, enjoying the thought that she had pulled something over on her usually astute older sister. Of course, Tina was so wrapped up in her pursuit of Willy, she would never have noticed anything else happening right beneath her nose.

"There's no one to meet," Tina said at last. "She's only the shell of who she was. She can't speak, she can't walk, and she lives in a nursing home."

"I'd like to meet her, anyway, to see what she looks like. After all, with two such lovely daughters—"

"There's no place to stay. We sold the house after her stroke."

"We won't stay. We'll go on Saturday morning and come back in the evening."

"But—"

"The plan sounds perfect to me," interjected Claudia, thrilled that he had offered to accompany her. "Perfect."

"Sure, why not?" Tina agreed. "I had no idea you two were so—so *close*."

Austin lifted Claudia's hand and laid it on the white tablecloth. He looked down again at her ringless fingers and placed his tanned hand over them. She felt the then-familiar current that flowed from his body to hers.

"Appearances are seldom what they seem," Austin said. "Are they, Tina?"

"I thought Harwood was married," Tina said in the ladies' room. They had left the table after drinking small cups of sweetened espresso subtly touched with elusive oil of lemon. Disapproval was obvious in Tina's voice.

"No, he's not married."

"Willy wouldn't give you his home phone number. Explain that to me, please."

"I've been to his home. There was no wife there."

"That doesn't mean a thing. He could stash a wife anywhere."

"Tina, he said he isn't married. What do you want from me? I choose to believe him." Even as she spoke the words Claudia realized how strangely chosen they were. Not "I believe him," but "I choose to believe him." Tina looked at her searchingly, concern written on her plump face. "Don't you think he's gorgeous?" Claudia went on defensively.

"I don't think he's gorgeous," Tina answered. "He's well dressed, he has a nice voice, but gorgeous? No."

"My goodness, how you disapprove of him! And aren't you imbued with morality all of a sudden? You're half in love with Willy because some charlatan fortune-teller told you that a man would come into your life. You think he's simply adorable, and believe me, Willy will never win any beauty contests. I suppose it only proves that beauty is in the eye of the beholder."

"That's different. Willy's a widower; he's fair game."

"Austin is fair game, too. And I maintain that he's the handsomest man I've ever seen in my life. The first time I saw him I was struck by his looks. I remember the morning vividly. I even remember how he smelled." She laughed, slightly embarrassed to reveal her intimate thoughts to Tina.

"When was that?"

"It must be more than a year ago now...last summer on the Connecticut train. I had been up to see Peter's parents in Darien."

"What was Harwood doing on the train? He said he lives in Manhattan." Tina's voice was laced with skepticism.

"I don't know."

"Visiting his parents, perhaps?"

"No, his mother lives in the West Indies."

"At home with his wife for the weekend, more likely. And you are naive, my dear, if you think differently."

"You sound like somebody's mother, Tina. I know what I'm doing." But Claudia's brow was wrinkled with an expression of doubt, and her voice lacked conviction.

"I'm trying to spare you heartache. Believe me, I know what I'm talking about. Try to be sensible."

"What shall I do?"

"Ask him right out what he was doing in Connecticut. And for heaven's sake, don't go to Cincinnati with him! That's much too compromising."

"I can't believe I'm hearing those words from your mouth! Didn't you go to Hong Kong with Jake? What about that trip to Mexico with what's-his-name? *They* didn't mince words about their wives and children on Long Island."

"Those were business trips."

"Monkey-business trips!" The sisters stared angrily at each other in the mirror above the row of sinks. Claudia dropped her eyes fist. Tina had always been able to make her back down. "Anyway, I'm already compromised," Claudia admitted in a quiet voice.

"Great!" Tina said with heavy sarcasm. "Well, don't say I didn't warn you. But for God's sake, don't take him home to meet Mother. Let's go. The men are waiting."

"I have an idea that I hope will meet with your approval, Cristina."

"Yes, Willy?" The innocence and docility that Tina feigned in front of Lindhurst turned Claudia's stomach. Tina was such a hypocrite, she thought, sitting there in that modest dress, acting as if she had lately emerged from twenty years in the convent and was still shading her eyes from the harsh light of a newly discovered world. The heated conversation with Tina in the ladies' room had left Claudia furious. How *dare* her sister stick her nose into Claudia's life—first with Lindhurst, then with Austin. She looked at Austin's profile in the fleeting light cast by infrequent streetlights. But what if Tina was right about him? The thought would not go away.

"There's a disco I know of in East Hampton," said Lindhurst. "I know you care for more serious music, my dear Cristina, but the place has—"

"I'd love to go, Willy. I've never been to a disco. Oh, how thrilling!" Claudia opened her mouth to speak, tempted to remind Tina that she had attended the inaugural parties at Xenon, Studio 54, and the new Regine's. She even felt nasty enough to add that Tina was a charter member of two private punk clubs on the Lower East Side.

"Let's beg off," Austin whispered in her ear. "I want to be alone with you." He squeezed her hand in the dark.

"Yes. I don't want to go." She would ask him as soon as they were alone and she would discover the whole truth. She knew Tina was wrong, but Tina was always so forceful in her logic.

"Come up to my room," he said when they reached the second floor landing. "I have the most fabulous bathtub."

"Austin, I want to talk to you," she said.

"We'll talk in the bathroom. We had a nice conversation in a tub once before, didn't we?"

"*I* was in the bathtub. You were not."

"Never argue with a high-priced lawyer."

He opened the door to his suite on the third floor. The room was in darkness as she walked in, and he followed her. The light of a full September moon streamed through the sliding glass door and cast long shadows through the living room. Claudia crossed to the door and looked out at the water shimmering in the ghostly light.

"You said you remember seeing me in Bergdorf's at Christmas," she began immediately.

"Yes, I do remember. I noticed your hair was covered with snowflakes. You were wearing a dark brown coat, and I thought you were beautiful. I think you are even more beautiful now that I know you." Austin walked up behind her and put his arms around her waist, pulling her close to him. Claudia leaned back against his hard body. She had meant to be cooler, but when he touched her...

"That's right. Tina got me the coat wholesale from the designer," she said in an attempt to keep the conversation rational. The warmth of his muscular body pressed against the length of her back and her thighs threatened to make Claudia lose her train of thought. "That day in December wasn't the first time I saw *you,* however."

"Really? When was?" He buried his face in her neck and kissed the hollow between her throat and her shoulders, sending shivers up and down her spine. She felt her nipples harden under the silk of the black dress she wore.

"On the Connecticut commuter train one Monday morning in August. You got on at Greenwich. I even noticed the Rolls at the station."

"And you remembered me all that time? How flattering," he whispered into her neck. "'Riddle of destiny, who can show/What thy short visit meant—'"

"'Or know/What thy errand here below?'" she finished. "I even remember your cologne. I stood next to you at the door when the train was coming into Grand Central. I loved the way you smelled, so fresh and clean. The way you always smell," she added quietly.

His lips were on the pulse point of her neck. She knew he felt the pounding of her blood, the erratic drum that echoed within her head.

"You have a special fragrance too. Did you know that?" He slipped his hands up and covered her rounded breasts, pressing his palms gently against them. "'A strange invisible perfume hits the sense...'"

Then—she had to speak then before the desire that grew within her febrile body took control of her, pushing away all caution, shutting out all reason. If she didn't ask him then, the opportunity would disappear. The words were on her tongue. *What were you doing on that train, Austin? Had you just spent the weekend with your wife? Where is your wife?* She opened her mouth to speak and she inhaled raggedly.

"Milton?" she asked.

"No Shakespeare. *Antony and Cleopatra.* You know— 'but she makes hungry/Where most she satisfies...'"

Claudia turned to Austin and searched out his mouth in the darkness. Already she was almost sick with desire for him. His hands were on her hips, beginning a slow, sensual stroking movement over their curves. Then he said against her lips, "Oh, yes, she makes hungry...."

Undiscovered muscles in Claudia's legs began to tremble, betraying her, and she could barely breathe. Where was the resolve she had cultivated? she wondered. Where was the caution? Where was the nagging doubt engendered by Tina's insidious questions? Gone— with the flowers of desire on his breath, which mixed with the same scent on hers; with the heat of his warm hands just the other side of the thin black silk of her dress; with the intense pressure of his hard chest on her soft breasts, a pressure that left her breathless. All thought was suspended.

"Come into the bedroom," he said. She obeyed without a murmur.

Afterward Claudia lay on her back in a half doze. Austin's hand was stroking her waist, his palm smooth against her skin. She inched closer to him on the wide bed.

"Is Antony still hungry?" She smiled.

"Temporarily satisfied, I'll admit," he answered with a grin. She saw the flash of his white teeth in the light that came from the open door of the bathroom. "Turn over," he ordered her, a mock-stern command.

"Why?"

"Just do as I say, seductive Queen of the Nile."

Something cold touched the skin of her hips.

"What are you doing?"

"You aren't the only artist around. I can draw, too. I doodled my way through law school, I'll have you know."

"You're drawing on me? What are you drawing?"

"You'll see."

"What are you using?"

"A pen I took from your supplies." She felt him hold up the pen in the shaft of light that shone on their naked bodies. "The label says 'Indelible black fine tip.' Do you think the ink is really indelible?"

Claudia giggled.

"Hold still. You'll ruin it!"

"I spilled a bottle of indelible ink once. It took weeks to get my fingernails clean. My shirt was ruined, and I had to use pumice to take the stain off my hands."

"You would never defile this gorgeous behind with a pumice stone, would you? Perish the thought!" Austin stroked the skin of her hips gently, running his fingers down the back of her thigh. "There, finished. Now to test the ink."

"Test the ink?"

"In the bathtub, of course."

"How dense I am." She laughed and rolled over to look at him. His eyes were happy and carefree. "Austin, you're not at all like what I thought you were."

"What do you mean?" He trailed his fingers down the skin between her breasts.

"Well, you look like such a serious lawyer, for one thing. At first you were so domineering, even cruel. And the way you embarrassed me in the restaurant downstairs! Then the blackmail you used to force me to go out to dinner with you the night of the ALMA meeting."

"Are you sorry?"

"No," she whispered.

"I never want you to be sorry."

"Then never lie to me."

"If you'll promise me the same."

"I promise." Then she thought of Tina's warning. "Have you ever told me a lie?" she asked him.

"Let me think." A long moment passed. "No," he said at last.

"You took a long time to answer."

"I wanted to be totally honest." He twined his fingers in her hair and held her head between his hands so she had to look into his eyes. "Now you tell me: Have you ever lied to me?"

She thought of Peter standing in the window. "Yes, once, but it was only a small white lie. Sometimes a white lie is better than hurting someone."

"Oh, so I can tell you white lies, is that it? Is that how the promise is going to work?"

"No, that's how it worked in the past. No more lies."

"Do you know what happens to little girls who tell lies? They get their mouths washed out with soap. But since you only told a white lie, I'm going to be lenient with you." He grinned. "I'm going to wash my artwork instead."

He turned on the water of the enormous bathtub full force. While he chose a spicy bath oil from the Lucite basket Claudia looked over her shoulder in the mirror in an attempt to see Austin's drawing, but he crossed quickly to her side and covered her eyes from behind with his hands.

"Not yet."

"Why can't I see?"

"Wait until you're alone," he said.

She rolled her long hair into a French twist and tucked in the ends. The tension of the heavy hair held the tresses in place behind her head.

"A neat trick," he commented. "Won't the hair come down?"

"Not unless I do something active, like playing tennis."

Austin eyed the rapidly filling spice-scented tub. "Tennis, you say? I wasn't thinking of tennis." He smiled impishly.

Claudia admired the muscles in his back when he leaned over the tub to adjust the control knob of the whirlpool bath.

"Your bath is ready, madam."

He held her wrist to help her climb over the side of the high tub and he kissed her hand before dropping it and entering the water himself, lowering his body and stretching his long legs on either side of hers. He then took a bar of soap and lathered it between his hands and began to wash her back and her neck, splashing water on her skin to rinse away the bubbles. He massaged the muscles of her arms, working down to her fingers, where he washed between each one.

"You have beautiful hands," he said quietly. "Your hands are one of the first things I noticed about you. I always look at people's hands."

"But my hands weren't the first part of me you noticed." She laughed, thinking that they had actually met in the same marble-walled room they were occupying then.

"No, not the first," he agreed with a chuckle.

Claudia turned the dial to increase the water's agitation. Strong impulses made the surface of the water tremble. She leaned back against him and he slipped his hands around to cup her breasts, which floated in the pulsating caress of the warm water. They sat silently. Claudia closed her eyes and gave herself over to the pleasure of the moment, inhaling the steam, redolent of Eastern spices, which rose from the water. They floated in a quiet world of slippery skin on skin, feeling only the fingers of the warm wetness, only their soft flesh vibrating. Every touch was a joy. Austin gripped her hips tautly against him with his thighs. Claudia ran her hands down his legs languidly, noting the texture of his long limbs beneath the trembling water. She already knew each inch of his body by touch, the density of every muscle and bone, and her eyes had memorized each tanned and golden variation of his skin. But then with closed eyes she committed to memory the feel of the hairs on his legs, the touch of his skin on hers beneath the warm pulsating jets from the whirlpool.

"Would you like me to wash your hair?" he asked.

"It takes forever to dry," she objected.

"I'll dry it for you."

She slid forward and loosened her hair, allowing its

length to fall into the water, and then she bent her head to wet the long auburn tresses. He poured shampoo into the palms of his hands and began to lather her copious hair. She felt his strong fingers massage her scalp.

"I'd like to take care of you," he said once. "That is, if you'd let me." He kissed the back of her neck.

"I'd like you to," she had answered softly.

When he had rinsed her hair, he left the tub and dried himself quickly, wrapping a towel around his waist. Then he held up a large bath sheet for her when she climbed out and stood next to the tub, allowing him to dry the drops of water that clung to her skin. He knelt before her and caressed her legs with the fluffy towel, running his hands up her legs again and again and around her hips. Then he buried his face in the skin of her thighs. She felt his warm breath and was so dissolved by it that her body opened to him, opened as if he had actually penetrated her once again. Without a word he raised himself up and stood behind her and caressed her back and her shoulders and her neck. He dried her skin as if she were an antique statue of finest Carrara marble, each lustrous crevice, each shadow of her to be polished gently and thoroughly by his tender, supple hands.

"You're very beautiful, Claudia... Claudia." He said her name twice as if he thought it was also beautiful, so beautiful it had to be repeated. Austin was tall and glowing from the warm bath and his eyes were so intensely blue that when they blinked, for a moment it was like some tiny flash of lightning, and Claudia felt a heady thrill in her breast each time she looked into their depths. "Stay here, my sweet. I'm going to get a hair dryer."

Austin left the bathroom. Only a moment had passed before he returned to her side. In his hands he held a portable blow-dryer.

"This is Willy's. He won't mind if we borrow it."

"Willy's! He hardly has enough hair to dry!"

"But what he has he takes good care of." He smiled. "Sit here," he said, drawing a stool out from underneath the shelf that served as a dressing table in the large bathroom.

"And Willy likes disco music," Claudia mused. "I find it hard to believe. He seemed so—so straight."

"Willy has all sorts of hidden aspects to his character. Do you think your sister's too serious for him?"

"I don't think so. She's not exactly what she appears to be at first glance, either." Claudia giggled, but her smile disappeared when she remembered her growing irritation with Tina. "She's walking a dangerous line," she added, thinking of the way Tina had created an entirely new personality for herself, fashioned in the image of what she thought would attract Lindhurst.

"Indeed she is," said Austin, and began to dry her hair.

Conversation became impossible with the noise of the blower, and Claudia was bewildered that the two of them were together like that while he combed and dried her long hair. The intimacy of the moment was strange to Claudia, who was only familiar with life with Peter, who never gave himself to any person, merely lent himself for the duration of his time with her or anyone. She was becoming aware of the intensity of her feelings for Austin. The physical attraction that had sprung to life between them she acknowledged freely, as one look into his eyes held the power to shake her to the core. Never before had she felt quite so intoxicated by the nearness of any man, yet something else worked within her when she was near him. She liked his gentleness and his quiet sense of humor. Certainly she admired the way he operated in the courtroom, but even more, she sensed an underlying compassion within him, a latent sadness that flitted like a shadow across his features. Its occasional specter made her want to take his hand and ask him about himself, ask him about the troubles she saw when she read the attractive lines in his strong face. Hadn't he once said that all his family had been unhappy? She longed to know more about him. And yet, despite the intimacy of the time they shared, she sensed a barrier around him, an almost tangible sign that proclaimed: "Don't pry." He might as well have said the words out loud. Perhaps Lindhurst would tell her what she longed to know.

"After we go to Cincinnati, will you stay with me for the rest of the weekend?" he asked, snapping off the dryer. "I have some work to do, but I can just as easily do it at home. We'll be together. It's the last time the house will be empty before—" He was having trouble wrapping the bulky cord around the handle of the dryer, and a small frown creased his brows.

"Before what?"

"Before my mother arrives from Jamaica," he finished.

Claudia shook off the half-formulated doubt his hesitation gave birth to, reminding herself of what she had told Tina about love and trust. If you love someone, you love him, you trust him, you accept him. Love...Was it love she felt for Austin Harwood? She eyed tanned hands next to starched cuffs as he pulled on his white shirt and tucked it into the waistband of his trousers. Once she had loved Peter, she mused, yet

Peter had betrayed her; not just once, but many times, she could finally admit to herself without emotion. She had promised herself during the agonizing months of the divorce that she would never again give away her heart totally. She wanted surcease from pain and she knew that if she held back a small measure of her heart, then no human being could penetrate the carapace of Claudia and bring with him the wrenching suffering that Peter had caused—that she had *permitted* Peter to cause, she amended, aware that she had made herself vulnerable to Peter. She vowed that as long as she had doubts about Austin, she would never indicate to him the depth of feeling she felt growing in her heart.

"You're suddenly very quiet, Claudia. A penny for your thoughts," he said, coming close to adjust the collar of the black silk dress she had slipped over her head.

"I was thinking how easily I might fall in love with you," she said without pause, astonished to hear the words come from her mouth. Who *was* this other Claudia who consistently spoke without permission, like a naughty child raising havoc at a formal tea party? "I mean, I mean—" she stammered and was quiet, unable to continue. A blush flashed to her cheeks. *I mean I already love you,* she said silently, admitting—at least to herself—the truth.

"I've been thinking the same," he answered, relieving her of a need to explain her inadvertent confession. He took her head between his warm hands and held her still while he kissed her softly on the lips. "Finding you seems too good to be true. I was certain I would never feel this way about a woman again. And that you could feel the same way about me..." A note of wonder filled his voice.

She kissed him, wrapping her arms around the starched white shirt at his waist.

They descended to the second floor hand in hand. When they reached Claudia's room, he opened the door with the key she handed him and he entered the room before she did, turning on the light as he did so. On the dresser stood a vase filled with showy yellow chrysanthemums. A card was pinned to the flowers. Claudia crossed the room to the dresser.

"Flowers! How lovely."

"Who are they from?"

"Probably my agent. He sold three of my pictures to the network news. I should send *him* flowers." She picked up the small white envelope and withdrew the card. "Thank you for Sunday night's warm welcome," it read. "You're the same in bed as I remembered. Ever, Peter." She dropped the card as if the stiff white paper had scorched her fingers. Austin picked it up from where it lay at her feet and glanced at it quickly. He looked into her eyes.

"That's—that's my ex-husband. He's very sick. The card doesn't mean what it seems to," she hastened to add.

"You don't owe me any explanations," Austin said in a normal tone of voice. But she saw a new, hard set to his mouth, the same grim expression she'd seen on his face when the prosecuting attorney succeeded in disallowing a juror the defense had counted on for its side.

"Austin, you don't understand."

"You don't have to explain," he said, giving her a tight smile that did not engage his eyes. "I'll see you in the morning." He left the room and closed the door quietly behind himself. Claudia stared at the door, then she picked up the heavy vase, undecided as to what to do. What she longed for was the nerve to throw the chrysanthemums against the wall, but the thought of the mess she would have to look at in the morning stayed her hand. Nor should the chambermaid be saddled with her temper, she reasoned. At last she opened the door and looked up and down the long corridor, which was then empty. She picked out another door at random and laid the vase of flowers in front of it. If only Peter were standing in front of her at that moment... If only she had a gun... Suddenly she understood why guns in the home were so dangerous, why, perhaps, Glenda Shorter had shot her husband. If the distraught Mrs. Shorter had felt but half the rage and hatred Claudia then felt for Peter, she deserved to be acquitted on the grounds of temporary insanity.

After she returned to the room, Claudia tore the white card into tiny pieces and flushed them down the toilet. How was she going to explain to Austin what had happened? She wished she had told him all about Peter's unwelcome appearance on Monday morning, when the Rolls had stopped at Gramercy Park for her. She realized that he had most probably seen Peter in the lighted window of her apartment. At the time she'd prayed he would be unable to guess which window was hers; after all, he'd been there only once. However, he had met Peter that first evening when they arrived home from dinner at La Colombe d'Or. Would Austin believe that Peter had literally forced his presence upon her? When it happened, she had lacked enough confidence to even attempt the truth, but too much time had passed. A small white lie, she had admitted. Ruefully she realized that Austin had been offering her an opportunity to extricate herself then, yet one small white lie had grown to enormous proportions. The lines of a Scott poem learned in high school came back to her as she tried to sleep, reverberating in her head like an unwelcome mantra in the still night. "Oh what a tangled web we weave,/When first we practice to deceive!"

In the morning she would explain everything. Or was it already too late?

Chapter Seven

Austin guided the rented car onto the new interstate highway that would take him and Claudia from the Cincinnati airport, actually located in northern Kentucky, to the Queen City, which clung picturesquely to hills and cliffs overlooking the wide Ohio River. Saturday traffic was light on the expressway. Although it was barely ten o'clock in the morning, the air was warm and moist and not at all like the crisp autumn dawn they had left behind in Long Island when they flew from Montauk Point to La Guardia Airport to make an early morning flight.

Claudia directed him over the river, through downtown, and past the sprawling University of Cincinnati until they were on a tree-shaded, winding road in Clifton, an older section of the city, which was distinguished by the presence of charmingly old-fashioned gas streetlights. The flames of the lamps still flickered dimly in the bright sunshine.

"Park right here on the street," she said.

"But this is a private house," he objected.

"Was. This house used to belong to a wealthy German family, but it's been a nursing home for twenty years or so. Hardly anyone can afford to keep up the old mansions in this part of town. Many have already been torn down."

"What a shame. Look at that stonework," he answered. Together they gazed at a southern Ohio recreation of a small Bavarian Gothic castle. Only unsightly fire escapes on either side of the gray stone mansion indicated that the building was no longer a private home.

Austin locked the car, and they entered the imposing structure together. The smell of a hundred years of floor wax greeted their nostrils.

"I'm a little scared," Claudia admitted to him as they climbed wide stairs protected by an ornately carved oak banister. "I'd never do anything to hurt my mother. You know that, don't you?"

Austin squeezed her elbow in reply. Since the night he had seen the flowers in Claudia's room she imagined that he had been slightly cooler toward her, but he had neither done nor said anything specific that could have led her to believe that he was angry. Nor had he withdrawn his invitation for the weekend at his house on Seventy-fourth Street. In fact, that morning as they left their luggage with his chauffeur, at the Montauk airport, Claudia had overheard Austin tell the driver to take both suitcases to his town house in New York City.

On the other hand, she may have misinterpreted his coolness of attitude for a certain preoccupation with the trial. She had hardly seen Austin since Wednesday evening, except in the courtroom. The following two nights he had been in conference until very late with Lindhurst and Glenda Shorter, although Claudia had shared dinner with both the men and Tina in the third-floor suite before their client arrived to talk on Thursday. Claudia had accompanied Tina to the tiny Montauk airport in the borrowed Rolls on Thursday night. Their time together had been slightly strained, but she had not given in to a natural inclination to ease the awkward silence with her sister. With Austin, she had found no opening to bring up the subject of Peter and his unwelcome visit to her apartment. As time went by she had ceased to look for an opportunity to broach the subject, and by Saturday her mind was too occupied with the visit to her mother even to think of Peter.

"I'm certain that if she loves you, she'll understand why your search is so important," he replied. "But how will you know if she does understand?"

"She blinks her eyes. And she has some very slight mobility in her left hand. I'll know if she understands. But what if she doesn't?" Tina's warnings came back in a rush that filled Claudia with a sense of dread and foreboding, and for a moment she thought of not mentioning the search at all, but she reminded herself that then, before she found her natural mother, was the optimum time. They had made the trip for only that reason. Afterward, too much emotion might go into play.

"This is the room," she indicated, stopping just before she reached the open door.

Austin took both of her hands in his. "Don't worry. Everything is going to work out. I don't want you to be upset, no matter what happens. I don't ever want you to worry about anything, do you understand?" As his blue eyes searched hers, Claudia felt the familiar lurch of her heart. He leaned toward her to kiss her lips, and she inclined toward him, but from the corner of her eye she saw a familiar figure descending upon them in the corridor. She drew back quickly, feeling the muscles of her neck tense. "My aunt Geraldine is coming toward us," she whispered to Austin. "She always means trouble. I'm going to apologize in advance."

"Well, Claudia! What are you doing here?"

"Geraldine, what a surprise! Are you visiting mother?" She tried to keep her features pleasant as she looked at Geraldine's gray hair falling here and there from a lopsided bun. When in a charitable mood, it was easy to feel sorry for Geraldine. After all, her adoptive aunt was more than neurotic—she was probably clinically crazy, although physically harmless to herself and others. However, her razor-sharp tongue and her unexplained tirades were hardly harmless. When her mood was not so generous, Claudia detested Geraldine and tried to keep as much distance between them as possible. All three of the Cleary women detested her, including the paralyzed Cynthia, who helplessly suffered her sister-in-law's frequent visits, unable to escape the unwelcome gossip and the self-righteous pronouncements of the meddlesome woman.

"Someone has to. Her *children* certainly never find the time." The stern-looking older woman wore a summery flowered dress that rippled over her ample hips, but despite the warmth and humidity of the day, around her neck and shoulders she sported a ragged fur boa of indeterminate origin. Claudia suspected that thirty years before, the fur had passed for fox. Two beady eyes, uncannily similar to Geraldine's, stared from a nearly hairless animal's head, which formed a clasp on the fur and seemed to be eating its own tail. Geraldine looked pointedly at Claudia's hands, still in Austin's grasp.

"And who is *this* young man?" She eyed him with her ever alert brown eyes. He dropped Claudia's hands.

"This is Austin Harwood, a friend of mine from New York. This is Aunt Geraldine, my mother's sister-in-law." She couldn't say "my father's sister," since she had never had a father.

"A friend of yours," Geraldine said scornfully, pointedly ignoring Austin's outstretched hand. "And what

does your husband say about you traveling with another man? What, young lady? Or perhaps he doesn't
know."

"Actually I'm Miss Cleary's attorney," said Austin
affably, stretching the truth for expediency.

"*Miss* Cleary? She didn't tell you she was married?"
she went on, not looking at him, bringing her face uncomfortably close to Claudia's. "Well, young lady? I'm
waiting for an explanation."

"Geraldine, I don't know why you're saying such a
thing. You know I'm divorced—I told you so myself
some time ago. I may travel with whomever I please. If
you'll excuse us, we'd like to see Mother now." Claudia tried to push by the straight-backed floral bulk that
blocked the doorway. She didn't have to tolerate Geraldine's rudeness. The spinster and her mouth were part
of the reason Tina had left Cincinnati. Tina had always
said that Geraldine was the female counterpart of her
father, only worse.

Geraldine's eyebrows seemed to take on a jumping,
quivering life of their own. While the eyebrows undu-
lated Geraldine sniffed and then rolled her eyes upward
as if to invoke the aid of the Lord in her mission. She
took a deep, rasping breath. "Divorced! You'll burn in
the fires of hell, young lady! You and Tina—you're just
alike. You and she will burn for all eternity for your
sins, mark my words. She was never any good, and
you're just like her. I warned Cynthia about you!" A
mottled purple blotch stained Geraldine's forehead and
her dark eyes flamed with righteous indignation. The
whole situation took on a surreal air as Claudia became
hypnotized by a tiny ball of saliva on the hair of Geraldine's upper lip. "The Lord is vengeful; he does not
forget! Tina killed her father, and you'll be the death of
poor Cynthia in there." She indicated the door to the

sickroom with an angry toss of her head, which caused her gray bun to shift slightly to the right.

"I think you're getting a little carried away," said Austin firmly, taking Claudia's elbow and attempting to lead her around Aunt Geraldine.

"Just a minute, Austin," said Claudia. She turned to her aunt. "What do you mean, Tina killed her father? That's a serious accusation, Geraldine." She asked the question despite herself, although she knew she shouldn't dignify Geraldine's ravings by acknowledging them. She knew that the abnormal fanatic was incapable of remembering Claudia's divorce, so why should she know an unheard and unsuspected truth about Tina? And yet, Geraldine held the fascination of a scandal sheet one sees at the supermarket checkout counter: "Woman Gives Birth on Flying Saucer," "Lose Twenty Pounds in One Week." She knew the stories within couldn't be true, and yet the headlines piqued one's curiosity nevertheless.

"She did. We all know what happened. Tina knew he had a heart condition. She goaded him into an argument, and he died screaming at Tina. She should never have gone to see him. She killed him. She killed my brother!"

"Claudia, this woman is hysterical. I'm going to find someone to take her away from here. She's upsetting everyone." Austin walked away in search of a member of the staff as Claudia looked around the hall. Elderly people had come to some of the doors and were staring at Geraldine and Claudia.

"I'm going, I'm going," Geraldine shouted at Austin's retreating back. "I won't be seen in the company of tramps like her and Tina." She marched down the hall, her sturdy black shoes making clicking noises on the polished oak floor. Austin stopped and watched her silently as she walked past him, then he retraced his steps to where Claudia stood shaking next to the door of her mother's room.

"Don't go in yet," he suggested, taking her by the hand and leading her to a solarium at the far end of the hall. "Sit down here for a minute and compose yourself." He guided her to a wicker chair set amidst ferns and he sat at her side in a matching chair.

"My heart is thumping! I can't believe she could be so hateful. She has no right, no right." Against her will Claudia burst into tears.

Austin offered her his snow-white handkerchief and patted her back awkwardly. "No matter what Tina did, she doesn't deserve that outburst. Anyway, it doesn't matter what your aunt said. Fanatics like that don't bear the time spent thinking about them. It's all right," he soothed.

"Geraldine's just mixed up, but she can be so cruel. Can you wonder that poor Tina left here to go to New York? People like Geraldine, like Tina's father, must have made her life miserable. Can you imagine getting so excited over something that never even happened? I'd forgotten how crazy Aunt Geraldine really is, just crazy! My mother never liked her, so we never saw very much of her." She sniffled.

"Good thing, too. Perhaps you'd like to ask the staff to keep your aunt from your mother? She's liable to be upsetting her every time she comes to visit."

"Of course. Do you—do you suppose Mother heard us? We were right outside her door."

"There's nothing you can do about it if she did. We won't mention a word when we see her. Can you act as if nothing has happened?"

Claudia wiped her eyes. "I can try." She smiled at him, as if to tell him she had regained her composure.

"Good. Are you ready?" He stood up.

Claudia hesitated another minute. "Austin." She laid a hand on his arm, persuading him to sit down again. "The things Geraldine said about Tina—"

"About killing her father?"

"No, I don't believe a word of that. I mean some of the other things." She was embarrassed to continue, but she felt she must. "Some of the words she called Tina. Austin, don't tell Willy what happened here, please? Tina has always been looking for the love she never got from her father. She's—she's looked in a lot of strange places. But people change. She loves Willy and she wants to marry him. She doesn't want him to know about her life. Please promise me you won't say anything to him?"

"I don't see what's so wrong with her life if that's all you're talking about. There must be something more she wants to hide," he answered.

"What do you mean?"

"Just that the scene your aunt Geraldine made has to be based on more than a fight with your father—I mean, Tina's father. Even if he did have a heart attack and die—well, for God's sake, I know that's a load of guilt Tina could be carrying, but it's not as if she stabbed him or anything. It wasn't Tina's fault."

"I don't know about anything else. There *isn't* anything else. I've never heard a word of a so-called scene, until now, and I don't believe Geraldine, anyway. If that were even remotely true, I would have heard about it before, don't you think? But will you promise not to say anything to Willy?" she asked him once more.

"Is this to be one of those expedient white lies you believe in?" He looked into her eyes, and she searched his face for some sign of humor, finding none.

"I don't believe in white lies anymore. I believe in the truth," she said seriously. "But in this case I feel we owe—at least *I* owe—Tina the right to operate on her own without intrusion from the past."

"The past will always intrude, as much as you prefer life to be otherwise." Austin said.

Claudia knew they were involved in a parallel conversation, one in which each word held a meaning unrelated to the topic in hand. She chose her words carefully.

"I'm in control of only my own life, no one else's. I can make only my own decisions, no one else's. I can't change my past, or Tina's, or yours. But I can limit what I allow of the past to influence the future. I'm not asking you to lie to Willy if he questions you. I'm merely asking that you don't bring up the subject yourself, just as I promised you I would not volunteer to repeat a certain conversation I overheard while taking a bath one night," she reminded him. "Will you do it? For me?"

"Lindhurst is a good friend of mine," he said slowly. "I know him very well and I know he's not as stiff-backed as you and your sister seem to believe. She has nothing to fear in telling him the truth."

"So you won't promise?" A feeling of disappointment settled over Claudia.

"On the other hand," he continued, "Tina's past—your past, for that matter—is none of my business." He smiled at her.

"*My* past," she said in surprise. "I have nothing to hide."

"Of course you don't. Neither do I. I promise I won't say anything to Lindhurst. Not unless he specifically asks me what Aunt Geraldine shouted in my presence at eleven thirty on Saturday morning."

"Very legal-sounding."

"That's how I make my living."

They walked back and entered the sunny bedroom at the center of the hall. Two high, narrow windows overlooked a valley behind Clifton. In a single bed lay Mrs. Cleary. Her eyes lit up at Claudia's entrance. She crossed the room to her mother's bedside and leaned down to kiss the frail woman on the forehead.

"Miss Cleary, how nice to see you." A nurse emerged from behind a screen set in one corner. "Are you in from New York for the weekend?"

"Just for the day, Mrs. Doherty," Claudia answered.

"Your mother is upset right now," said the nurse. "I can always tell by her eyes. I think the visit from Miss Cleary—the other Miss Cleary—was too much for her. I know you came a long way to see her, but don't stay too long, dear. She needs her rest."

Claudia pulled a chair up to the side of the bed and sat down, taking her mother's left hand in hers. The skin was translucent, and she could pick out each spidery vein beneath the tissue-thin covering. She felt as if she held the bony body of a bird in her palm.

"Mother, this is Austin Harwood. He's—he's someone very special to me," she said. She felt a faint pressure as her mother squeezed her hand. "We've just seen Aunt Geraldine. Would you like me to ask the staff to keep her away? Just blink once if you want me to speak to someone."

Without hesitation her mother blinked her pale, almost colorless eyes. Claudia felt rather than saw that Austin had taken a seat in the corner. "I'll take care of it," she promised.

She spoke to her mother for a few minutes, telling her about the trial she was working on, about Tina's ideas for the new spring collection she was designing, about how she was decorating her apartment. Before long she had run out of chatter, as it was so difficult to talk to someone who could not respond. Cynthia Cleary's eyes were alive, however. Claudia knew she heard and registered every word. Claudia hesitated. The time had arrived to bring up the subject that weighed so heavily on her, yet although the words were formed and ready on her tongue, she could not force herself to say them. She turned to Austin for guidance.

He nodded gently at her. She took strength from his eyes and reassurance from his presence. She turned back to the frail figure in the bed. Her mother's eyes were watchful, waiting.

Claudia swallowed. Her mouth was dry and her throat suddenly began to ache. "Mother, I love you very much. You've been a good mother to me. I know how hard you worked to see that I had nice things, how you did without so that I could go to college for two years and then to art school. No child could ask for a more loving and devoted mother than you." Cynthia Cleary squeezed her daughter's hand.

"Now, I don't want you to think I'm ungrateful when I tell you this." She searched her mother's eyes and saw that they were blinking rapidly, indicating her agitation. Who wouldn't be agitated after such a prologue? thought Claudia. "For some time now I have had an overwhelming desire—Tina calls it an obsession—to know who my birth mother is. I'm not looking for another mother," she hastened to add. "Do you understand?" The bony hand squeezed hers faintly, but thin, red-veined lids hid the eyes from Claudia's scrutiny. "It's more a genetic curiosity. I'm not looking for a mother," she repeated. "*You* are my mother, and I love you dearly."

Cynthia opened her eyes. They were so hard to read,

thought Claudia. The formerly gold-flecked hazel pupils were faded to a midtone gray, and milky blue rings surrounded them, but she saw understanding in her mother's eyes. Certainly there was no hurt there. Understanding, yes, and—what? A touch of fear?

"I'm afraid, too," she said, squeezing the skin-covered bones lightly. Her mother blinked once.

"Mother, do you know who this woman is?"

The question lay between them in the sunny room, echoing in Claudia's head. A long moment passed. Claudia was afraid to close her eyes for fear she might miss the answer.

One blink.

Thank God, thank God, she was going to help. Claudia leaned over and kissed her forehead.

"I know this is painful, Mother. Is she here in town, in Cincinnati?"

Two blinks, no hesitation.

"Is she— Do you know if she is still alive?"

One blink—still alive, Claudia realized she had been holding her breath. She let out a sigh of relief, shocked at how tense the muscles in the back of her neck had become. Perhaps she had allowed herself to be influenced by all that hokum from the fortune-teller. She looked over her shoulder at Austin and saw joy and encouragement for her in his blue eyes.

"Can you—will you tell me who she is?" How Cynthia would tell her was another matter to be worked out later. They could go through the alphabet together, or something. Claudia would devise a way....

Her mother was blinking rapidly, blinking away the two large tears that had suddenly formed in her rheumy eyes.

"Mrs. Cleary, honey, what's the matter?" Mrs. Doherty was back, rapidly walking around to the other side of the bed. "What's going on here? You're all upset, honey!" She looked accusingly at Claudia. "I warned you not to upset her. You want her to have another stroke?" She began to bustle, straightening out the coverlet and the pillows under the thin wisps of gray hair. "You'd best be on your way, young lady. There's been altogether too much excitement today."

"Wait, wait—I need to ask her one more question."

"No more now. I told you she needs to rest. She always needs a rest after that harpy comes to visit. And now her own daughter's got her crying, and all."

Claudia felt a faint pressure on her hand.

"I think she wants to answer your question," said Austin from his chair in the back of the room.

"Do you, Mother?"

One blink.

"If I found a method of asking, would you tell me who she is?"

Two blinks. Two more tears.

"You won't tell me?"

Two blinks.

"She means she can't. She promised—she can't tell," said Austin, approaching the bed.

Cynthia blinked once, then closed her eyes.

Claudia burst into tears.

In the solarium Claudia sat and cried. Austin didn't try to stop her. He took the chair next to hers and waited until the tears were exhausted.

"She's always known. Always. They all know, I bet. Everyone but the person most concerned."

"Do you think Tina knows?" he asked her.

"No, I don't think so." She blew her nose. "She would have told me a long time ago when I first started looking. She wouldn't have let me go on and on."

"What makes you so certain?"

"It's too cruel. Tina's not cruel."

"But she's very protective, isn't she? Perhaps she thought she'd be doing the best thing in not telling you. Has she always tried to discourage you from your search?"

"Right from the start," she admitted. "But that's natural. People who aren't adopted think you're ungrateful to your family if you search. They consider it a form of rejection. Tina's always warning me that I might find out things I'm better off not knowing."

"Perhaps she's right."

"Not you, too. I thought you understood!" Claudia began to cry again.

Austin pulled his chair closer to hers and put his arms around her. "I do understand. I know finding your birth mother is the most important thing in the world to you. I want what you want, but I don't want you to be unhappy. I want your life to be perfect—no problems, no unhappiness, no suffering."

"You do?"

"Yes."

"Funny, that's what I want for you, too."

"You do?"

They smiled shyly at each other.

"Come on, let's have lunch somewhere. This place is getting me down." He stood and pulled Claudia up from the chair. She stumbled and fell into his arms.

"Don't you think perfection is too much to ask from life? Kind of daring the gods, if you know what I mean." She tilted her head back to look up into his eyes.

"In the theological sense, perfection is reserved for the gods," he admitted.

"Do you always talk this way? How did I ever get involved with an attorney?" She smiled.

"I'm serious. Of course, our lives will never be perfect, but if you're with the right person, that's as close to perfection as any human has a right to hope for. All the necessary tedium of life fades away to unimportance. Remember: '*Il n'importe qu'on vivre, mais comment.*'"

"Good lord, you'll have to translate. I hardly remember my high school French."

"'It matters not how long we live, but how.' You might keep that in mind when you reach the end of your search."

"Will you remind me if I'm devastated by what I find?"

"I promise." He kissed her. "Do you think that finding this woman will change you into something horrible? You are already who you are—nothing can change that. And personally speaking, I like you this way—more than like you. I feel privileged to know you."

"The feeling is mutual, Counselor." Claudia took his arm, and they walked down the hall together. Perhaps she should have responded more seriously to him, she thought, but his comments had embarrassed her slightly. She wanted to tell him that she loved him, but shyness stopped her. She felt that he was about to say the same to her, but he had not. He said he felt privileged to know her, an odd comment. She would rather have heard him tell her that he loved her. Perhaps he too was shy, or perhaps he too feared rejection. She imagined nothing was worse than to say "I love you" to a person and have the object of your love not reply in kind. Or not reply at all...

"Let me say good-bye to my mother," Claudia said as they reached the door to her room.

"I'll wait here," Austin replied.

Mrs. Doherty sat dozing in a chair by the window. Claudia crossed to the bed and leaned over Cynthia Cleary's frail torso, taking her hand once more.

"Mother, I'm leaving now," she whispered. "Mother, I didn't mean to upset you. I love you—I'd never purposely hurt you. Tina will be here next month to see you, as usual. I'm leaving instructions at the office not to let Geraldine in anymore." Mrs. Cleary's hand squeezed gently. "Mother, I love that man I brought here today. He's a very wonderful man." Her hand squeezed again. "I knew you'd like him—it's impossible not to."

After kissing her mother's brow again, Claudia left the room quietly, so as not to awaken the nurse.

"Your mother is older than I thought she would be," said Austin, replacing a magazine he had just leafed through in the pocket of the seat in front of him.

Claudia turned her gaze from the aircraft's window to his handsome face. The clear daylight emphasized the scar near his eye. "She must be at least seventy. She's aged terribly since the stroke, but she used to be such a beautiful woman. When I was a child, I thought she was one of the most incredible-looking women I had ever seen, even though she was much older than all my friends' mothers. She's Tina's mother, after all, and Lord knows Tina's real age—she always lies about it, even to me. Don't tell Willy, okay?"

"No, I won't tell Willy." He laughed. "Tina doesn't look like her mother at all."

"No, not at all. My mother was very tall and thin and she had beautiful white skin. She *never* went out in the sun without a big hat to protect herself. Here, I have a picture of her somewhere." Claudia dug a wallet out from her purse and extracted a black-and-white photograph from one compartment. The edges of the faded picture were brown and wrinkled. Austin took the picture from her hand and studied it.

"Who is the man?" he asked, indicating a dark-haired heavy man wearing a fedora. The shadow cast by the hat did not hide the scowl on his face.

"That's her husband."

"So this child isn't you? I thought it was."

"No, that's Tina. She must have been about ten when the picture was taken. There's a date on the back, I think."

"Yes. I see."

"Wasn't she beautiful?" Claudia asked referring to the fine-boned woman at the side of the scowling man. In one hand the woman held a wide-brimmed sun hat as if she had just removed it at the photographer's request.

"Yes, beautiful. Not as beautiful as her daughter, however." He leaned across the armrest that divided the seats to kiss her tenderly.

Claudia smiled happily.

When the plane landed, they debarked first, since they were the only passengers in first class on a slow Saturday afternoon. As they didn't have any luggage, they left the terminal quickly and found a taxi that brought them to his house on Seventy-fourth Street in record time.

"There's nothing to eat," Austin said. "I gave the cook the week off, because I was going to be in Montauk, anyway. I'll have to go out and find us some food."

"I'll go with you," she offered.

"No, you stay here and rest. You've had an emotionally draining experience. I'll be back as soon as possible. There's a place on Third Avenue that has all sorts of delicious food. I have a confession to make: I love to eat in bed." He wrapped his arms around her. "Will you join me?"

"Absolutely."

After Austin left the house, Claudia made her way to the top floor, intent on changing her clothes and washing up before he returned. She stopped to peer into the open doors of the two other bedrooms that shared the top floor of the house. One was obviously a guest room and had the soothing, anonymous look of a gracious hideaway provided for the occasional visitor. A glance into the other bedroom, however, caught her interest immediately.

Claudia entered the open door of the room, the windows of which overlooked the changing leaves of the plane trees on Seventy-fourth Street. A graceful canopy bed dominated the room. It was draped in a pale turquoise silk and covered with an antique spread of intricate crewelwork. Matching silk swags hung over the two tall windows, which were covered by sheer curtains. She looked admiringly at the wallpaper, which at first appeared to be an exaggerated marbelized print of turquoise and sable beige, but on closer inspection proved to be a covering of silk moiré. It was a beautiful and extremely feminine room, she told herself. There was an intricately designed Chinese desk in one corner of the gracious bedroom. Claudia crossed a rug of darker turquoise spotted with pastel heron and pagoda motifs and picked up one of the two sterling silver picture frames on the delicate desk.

It was a wedding picture of a younger, more carefree Austin and a blond woman who looked vaguely as Claudia imagined Glenda Shorter must have appeared about ten years before, with sun-streaked blond hair, high cheekbones, and a long, straight nose.

She replaced the photograph on the desk and picked up the other, which was of the same two people, but some years had passed between photographs. They were looking at each other and laughing. The woman was heavier, Austin thinner and more lined than on his wedding day. They seemed to be on vacation in the tropics. Palm trees and hibiscus were visible in the background. Jamaica? she wondered. Could his wife be dead? If she was dead, why didn't he simply say so?

Claudia replaced the frame with an ice-cold hand, leaving a fingerprint on the heavy silver. She went to an adjoining bathroom for a piece of tissue to remove the smudge. On impulse she opened the cabinet and discovered that it contained an array of fashionable cosmetics and expensive perfumes. She closed the door softly, catching a glimpse of her pinched mouth in the mirror above the sink.

"You've been a stupid fool," the ashen face told her.

She went back to the desk and picked up the second photograph again. Where was this woman? No doubt remained that Austin had a living wife, a wife who wore Patou perfume and made up her face with foundation by Elizabeth Arden. A cold, hard ball of pain filled the space just below her breastbone. She looked again at Austin's smiling profile in the photograph. Something was missing, she realized. At last it hit her: Where was the scar? The right side of his face was to the camera, making her wonder if the negative had been reversed in the printing process. She looked at the wedding picture, but there was no scar there, either. He looked so young, so untouched by life.

Claudia left the room in a daze. Now what? Should she walk out without a word? She could go before he returned from the store. Her suitcase lay still unopened in the hall where she stood. She could hail a taxi right outside the front door on Seventy-fourth Street, go home, and not answer the telephone. However, when Monday rolled around, she would have to look at the pain and confusion in his blue eyes, and she would be unable to hide the pain in her own eyes when he looked across the courtoom at her.

Claudia wandered into Austin's bedroom, at the back of the house. No pictures of his wife were there, but of course not. How could he leave the telltale evidence around when he brought another woman into his house? Another woman—*Claudia* was the other woman. How often she and Tina had talked about the married-man problem. "All the best ones are," she remembered.

When Claudia crossed to his desk, she found that the lid was open as she had seen it before, books and papers piled everywhere on its surface. The pigeonholes overflowed as well. She had never snooped in anyone's possessions, not even in Peter's when she had suspected him of the worst, but the situation with Austin was different: He had lied to her, had led her to believe that he was single. His lie canceled any sense of fair play, any ethics. A woman had the right to protect herself, hadn't she? Her hand went out to the papers, but she drew it back. Reading another person's mail simply wasn't in her repertoire. Her hand then settled instead on a stack of books on the desk. *Bleak House, The Pickwick Papers,* and *Crime and Punishment* lay beneath biographies of Louis Nizer and Learned Hand. *The Brethren,* a story of the Supreme Court justices, was at the top of the stack, and a piece of blue stationery protruded from it, marking a page in the book. Claudia couldn't stop her hand from picking up the book and allowing the pages to fall open to the spot marked by the heavy monogrammed writing paper.

Dear Rem,
I don't see why we have to be apart like this. I'm sick of being stuck up here in New Canaan while you travel around and have all the fun. Even if you don't want a real marriage, is there any reason I can't come to the city now and then? Or are you so busy with other people—other women—that you don't care to see me? Thanks for the books. I liked the biography of Zelda Fitzgerald, but Kissinger's book left me cold.

Evangeline

The letter was dated "New Canaan—Wednesday." As if to dispel any lingering doubt, Claudia fingered the sharp edges of the engraved EH at the top of the page. The only incongruity was that his wife called him Rem. The name sounded ridiculous to Claudia. Its false-macho ring didn't fit the Austin she knew at all, the gentle, quiet man who hid his power beneath his civility, who hid his sensuality beneath his finely tailored English clothes. The again, maybe the name fit him perfectly, but then she would never know. *How could I have been so wrong?* she berated herself. *I was duped by a master.*

She replaced the letter between the pages of *The Brethren* and took her suitcase down to the entrance hall. She found her mohair cape in the hall closet and threw it over a chair next to the suitcase, then she went into the kitchen to wait for Harwood to return.

Claudia didn't have long to wait. He came through the door between the garage and the kitchen within ten minutes.

"Did you have a rest?" he asked, setting down two brown grocery bags on the counter.

"Oh yes. The whole world looks different to me now," she answered dully.

"I got some potatoes. Did you ever have baked potatoes with sour cream and red caviar on them? Delicious and easy to cook. Even I can—" He stopped. "What's the matter? You're staring at me in such an odd way."

"Was I? You look different to me, that's all. Tell me, where did you get the scar on your face?"

His fingertip went up to the scar and drew a line down his cheek. "This? Oh, a childhood accident. I would love to tell you a romantic story, but the truth is that a little girl ran into me with her sled. They kind of botched the stitching, didn't they?" He began to unpack the groceries.

"You're lying to me."

"What makes you think so?" He turned slowly to face her.

"I don't think, I know. You promised never to lie to me."

"And you promised not to pry into my past."

"I promised you that before... before we got so close to each other. I have a right to know some things."

"Like what? What do you want to know?" He leaned back against the counter and folded his arms over his chest. He stared at her with angry eyes. Claudia felt a ripple of fear when she looked at his face.

"I want to know about your wife in New Canaan. I want to know why you didn't tell me about her before."

"Because my wife wasn't any business of yours before," he said harshly. "Nor is she now."

"How can you say that? You promised you had never lied to me. You promised you never would. I know you're lying about the scar, so how can I believe anything else you've told me?" Her eyes filled with tears.

"Look, I don't pry into your life."

"What are you talking about? My life's an open book. I've told you everything about me. You've met my sister. You've even met my mother. Ask me anything—I'll tell you the truth!"

"Just as you always have, no doubt," he said coldly.

"Of course. I've never hidden anything from you."

"Not your husband at your place last Sunday night? I saw him. I also saw the loving message he sent you with the flowers, or have you conveniently forgotten? You've chosen not to explain yourself, and I haven't asked you to, have I?"

"Yes, but—"

"Yes, but what? That's different, right? You can tell or not tell what you want, but from me you demand something else."

"But I'm divorced from Peter."

"From where I stand you don't look divorced. You left my bed to go to his—that's what it looks like to me!"

"Austin, you don't understand, I tried to tell you about him. He's—"

"He's an obsession with you, that's what he is. You and I don't have a chance together until you get over him. We met at the wrong time, that's all." There was a note of finality in his voice that pierced her, but she was angry that he had misconstrued the facts so totally, not to mention that she was getting another dose of amateur psychology—but then from an attorney who had no idea of her true feelings instead of from a psychologist who thought he had the right to tell her how to feel.

"How dare you accuse me? How dare you put *me* on the defensive. You're the one who lied to me, remember. I don't have an obsession with Peter. You're out of your mind. You and I don't have a chance together, anyway, because you didn't tell me about Evangeline. Our whole time together was built on sand, and that's *your* fault, not mine."

"I still don't see what Evangeline has to do with us," Austin said, bewilderment evident in his voice.

"A hell of a lot more than Peter does!" she shouted.

Claudia turned and ran up the stairs that led out of the kitchen, blindly stumbling toward the entrance hall, where her suitcase lay. She fumbled with the lock and ran out the door, oblivious when the mohair cape dragged in the gutter as she ran down the street, looking for a taxi. She found one on Park Avenue and was just throwing her suitcase in the backseat when she saw Austin racing toward her on the leaf-strewn street.

"Wait, Claudia, wait!" he shouted. "Wait for me. I understand now. You've made a terrible mistake!"

"You bet I have!" She threw herself into the backseat of the yellow taxi, locked the door, and rolled up the window. He was within ten feet of the cab.

"That man just escaped from Bellevue," she said breathlessly to the driver. "He's dangerous. You'd better get out of here before he does something violent."

The driver slammed his foot on the accelerator.

"We had a problem like that with my kid sister's husband once," he began.

"I don't want to hear about it, if you don't mind. Please take me to Gramercy Square." Claudia began to cry in earnest.

Chapter Eight

"Hey, Arnold. How are you? You're lucky to be out at the beach," said McLaughlin. "It's one of those quirky fall days in the city. Feels just like August. The streets are already gummy from the heat."

"Yes, I know. I'm in the city."

"What about the trial?"

"I'm withdrawing from the trial. I'm terribly sorry, Mr. McLaughlin, I really am. A family emergency. My— my mother has had a stroke, you see." She was so glad she wasn't talking to McLaughlin in person, so glad the telephone protected her from his all-knowing eyes. "I've spoken to my agent. He has a young artist who's free to take over. Just say the word, and he'll be on the next train to Montauk."

"I don't know, Arnold." The hesitation in his voice was evident.

"Cleary," she corrected mechanically. "He's good." She mentioned several publications in which his work had appeared recently.

"But no courtroom experience—"

"Give him a break. Come on, everyone needs to start somewhere."

"And I'm desperate," he agreed. "Listen, I'm really sorry about your mother. I hope she'll be well soon."

"Keep me in mind for the next time, please. You won't hold this against me, will you?"

"Hell, no. You worked for me for years. I know how reliable you are. So long, Arnold."

"Cleary," she said to the dead receiver, feeling guilty as sin that she had lied to McLaughlin.

What did people ever do before telephones to mask their eyes when they lied? Before telephone answering machines to screen their calls as they sat in misery next to the tinny speaker, waiting for the right voice to come out of the box? She remembered the days when she and Peter were courting—and fighting—and how she had been afraid to go to class or to the Laundromat for fear she would miss his call after they had had a disagreement.

Idly she flipped the switch on the machine to play back the tape of all the calls that had come in since she had departed for Montauk.

Beep. A hang-up.

Beep. "This is Peter. It's Thursday night. Just checking," said the voice of her former husband.

Beep. "Peter again on Friday. Leaving for California tonight. Thought I'd say good-bye and see if things were still the same." Inane little chuckle. *Click.*

"And good riddance," Claudia said out loud.

Beep. "Alex Gómez here. It's Saturday afternoon. Was going to ask you to join me to see an Off-Broadway revival I have tickets for, but you're obviously busy. See you in court." Another inane chuckle. *Click.* Some people couldn't talk normally on an answering machine. She supposed she'd never get rid of Alex, since he knew she was divorced.

Beep. Another hang-up. They were so irritating.

Beep. "The waves are breaking right outside my window and there's a glorious sunset. I thought you'd be in bed by now, due to the time difference. You probably are, but not at home. Come out and try my waterbed!" Maniacal laugh. *Click.* Would he never leave her alone? she wondered. Why in heaven's name was he calling her daily? She hadn't heard from him for the past ten months, and then in the last fortnight he'd come back to haunt her life with a vengeance.

That brought the messages up to Sunday. She sat and listened for the fourth time to the call she had heard come in while she was struggling to find the apartment keys in her purse in the hall right outside the door.

Beep. "This is Austin. Obviously I had the wrong number." *Click.*

"No, *I* had the wrong number," she said softly to the speaker and she began to cry. What a beautiful voice he had, even icy cold with anger as it sounded. With a twinge of regret from the knowledge that she would probably never hear his voice again, she erased the entire message tape and set up the machine to take incoming calls once more.

After Claudia called her agent and told him of McLaughlin's decision, she returned to the package that had arrived by messenger an hour before. She opened the thick envelope and riffled the photographs, sketches, and memos of instruction contained within, deciding how to approach the rush job for one of the large New York department stores. It was an assignment her agent had arranged when she told him she was withdrawing from the trial for personal reasons. He never asked her a single question. The tone of her voice had told him that she was not to be dissuaded.

Claudia wasn't keen to return to fashion illustration, although she knew she was good and would never lack work if she chose to pursue a career devoted exclusively to its confines. Primarily she disliked working alone all day with only the sound of the television for company. Variety and the ability to meet people had led her to courtroom art. In addition, she didn't care for the people involved in the fashion business, including the people she knew from Tina's company—including Tina at that moment, she told herself bitterly. Tina the phony, who couldn't keep a hand out of Claudia's life. Tina was hardly capable of running her own mixed-up life, and she sorely resented Tina's nosing into hers. That Tina had been right about Austin was more than she could bear thinking about.

Those thoughts kept her from thinking about A. Remington Harwood IV, known as Rem to his wife and Austin to his lover. She closed her eyes and tried to evoke the searing shock and anger she had felt on Saturday evening, but all she felt was a hollow sense of pain and loss. She tried again to hear the harshness in his voice when he had said, "Because my wife wasn't any business of yours..." but instead she heard him say "I want your life to be perfect—no problems, no unhappiness, no suffering." She had indeed tempted the gods when she became involved with him. She had known. Blithely she had passed all the warning flags, the yellow pennants fluttering in the breeze of experience and said "Slow down—married man ahead." She had known and she was suffering. Whose fault was it, anyway? Certainly not all Harwood's. Being single in New York was a clear case of caveat emptor—let the buyer beware. She was as much at fault as he.

Time, time. Time was all she needed. She hated the trite answer, but she knew its truth.

"What are you doing here? How did you know I was home?" Claudia stood in the foyer of her apartment, dressed in blue jeans and a paint-stained work shirt.

Tina's floral perfume rolled through the front door like a fogbank.

"Willy told me. Why aren't you out in Montauk?"

"I withdrew from the trial."

"Why?"

"Something more lucrative came along." She indicated her drawing board set next to a window overlooking Gramercy Park in one corner of the living room. A nearly finished fashion layout was tacked to the ink-stained wood.

"I didn't realize the money was that important."

"My new couch arrives tomorrow."

"I see. Aren't you going to ask me in?"

Claudia stepped back. "Come in," she said stiffly. "Come into the kitchen. I have some chairs there."

"You've been back from Cincinnati for five days. How come you haven't called me?"

"I've been busy. It's a rush job."

"Too busy to pick up the telephone? You could dial with your left hand and still draw with your right. How come you're mad at me?"

"I'm not mad, Tina."

"Sure." Tina sat on a pressed-back oak chair at the kitchen table. She laid her handbag on the floor.

"You're wearing a new perfume. What's it called?"

"Calandre. Willy gave it to me because he thought the Jungle Gardenia I used to wear was too heavy."

"I like it. He has good taste. It's getting serious, huh?"

"Seems to be going well. I'm having dinner with him tonight."

"Isn't he in Montauk?"

"The trial has been postponed for ten days. New evidence or something, I don't know. The prosecution asked for a delay. I told Willy to pick me up at your place on his way back into the city."

"Is he—is he coming alone?"

"I assume so. What happened with you and Harwood?"

"Willy didn't tell you anything?"

"No. You know him, he's probably the most closed-mouthed person in the world."

"Nothing happened. Nothing. Please never mention Austin's name to me again." She would bite her tongue off before she admitted to Tina that Austin was married, just as her older sister had predicted. Tina would find out soon enough, if she didn't already know. Claudia could hear the *I told you so's* already. Every girl in the world should be an only child if just to be spared the existence of a know-it-all older sister, she thought.

"But—"

"Never again."

"All right. What happened in Cincinnati? How is Mother? Did you tell her?" Tina stared at the scarred top of the oak kitchen table and chewed at the cuticle of one manicured fingernail.

"I told her. You were right—she was upset. But she was also supportive, just as I predicted. She told me a few things, too. She knows who my birth mother is."

"She told you?" Tina looked up quickly, a note of astonishment in her voice.

"No, she wouldn't tell me. Austin thought—" She hesitated, finding it painful to even utter his name. "Austin figured that Mother had promised not to tell, but she did admit that the woman is alive and that she is not in Cincinnati. So much for your fortune-teller, Tina."

"What the hell. I'm on my way to see her now. Want to come?"

"Whatever for? She was wrong about everything."

"For you, maybe. Not for me."

"What about Willy? When are you coming back?"

"Give him a drink. I'll be back by seven." Tina stood and smoothed out the skirt of her suit. "Don't be angry with me, Claudia." She placed a manicured hand on her sister's shoulder and looked her directly in the eyes. "I only want what's best for you. That's all I've ever wanted."

"I know that, Tina." Tears filled Claudia's eyes. "It's just that you treat me like a baby at times. You act as if I can't take care of myself. I know what I'm doing, you know."

"Sometimes I'm not so sure. I have to learn to let go, I suppose. It's very hard to let you make your own mistakes, take your own lumps. I wanted to spare you the pain. Believe me, I know what I'm talking about."

"I know you do." She put her arms around Tina's plump waist and kissed her on the forehead. "Go on to your fortune-teller. See if she can set the date for your wedding."

"I've got other things on my mind," Tina said morosely.

"Trouble with Willy?"

"Not yet."

"Have you come straight with him? Told him everything?"

"Not yet."

"Just be yourself, Tina. If he loves you, he loves you. Austin says—" She'd accidentally said his name again. "Well, Austin says he's not as stuffy as you think."

"Really?" Tina's voice showed no enthusiasm. "Bully for Austin."

Claudia returned to the drawing board. At seven the doorbell rang and she put on her glasses to look out the window. The blue Rolls-Royce was just pulling away from the curb. With Austin inside? she wondered. She rang the buzzer to let Lindhurst into the building.

"Are you alone?" he asked, peering around as he removed the raincoat he wore and handing it to Claudia, who hung it in the hall closet.

"Yes, Tina had an errand to do. I expect her any minute. A drink? Dubonnet, right?"

"If you please."

"There are no living room chairs, Willy. Do you mind sitting on a pillow? I have a new couch coming tomorrow, but until then..." She pulled two large pillows made from remnants of Oriental rugs to a spot in front of the fireplace. She poured two Dubonnets in the kitchen and brought them to the living room, lowering herself onto a pillow facing Lindhurst.

"Cheers," said Claudia, holding up her glass.

"To your search," rejoined Lindhurst.

They sipped the aperitif.

"What's happening with the search?" she asked him.

"I really don't know. I've been removed from the case, so to speak."

"Removed from the case? I don't understand."

"Austin has taken over. The investigators have been told to report directly to him—to no one else."

"Whatever for?" she asked him.

"To protect your privacy, I would imagine. The fewer people involved the better. It's the first time such a thing has ever happened between us. Perhaps he feared I would tell Cristina before you—"

"Willy, you'd never do that! I can't imagine anyone

more discreet than you. How could he think such a thing? What an insult to you!" His pain was obvious simply from the set of his shoulders. And Austin was not the man Claudia had thought he was before. How cruel could one be?

"Nevertheless, he's the boss," said Lindhurst dejectedly. "Since you are alone, I have something for you," he said, changing the topic quickly. He reached into the outside pocket of his dark gray suit and pulled out a small box from Van Cleef & Arpels, the Fifth Avenue jeweler.

"Is this from Austin? I don't want it."

"Take it. It's sent in good spirit."

"How do you know? Is there a message?"

"No, no message. I know that he cares for you very much, however. He's sorry about the way things turned out."

"Did he tell you that?"

"He didn't have to tell me. He and I have known each other a long time. I know how he feels."

"He hasn't thought too much of *your* feelings lately, has he?" But she had said too much. She hadn't counted on the years of friendship between the two men, and then she saw that the words were a mistake by the way Lindhurst's eyes clouded over behind his glasses.

"One of the things about Austin is that he always does the correct thing, even if what he thinks is right seems to be unpopular or uncomfortable. Above all, Austin is an ethical man." What a true friend said in defense of the absent party, she thought. How ethical was a married man who knowingly began an affair? Who lied about his wife?

"Why didn't Austin tell me about his wife? Can you explain that, Willy?"

"He *never* discusses his wife. No one is permitted to bring up the subject—ever." Lindhurst was using his best lawyer-in-court voice—cold, stern, forbidding. Claudia knew she had committed a faux pas and although she wanted to press on anyway, she saw from the look on his face that she would learn nothing more from the discreet Lindhurst.

The buzzer from the downstairs lobby rang. Annoyed, she stood to respond, throwing one last barb over her shoulder as she crossed the room. "I don't call neglecting to mention something as important as a wife terribly ethical." She listened to the intercom and pressed the buzzer. "It's Tina," she explained, returning to the living room.

Lindhurst stood and set his empty glass down on the mantel. "I think you've gone a bit far, Claudia. After all, *you* haven't been all that honest with him. You have no right to complain about Austin's foibles. May I use your bathroom? I'd like to freshen up a bit. It's a long drive from Montauk."

"Me! *I* haven't been honest? Willy, what are you talking about?" she asked indignantly, but he was already on his way toward the bathroom, in the direction she had indicated. The bell of the front door sounded. She stamped to the hall, muttering under her breath, "Austin's foibles, indeed!" She attempted to compose herself before she saw Tina, knowing her sister's ability to read every emotion on her face. What difference did it make what Willy thought? It was all over with Austin Harwood, anyway.

"Is Willy here?"

"He's in the bathroom."

"Good. We'll be late if we don't leave right now. We have reservations for eight thirty."

"How was the fortune-teller?" asked Claudia.

"Shh—he doesn't know about her. She was fine. It's all going to work out if I play my cards right."

Claudia rolled her eyes heavenward.

"What's your problem? You look furious," said Tina, inspecting her closely.

"Me? I don't have any problems. I seem to be the only person in the world who doesn't." She opened the closet door and took Lindhurst's raincoat from a hanger. "Here's Willy's coat."

"Do you want to come with us?" It was Lindhurst who invited her. He and Tina smiled at each other and kissed quickly on the lips.

"Thanks, anyway, Willy, but I have to work." She knew he meant the invitation as a tacit reconciliation and she appreciated his gracious gesture. Yet her argument had not really been with Willy, she realized. "Thank you for the invitation," she repeated.

Tina went out the door, but Lindhurst lagged back and said quietly, "Evangeline doesn't have to come between you two, you know. Everything can be worked out with a little discretion, a little sensitivity. Why don't you reconsider? Get yourself free first and then see what happens."

"I don't understand. You of all people to suggest such a thing—"

"Willy, come on! We'll be late," Tina called from the hall.

"Think about it," he suggested.

"There's nothing to think about! What kind of woman do you take me for, anyway?"

"A very nice woman. A bit short-sighted, perhaps, a bit mixed-up, if you don't mind my saying so."

"Yes, I mind. I mind very much!"

"Will-ee!"

"I'm coming, my dear. Good-bye, Claudia."

Good lord, they'd all gone crazy, she thought as she took the two glasses to the kitchen sink. She poured the dregs of her cocktail down the drain, because she'd told Willy the truth about having to work. Crazy! First Tina charting her life by the stars and then the pronouncements of a fortune-teller with one blue eye and one brown eye. She should have let Tina spike Willys' drink with the voodoo love potion. He deserved a stomachache for suggesting such a tawdry arrangement between her and Austin. She'd rather be celibate for the rest of her life than be someone's mistress, some man's second best anything. She wasn't mixed-up; on the contrary, she was in good shape, except for the pain in her breast that hadn't abated one iota since the previous weekend. But the pain would go away, she told herself. Even in the middle of the night, even when she couldn't sleep because she hurt so much, she knew that after a time the pain would fade and only a dull ache would be left, a scar to remind her of the short, but wonderful days with Austin.

Claudia returned to the layout on the drawing board and picked up a pen, dipping it into a bottle of black india ink and blotting her finger in the process. She swore in annoyance and wiped off the finger. The stain would be on the skin for a week at least, even if she washed up right then. India ink was—

She ran into the bathroom and threw open the door of the closet. She unzipped her jeans and kicked them off, at the same time pushing down the bikini panties she wore to reveal the skin of her hips. She twisted around to see her reflection in the full-length mirror on the back of the closet door.

"I love you," the message read. The words were written backward so that they would be legible in a mirror. The mole on her hip formed the dot above the I. A ring of doodled flowers encircled the message.

He had never told her. She had never thought to look and she had never responded to his message.

Leaving the blue jeans on the floor, she went back to the living room and picked up the small box from Van Cleef & Arpels. The silver box, heavy for its size, was sealed with circular silver tabs. If she opened the gift, she would have to keep it, but if she was going to send it back it should go back with the seals intact....

She slipped her thumbnail under the seals and broke them. In white tissue paper lay a heavy ornamental gold comb for her hair. Her monogram was carved deeply into the lustrous metal—CNC, the initials of her maiden name. She held the cool ore in the palm of her hand. She would be afraid to wear such a valuable piece of jewelry on the streets of New York City. After all, people had been killed for the chains they hung around their necks, and the comb in her palm was heavier than ten necklaces. On the other hand, who would believe a hair ornament was actually fashioned of eighteen karat gold? She took down her hair and redid it, replacing the mother-of-pearl combs she wore with the mono-grammed gold one. Later she slept with the comb under her pillow, her fingers gently curling around its warmth.

Beep. "Peter again. It's noon on Monday, your time. Just checking up on things." *Click.*

Beep. A hang-up.

Beep. "Altman's loved the rush job. There's another here if you want it. Give me a call when you get in." *Click.*

Beep. "It is Monday, two P.M. This is Mr. Austin Harwood's office calling. Mr. Harwood has the information you requested. Please advise if it is possible for you to be at our offices at nine o'clock Tuesday morning. Thank you." *Click.*

"Is Mr. Harwood there? This is Claudia Cleary."

"Mr. Harwood is with a client right now. May I take a message?"

"Please tell him I'll be there at nine o'clock tomorrow morning." Better not to talk to him. Better not to hear his voice. Better to keep everything strictly business. But she would wear the gold comb, anyway. She would never mention that she had seen the drawing he made, but she would wear the gold comb.

"Claudia Cleary. I have an appointment with Mr. Harwood."

"Have a seat, Miss Cleary. He'll be with you in a moment."

Claudia sat on a nubby gray-striped sofa in the reception room and stared at the minute hand of an antique grandfather clock on the opposite wall. Her stomach churned with apprehension. She was unable to decide what would upset her more, seeing Austin or hearing the information he had uncovered. She rubbed her palms on the rough wool upholstery to dry them. *I should be happy,* she told herself. *After all this time, being so close to finding my birth mother should elate me beyond reason.* But she was not elated; she was filled with fear. Her fingers pressed the pleats in the coral-colored wool skirt she wore. From time to time her hand touched the gold comb in her auburn hair. Fifteen minutes passed. Twenty. The receptionist offered Claudia a cup of coffee, which she declined. How dare he make her wait half an hour!

"Mr. Harwood will see you now." Claudia followed the woman's trim ankles down the ribbon of gray carpet to Austin's corner office. The rooms to her left and right virtually hummed with activity. They approached the end of the corridor, and the woman opened the door and stood back against it, allowing Claudia to enter the office. Then Claudia was inside the glass-walled room, and the door was closing behind her.

Austin stood behind his wide desk of lustrous wood. A manila folder lay closed on the desk in front of him. He wore glasses and a three-piece suit and his blue oxford cloth shirt mirrored the sky-blue of his eyes. The room was filled with the clear morning light that shone like crystal on a perfect New York day in early October.

"I don't want to be disturbed, Mrs. Ryder," he said to the closing door.

"Very well, Mr. Harwood."

Claudia stood still, unsure of what to say. A chair upholstered in maroon leather was placed in front of his desk. She approached the desk and felt the muscles of her stomach tighten.

"Please sit down, Claudia," he said formally. At least he hadn't called her Miss Cleary as she had expected from the strong and determined set of his jaw. The gloomy look on his face was just short of anger. She sat blindly, thankful for the width of the antique desk that separated them. She longed to touch him, to inhale his scent, to feel the special texture of his tanned skin beneath her hands. She longed to tell him that Lindhurst's suggestion no longer seemed so bizarre and shocking since she had turned his unwelcome words over in her head. Over and over, in the quiet empty hours of the early morning while she lay under the blue quilt, watching the shadows the streetlights cast on the ceiling of her lonely bedroom, she had thought of what a life with Austin in it—but not truly part of it—would be like. She needed him more than she thought another human should and she knew her need for him was unhealthy and that her longing was dangerous. She had considered a life with Austin as he was, just out of her reach, legally belonging to another woman. She had considered, rejected, weighed again, rejected—yet the thought returned.

Austin regarded her silently; perhaps he noticed the new, dark smudges beneath her green eyes, telltale evidence of sleepless nights. She looked into his eyes and was conscious of the most extraordinary sensations in her breast and a gelatinous weakening of her legs.

"Why did you make me wait so long? I had a nine o'clock appointment." Her petulant words, purposely chosen to create a barrier of ice between them, broke the trance in an instant. He turned to the transparent wall behind him and stared out at the steel and glass of Park Avenue.

"We've made contact with your mother," he said.

"Contact," she whispered. "You've made contact with her?" she said aloud, rising to her feet and taking a step toward him, although she still stood before the desk. "Why would you do such a thing when I only wanted her name? I wanted to make contact myself. Why did you do that?" How dare he! Treating her like a child, ignoring her rights, infringing on her innermost self!

"The contact was inadvertent. She discovered that inquiries were being made and she surfaced." He turned to face her and he seemed to be awaiting a reply from Claudia, but she was so stunned and angered by his news that she stood silently, listening to the echo of his unexpected first statement. His eyes fell on the manila folder.

"Who is she?" she managed to ask at last, following the path his eye had taken. "What's her name? Where is she?" She thought she might faint. The edges of her vision blurred, and she was barely aware that Austin had moved around the desk and was standing close enough to touch.

"I'm sorry. I can't give you that information."

"What?"

"I can't tell you. I'm sorry." The pain in his voice was reflected in his eyes. She heard his words from far away, as if from the other end of a tunnel, but she remained unmoved and nearly unaware of his presence. She was back in Ohio in a room as austere and institutional as Harwood's office was luxurious and studiedly comfortable. The pinched face of a bureaucrat sat across from her at a gray steel desk and intoned, "I'm sorry, that information is privileged. I'm sorry, I'm not at liberty to divulge those details."

"Claudia, are you all right? Are you going to be sick?" He stepped closer and put an arm out to catch her as she swayed on her feet.

"Don't touch me! Get back, don't touch me!" She clutched her handbag to her breast and stared down at the thick gray rug, irrelevantly marking the shadow the loops cast as sunlight from the window combed through the weave.

"You're going to faint. All the blood is gone from your face. For God's sake, sit down." He pulled the chair over until it was behind her and gently he touched her shoulder until she felt herself falling back into the maroon leather seat. He threw himself to his knees on the floor in front of the chair and buried his head in her lap. "Oh, my God, I didn't want to say those words to you. My darling, I'm so sorry."

Claudia looked down at the back of his head, the

back of a stranger's head, in her lap. She shook her head to clear her brain. Why was he kneeling on the rug? Was she losing her mind? She meant to push his head away, but her fingers went through his brown hair in a distracted caress instead.

"Why? Why can't you tell me? How can you not tell me? You, of all people, you know how much I need to know." When he was that close her head swam. "Austin, you love me, you love me—you told me so. If you really loved me, you wouldn't do this to me. I can't stand the pain anymore. You don't know, you don't understand—"

"I know, I know."

She grabbed his head between frantic hands and pulled him around until he looked at her. There were tears in his eyes. "Then tell me!"

"I can't. She came to me in confidence, she came as a client—"

"I thought *I* was your client. I thought I was *more* than your client. If it's a question of money, I'll give—"

"No! No, it isn't money. I have to do what's right, what I think is right for everyone concerned, do you understand? I can't give you the name unless she allows me to."

"Does she have a family? A husband? Children? I won't embarrass her in front of them, you know I won't. Austin, please! Don't do this to me." She swallowed painfully, making an enormous and futile effort to control her raging emotions. Tears rolled down her cheeks.

"Yes—yes, she has a family," he answered quickly, obviously grasping at the explanation she herself had just provided. "She doesn't want her family to know."

Claudia tore her eyes away from the deceit she read in his usually clear blue eyes. She caught sight of the manila folder on the desk.

"Get up, Austin," she said coldly. "Get up."

He got to his feet and brushed at his knees absently. He stood awkwardly before her while she secretly weighed her chances of reaching the folder before he did. He followed her gaze, but he stood immobile.

"I know what you're thinking and I want you to forget it," he said sternly.

"There's no way? Are you willing simply to step outside to speak to your secretary for one minute? For thirty seconds?" She hated herself for groveling; she hated him for making her grovel.

"No, but listen: I have a letter for you."

"From her?"

"Yes."

He walked behind the desk and opened the manila folder. Before he quickly slipped the top document to the bottom of the thin stack of papers in the file, she had a fleeting glimpse of a photostat, a line drawing of a setting sun, a sheaf of wheat: the official seal of the state of Ohio. He extracted a sheet of plain bond paper and closed the folder.

"Was that a copy of my true birth certificate?"

"Yes." The word was loud in her ears in the quiet office.

"Oh, my God." She closed her eyes and a minute passed.

"Shall I read you the letter? Or would you rather—"

"Read it to me." What was the difference? Austin already knew what the letter said. He knew everything, everything she longed to know.

"'My dearest daughter Claudia.'"

"She knows my name. Did you tell her?"

"No, she already knew your name."

"'My dearest daughter Claudia,'" he began again. "'I know of your search for me and I know how important the discovery of my name seems to you. For you to know who I am is the most important thing in your life. But for me and those I love that discovery would have disastrous consequences. I have lived a lie about you for so long that to extricate myself at this stage of my life is not simply difficult or inconvenient, it is impossible. Since your adoption I have known where you are and I have followed your life closely. I know of your schooling, of your career in art, of your failed marriage, and, by the way, I always thought that Peter was a schmuck and I considered your divorce a success, not a failure—'"

Claudia opened her eyes. "Wait. She wrote *schmuck*?"

"Yes," he said, looking over his horn-rimmed glasses at her.

"She lives in New York," Claudia said, smiling faintly.

"That's right," he conceded. He adjusted his glasses and continued. "'...considered your divorce a success, not a failure. I know you well; you will be angry and hurt because I lack the courage to own up to the truth, but please have compassion for your mother, who loves and respects you and who tried to do the best for you under extreme difficulties when you were a baby. All my love, Your Mother.'"

"She knows a lot about me," she said softly. "Am I like her? Do I look like her?"

"Some parts of you. Your hands, your gestures are just the same. Your voices, too. When I first heard her speak, I could have sworn it was you. But you are much more beautiful than she is, much more beautiful."

"Well, I'm younger, that's all," she said, blushing.

"She's not old. She's younger than you imagine."

"No, she's older than I imagine. We adoptees all picture our birth mothers as perpetually stuck at the age they gave us up. But what am I saying? What do you care?"

"I care a lot," he said gently. "You know I do."

"I doubt it." She stood up. "Look, Austin, you and I had an agreement. How would you feel if I said I no longer felt bound, since you weren't forthcoming with the information you promised me? You knew I would never have gone against my word before, not for anything. You know me better than that. And I thought you were a man of your word. You and I—" Her voice broke with pain, and then she was silent.

Austin walked around the desk and attempted to put his arms around her. The citrus scent of his cologne filled her nostrils and evoked an assult of sensual memories that made her draw in her breath quickly.

"Please don't come near me. I can't stand to have you so close to me." *Because I can't help what I do when you are near me.* She clutched her handbag to her breast again as if the brown leather would protect her from his heady presence.

"Claudia, I know how you feel right now. Too much has happened too fast, but please reconsider before you—"

"Are you afraid you'll lose your precious case? Is that all you ever cared about?" She felt totally betrayed, both by Austin and by her natural mother. "If Mrs. Shorter shot her husband, she deserves to be punished," she lashed out, but she knew her threat was an idle one. Long ago she had decided she could not bear the responsibility of revealing what she had heard Glenda Shorter admit.

"I won't dignify your first question with an answer—you know how I felt about you before, quite aside from the case. As for the second, Glenda doesn't necessarily deserve to be convicted. Yes, she shot him, but there are others to consider. Not only did Shorter cheat openly on her, he beat her and he beat their twin five-year-old boys, too. Have you seen her little boys, by the way? He beat those poor, helpless children. The twins will be taken away from Glenda and made wards of the state if she's convicted. They will probably grow up separated from each other, grow up raised by strangers. You know what that feels like, don't you, Claudia?"

Of course she knew. What was her search all about? He was asking her to spare two children the agony she knew intimately. "Bring those facts out in court. They can only help her case," she persisted.

"She doesn't want the publicity to come back to haunt her children later. Whatever you may think of her, she's a good mother. Claudia, think of the children."

"That's unfair, Austin. You're manipulating me." No wonder he won the most impossible cases.

"Those are simply the facts. Nothing in the world looks the same when you're in possession of all the facts. Before you do anything hasty please consider the fate of two helpless children who have no say in their own destinies."

A moment earlier an overwhelming desire for revenge against Austin had burned within her, actually tempting her to reveal her knowledge. She never would have, but she allowed Austin to think he had convinced her.

"I'll do something for you," he said.

"Isn't this where I came in? What will you do for me? No, never mind. You can't do anything for me."

"I will speak to your mother and try to arrange a meeting. I can't promise anything, except that I'll try."

"She'll never do it. The letter said—"

"I know her. I think she'll listen to me," he interrupted.

"Are you doing this for me? Or for the children?"

"It doesn't matter. I'm doing what I think is right."

Chapter Nine

"Nolo contendere. Isn't that what you lawyers say when there are no arguments? When the defendant gives up?" She walked to the window and watched the blur of yellow taxis below on Park Avenue.

"Yes, that's what we say. Unwilling to continue the defense."

"I couldn't be part of anything that would hurt those children." *Nor could I break a promise to you.*

"I knew that."

"And you used it. Shamelessly."

"Yes," he admitted, but he didn't sound victorious.

"Did you tell me the truth about Mr. Shorter? Was he really that bad?"

"Worse. You don't want to know."

"No, don't tell me anything more. I feel terrible already. I can't take any more bad news today." The ache in her breast was dull, but steady, and her entire body was tired. Her mother had rejected her—again. Austin had betrayed her and he no longer loved her. He had said, "You know how I *felt* about you." No longer...

"He had everything—blue blood, millions of dollars, that estate at Hither Hills. How can a man like that—"

"Claudia, do you really think good family makes a person perfect? Nice people like the Shorters are just as apt to beat their spouses or be promiscuous or be alcoholics as anyone else. Don't tell me you believe that a so-called patrician bloodline protects people from human weaknesses, because if you believe that nonsense, you're hopelessly naive. You're so caught up in your own lack of family origins that you've idealized everyone else's. Wake up and look around you, for God's sake. You'll see what's obvious to anyone else with a brain, what's staring you right in the face."

"You're a fine person to talk!" She whirled around to face Austin. "What do you know about real life? You're a rich man. You've had everything handed to you on a platter, including a pedigree that didn't hurt your chances in life. You can have almost anything you want in this world by dint of money or connections. And what doesn't fall into your lap that way, you manipulate—just as you think you manipulated me into doing what you wanted by using those poor little children." She reached behind her head and tore the gold comb from her hair. Her heavy auburn tresses tumbled down her back. "I don't want your damn presents. I don't want to see you ever again. I want to forget I ever set eyes on you." She threw the comb on the desk and watched it skid across the burnished wood and leave a deep gouge in its wake. Claudia covered her eyes and burst into gasping tears. The morning had been a hurricane of emotions.

Austin picked up the comb calmly. "Please keep the comb. It can't be returned; it has your monogram, you know."

"The initials mean nothing to me. They aren't mine, anyway. They're just a name Cynthia Cleary made up."

"It's your name," he said patiently. "I want you to have it."

She shook her head.

"At least wear it home. I know you hate to go out with your hair down. Wear it for a while." She felt the warmth of his body behind her. He lifted her heavy hair and twisted it gently, rolling it back against her head. She felt the comb's heavy teeth slide into her hair. Austin's lips touched the back of her neck, and the kiss burned on her skin.

"Austin, don't." *Don't, because I'll tell you that I love you, even if you don't love me anymore, even if you have a wife, even if you have betrayed me. No matter what, I love you—I can't help myself, I just do. But I can control what I do about the love I feel. At least I'm in control of that part of my life, if nothing else.*

She stepped away from him deliberately.

"Thank you, I'll send it back to you soon," she said coldly, as if she had borrowed his umbrella in an unexpected rainstorm. "By the way, may I have the letter?"

"Of course," he answered. He went to the desk for the letter. He kept his eyes down when he handed her the single page.

"The letter is typewritten!" she said in surprise. "Everything but the signature."

"There's something wrong with her hands," he mumbled.

Claudia looked at the top of his bent head. She recognized the catch in his throat and she knew why he refused to look at her. Men were not supposed to cry. It tore her heart to act with such cruelty and coldness toward him. The same tears choked painfully in her own throat and threatened to spill from her eyes. She turned quickly and left the office.

Beep. "Peter calling. I know it's Thursday, and you're no doubt at ALMA, but I wanted to hear the sweet

voice on your message tape before I left on a two-week
lecture trip to Hawaii and Japan." Strange laugh. *"Say-
onara."* *Click.*

Beep. "Austin Harwood here. Your mother will meet
you at two thirty Friday afternoon, Café des Artistes,
One West Sixty-seventh Street. I'm sending Lindhurst
over at lunchtime Friday with some papers for you.
Please advise if the arrangements are inconvenient,
otherwise I'll assume everything meets with your approval." *Click.* Claudia erased Peter's message and re-
played Austin's cold, formal words—words that fairly
dripped controlled anger. What right did he have?
Claudia hadn't betrayed him, lied to him, mistreated
him—just the opposite. She was the one suffering. But
Austin had kept his promise to arrange a meeting. At
last she was to meet her mother.

"Come in, Willy. I'm just making a grilled cheese sand-
wich, but I know I'm too excited to eat it. Will you join
me?"

"I'd like that very much," Lindhurst answered, removing his raincoat. "I see your new couch is here.
Very nice."

"Thank you. Come into the kitchen and sit down.
What papers do you have for me?"

Lindhurst sat at the oak table and removed a manila
envelope from his briefcase. "Austin has a house on
Block Island he'd like to lend to you for as long as you
like. Here's a map to show you how to get there, car
registration for the MG, instructions for turning on the
water pump—"

"Whatever for? I mean, that's very nice of him, but
why is he doing this for me?" She flipped the cheese
sandwiches in the frying pan and then sat down at the
table with Lindhurst.

"He told me you are to meet your birth mother this afternoon."

"That's right."

"I'm very happy for you, Claudia. Austin thought you might want to get away afterward, to be by yourself. His place on Block Island is quiet. You can be alone there."

"I can be alone here in my apartment, Willy. What's all the fuss about?"

"He meant really alone, where no one will bother you, call you on the phone—you know."

"To get over the trauma, I suppose? My, aren't you all paternalistic! Doesn't anyone think I can take care of myself? Today is a happy occasion for me, Willy. I've been looking forward to this day for most of my life. I don't need Austin's protection, but thank him for me, anyway."

"The car is in a garage on Nineteenth Street. I'll leave the envelope in case you change your mind. You can always return the car later if you decide not to go."

"All right, Willy, I give up! I know you're just doing your job. Have you seen my mother? Do you know anything about today? How is she going to recognize me?"

"I know nothing of the arrangements, nothing at all."

She served the grilled cheese sandwiches and two glasses of iced tea, and they began to eat.

"Claudia, may I ask you a question?" Lindhurst asked shyly, wiping his mouth with a napkin.

"Go ahead." She watched his serious eyes.

"Do you think—do you think Cristina would marry me if I asked her?" He blushed up to the bald spot on the top of his head.

"Why don't you ask her? Personally, I believe she'd

say yes, Willy. In fact, I'm certain she'll marry you.''

"Really? Oh, I'd be such a happy man. I know we haven't known one another for very long, but she's brought me an entirely new outlook on life. I feel eighteen years old.''

"Tina's certainly alive, Willy. You deserve to be happy. Go ahead and ask her.''

Claudia dressed carefully for the afternoon appointment. The October day was cool and sunny, so she chose a violet wool flannel suit that Tina had designed. The suit was elegant and serious with a two-button padded shoulder jacket and an inverted-pleat skirt. She knew its softly draped lines were perfect for the meeting. She decided to wear no jewelry except for the gold comb from Austin, which she had not yet given back to him. She hated to part with the beautiful ornament. She held the heavy gold in her hand a moment and regarded its lustrous color with regret before she arranged her hair.

One last check in the full-length mirror of the bedroom closet satisfied her critical eye before she descended the stairs to the street in search of a taxi, purposely shoving from her mind the wild and fearsome speculations about the two thirty meeting, which had continuously assaulted her since Austin's message had come in on the answering machine the night before. The only thought she allowed herself was that her birth mother might live on the West Side and had chosen the Café des Artistes for convenience. Most adoptees she knew had made contact originally in restaurants or some equally neutral place. Imagine, her mother was one of the millions of faceless New Yorkers! Possibly she had seen her before—sat next to her on a bus, stepped over her ankles en route to a seat at the Metropolitan Opera, even asked directions from her on the street.

Claudia paid the driver when the taxi rolled to a stop at the corner of Sixty-seventh Street and Central Park West. The door opened while she was still waiting for her change.

"Claudia?" Her sister stood awkwardly at the door to the taxi. Anxiety clouded her familiar eyes.

"Tina! What are you doing here?"

"I didn't think you should come alone," said Tina quickly. "You need support. I thought—"

"Support! You've fought me all the way in my search and now—the one time I have to be alone—you want to give me support. You treat me just like a baby, Tina, you always have. You don't understand anything about what's going on, do you? I have to do this alone. This is a private part of my life. Private, do you hear me? How did you know I'd be here, anyway? Who told you?"

"Willy told me. I just had lunch with him. He said the meeting was going to be traumatic, that I should come along in case—"

"Tina, you're lying. I don't know why, but you're lying to me. *I* had lunch with Willy, and he doesn't know anything about this afternoon." She eyed Tina's pale cheeks. "I'm going to be late. Get out of my way, Tina, and don't follow me inside, do you understand? I don't want you here. I have to go through today by myself.

Claudia brushed past Tina and went into the restaurant alone. At mid-afternoon the elegant room was nearly empty; only late lunchers remained dawdling over their coffee.

"One madam?"

"No, two. I'm waiting for—" She didn't have a name to give the maître d'. "I'm waiting for a lady."
At least I hope she's a lady, she prayed silently, trying to

push away the unwelcome vision of a subway bag lady or a stridently made-up streetwalker that floated before her mind's eye. The tuxedoed man led her to a table under lead-paned windows overlooking the orange- and brown- and red-painted leaves of the trees in Central Park, across the street. Ignoring the view, she took a seat that would allow her to see anyone entering the door. She ordered a glass of white wine and peered around at the greenery and the many empty tables under the sensuous sylvan murals painted by Howard Chandler Christy. She knew that under other circumstances she would have loved the charming room, so reminiscent of a European café, but that day she was filled with fear, and icy butterflies seemed to be imprisoned just under her rib cage.

A dark-haired woman was crossing the room toward her. She whipped her glasses out of her handbag to bring the newcomer into focus. Tina—Tina, with that determined set to her jaw that had always announced "Now you're going to do as I say, young lady."

"I told you I don't want you here, Tina," she hissed as her sister arrived at the table. "And don't give me the line that you know better. Look, even if you were right about Austin's wife—"

"What about Austin's wife?" Tina asked innocently, taking the chair opposite Claudia.

"Tina, get out of here. I'm really angry! Leave me alone, can't you hear me? I don't want you here!"

"I hear you, but I'm staying. Nothing you can say will make me leave. I know what I'm doing."

Claudia squeezed her hands together under the table. She knew that streak of stubborness, that vein of all-out determination in Tina. Claudia recognized that she and Tina, unlike anyone else in their family, had been uncannily alike in their blind perseverance of a.

goal. Her fingernails dug into the skin of her palms until she thought they would bleed. After a moment of silence during which frustrated tears filled her eyes, she crumbled and uttered in a voice fairly aquiver with rage and pain, "At least sit in the other chair so I can see the door."

"That's better," Tina said, moving to the chair next to Claudia, who anxiously continued to watch the entrance to the restaurant.

"Willy is on the verge of proposing," Tina announced after the waiter had taken her order for a martini and left them alone. Claudia never removed her eyes from the door. How could Tina act as if they were meeting for an ordinary lunch, as if today were like any other day in her life? Because it *was* an ordinary day for Tina, she realized.

"I know. He told me today."

"Did he?" Silence.

"Well, aren't you happy?" asked Claudia distractedly.

"No, I'm scared to death."

"Why?" An elderly woman was walking through the door.

"I've gone through all that with you before. You know I've fallen in love with Willy. I don't want to live without him in my life. I'm scared, because he's going to find out everything about me. Everyone is going to find out. Because Willy won't marry me when he does— you'll see, he won't. But worse, I'm going to lose *everyone* I love. What can I do?" She looked at Claudia, who didn't appear to have heard her, watching the progress of the elderly matron through the café. The woman stopped at a table in the center of the dining room and joined a couple already there. "Did you hear me? Look at me. Please pay attention to me, Claudia."

"What? What?" snapped Claudia, annoyed. "Tina, I'm watching for my mother, for God's sake. If you won't go away, at least stop nattering on. You're talking inanely. What could you have possibly done to Willy to make him not want to marry you? Your past is your own business. You don't owe him any explanations." Tersely she dismissed Tina's worries. She checked her wristwatch after two other women entered and, never looking her way, continued into the bar. Her birth mother was really late. Perhaps she had lost her nerve, after all. "I don't want to miss her when she comes in. Oh, God, what if she doesn't come?" She spoke out loud, but more to herself than to Tina.

"It's not what I've done to Willy. It's my life—my whole life's been a lie." Tina hesitated, then seemed to make up her mind. She drew in a deep breath. "You're not going to miss your mother, Claudia," said Tina. "She's already here."

Claudia turned her head slowly to the left until she was looking fully into Tina's face. She stared at dark eyes dancing with fear, at plump cheeks, at pale lips where Tina was chewing away her plum lipstick from nervousness. Her stunned mind whirled like a tape recorder in reverse, even to the accompanying strange high whine that pierced her eardrums. Her life seemed to play backward in a speed faster than sound, faster than light itself. Diverse wisps of memory, whispered hints of long-ago years, a snigger, a sideways look at a half-forgotten family funeral—all flashed across her brain like moths fluttering against a screen on a still summer night, bumping, seeking entry to the place where the light shone. She thought of a roulette game she had played in a London casino, of the red ball spinning and spinning around the wheel almost in slow motion, whirling and whirling in the bowl until at last the small ball hesitated, hung for a millisecond, and finally dropped with a crisp click into the numbered slot.

"She's here? You?" she whispered. "You?"

Tina nodded her head, agony written all over her features. Her eyes burned as she stared into Claudia's.

"Oh, my God. You!" Claudia threw her hands up to her face and covered her eyes. She felt all the blood drain from her head. Tina, her sister, her mother! Tina, Tina. All those years a lie. Tina...

"Are you all right?" Tina's hand closed on the violet wool of Claudia's jacket, closed around her arm near the elbow. Claudia pulled away from Tina with a rude jerk.

"Don't touch me," she mumbled behind her hands. "I don't want you to touch me!" Her mother, her mother all along. She didn't want to be touched by the woman who had so basely betrayed her; she didn't want to be touched by anyone. She was isolated from everyone. Deceit and betrayal had left her alone and in such pain that every inch of her skin suddenly felt exposed, felt flayed, felt turned inside out to the cold air. All these years had been a monstrous lie!

Claudia looked through her fingers at Tina's hand where it lay on the white tablecloth and she knew that what Tina had said was true. True. Tina's hand and hers... She lowered one cold, trembling hand and laid it on the snowy-white linen next to Tina's. The two hands were nearly identical in length and in the shape of the fingers, identical in skin tone, in gesture. How had she been so long ignorant of their similarity? Unconsciously she rubbed at one temple with her other hand, a dazed frown on her brow. The image of Tina's carefully polished plum-colored fingernails swam before her eyes. Her head had begun to pound, her breast to ache, and her mouth filled with a metallic-tasting saliva.

"Austin saw it, too. Our hands," said Tina in a low voice. "He knew the first time he met me. He kept staring at my hands all night, and I realized immediately that he knew."

"He never said a word to me," Claudia whispered, meeting Tina's anxious eyes at last. The murals of the high-ceilinged room seemed to spin when she raised her head. "He never told me anything. Oh, my God, I think I'm going to faint." Her legs were suddenly heavy and her head felt as if someone had pumped it full of helium.

"Here, smelling salts." Tina broke open a thin purple ampul and waved the vial under her nose, causing fumes of lavender and ammonia to rise and sear Claudia's eyes. She coughed and sputtered, but her head cleared. She pushed it away. When she had composed herself, she looked at Tina's face and read the mute cry for understanding and compassion that clouded her sister's dark anguished eyes. The silence lay heavily between them as they looked at one another steadily, each waiting for the other to speak. It was Claudia who at last broke the impasse.

"I hate you, Tina," she said finally, enunciating each word with her pain. "I hate you for what you've done to me. And the sad thing is, you don't even realize the enormity of it all. You've robbed me of everything. You've robbed me of a mother, of a birthright, of an entire heritage. You've allowed me to live nearly thirty years as an incomplete person. You can't imagine what it is to be adopted. There's no way you'll ever understand. You feel like a piece of you is missing, like an incomplete jigsaw puzzle. Like a pie that's had a slice stolen by a stranger. It shadows your whole life. I can never forgive you for this—this lifetime of lies!"

She stood up to leave, but another wave of dizziness assaulted her senses.

Tina pulled her roughly by the sleeve. "Sit down," she ordered harshly. "You're in no condition to go anywhere right now!" Claudia obeyed mutely, obeyed the voice of command more than the logic of Tina's order. But Tina was right; she was too dizzy to walk across the large room.

In a conciliatory tone Tina went on. "Look, I know you're angry, I know you're more than angry. I know you're hurt. I'll understand if you can never find it in your heart to forgive me. I realize the whole idea is a lot to take in all at once, but I want to tell you what happened. Please hear me out, hear the whole story. You must have some questions, haven't you?" Tina picked up the martini in front of her and drained the glass. She signaled the waiter to bring her another, not bothering to consult with Claudia, since her wineglass still sat virtually untouched before her on the table. "So let me talk, and then, if you never want to speak to me again, at least you'll be aware of the facts."

Claudia was silent, vowing she would not speak. She had already promised herself that she was through with Tina, that nothing Tina said could possibly explain away the years and years of lies. Tina was unaware of the import of such a colossal deception. There she sat, smiling politely at the waiter, nodding a gracious dismissal to the man who had just set an icy straight-up martini on the white tablecloth in front of her, acting as if the world were still placidly spinning on its axle, while in truth the bottom of Claudia's universe had just fallen into an endless void. Claudia was no longer the person she had been just ten minutes before—not that she had known who that person was. She was no longer the nameless stranger brought into the bosom of the Cleary family for an unfathomable reason—charity or expedience? She was a living part of them—flesh of their flesh, blood of their blood, with all their weaknesses and defects, all their history and pain, all their—

"You drink too much, Tina," she said in a flat voice, wanting to wound in any way possible.

Tina ignored her and picked up the stem of the martini glass with trembling fingers. She took a small sip, then a hefty gulp, and set down the glass.

"What I'm about to tell you is the truth, Claudia. I swear. First of all, I've lied to you about my age—hell, I've lied to everyone about my age so long, I can hardly remember the right year myself—but the *real* truth is that I'm actually eighteen years older than you are. When I was in high school, I loved a boy. He loved me, too. He was going to be a musician, a classical pianist— he was very talented—and I was going to be a famous designer. We were going to get married and go to New York together, get away from Cincinnati, away from our families—you know, take New York by storm. Oh, we had big plans." She gazed out at the red-and-gold trees in the park with a faraway look in her eyes. "Of course, my father would never have allowed it. I was only a kid, after all. He had beautiful dark red hair just like yours," she added.

"So what happened?" Claudia asked despite herself, not lifting her eyes from the tablecloth. Sitting listening to Tina was agony. Waves of nausea swept over her, weakening her and shaking her internally. She longed to be outside, breathing the crisp autumn air, but a consuming curiosity, an undeniable need to know, kept her rooted to the chair.

"He got drafted. There was no war, but they got him, anyway. You probably don't know it, but they used to draft everybody. He had no business in the army. He was an artist—a sensitive, gentle man."

"I suppose he died some glorious hero's death," said Claudia caustically. If Tina confirmed her statement, if Tina told her some sentimental claptrap, she'd know she was lying.

"No. So ludicrous, he was killed in a traffic accident in boot camp at Fort Leonard Wood in Missouri. He never even knew about you."

"Very inconvenient for *you*," said Claudia coldly.

"Oh, my heart was broken!" said Tina, seemingly unaware of Claudia's sarcasm. "I thought I would die, I was so sorry about his death, but not as sorry as when I found out I was pregnant. I don't mean that as it sounds. I wanted his baby, don't misunderstand me. I wanted *you*. But my father! When he realized I was pregnant, he kicked me out of the house, screaming that as far as he was concerned his daughter was dead. I went to live with an old friend of Mother's, and after you were born, I put you in a foundling home—temporarily. I didn't give you up, Claudia," she added hastily. "I couldn't, I loved you. I planned to keep you, but I had to go back and finish my last year of school so I could support us. I worked as an apprentice for a dressmaker. I worked after school and all day weekends, except for Sunday morning, when I used to visit you." She sipped her drink.

"But I don't understand," said Claudia, forgetting her vow to keep silent. To her stunned dismay she was beginning to realize that there *was* a resemblance between her and Tina, not in their features, but in their gestures, in the timbre of their voices. "Didn't he have a family? Why didn't you go to his family?"

"I did at first. They didn't believe me. They were much better off than our family. I suppose they thought I wanted to take advantage of their financial position." Tina's tone indicated that she had never held their attitude against her lover's family. Claudia caught a glimpse of a scared young girl—pregnant, alone, and penniless—and for a fleeting moment her heart softened.

"Then Daddy had a heart attack, then another. Mother and I were always in touch. She told me he was very bad. I went to see him, because we thought he was going to die. I wanted to tell him that I loved him. Maybe I hoped he would forgive me, although in my heart I knew he never would—"

"And when he saw you, he got so angry, he had another attack and died," Claudia said.

"Yes, how do you know that?" Tina stared in surprise.

"Geraldine told me." And suddenly Claudia understood why she had been lumped together with Tina, why Geraldine had called her a tramp. "Geraldine knows you're my mother, Mother knows, Austin knows. Who else knows? Peter? *The New York Times?* The *Guinness Book of World Records?* Everyone but me, right? Tina, how could you *do* this to me?" Claudia's eyes filled with tears.

"Geraldine doesn't know," said Tina in a soothing voice. For a moment she looked as if she would lay her hand over Claudia's, but she seemed to think better of it. Instead she toyed with the stem of her martini glass, turning it around and around on the tablecloth. "Geraldine has always suspected, it's true. But she's so crazy, nobody believes anything she says, anyway. As for Mother and me—well, we thought it was for the best. When Daddy died, there was no money. Mother begged me to come back with her, and we did, you and I. It was she who suggested that she adopt you, save you from the stigma of illegitimacy—"

"The stigma of illegitimacy! What about my imaginings? Can you imagine the scenarios that have gone through my mind through the years? What about a lifetime of lies? Illegitimacy would have been preferable to this sham.''

"That's easy for you to say now, thirty years later. But this all happened a generation ago, remember. Attitudes have changed, you know. Anyway, after a while I made a good reputation for myself in town as a designer-dressmaker and I got an offer in New York for much more than I would ever have earned in Cincinnati. I took the job—I had to. I didn't want to leave you, but I was the sole support of all three of us. What could I do?

"But what about the insurance money from your father? Mother always said she had enough for college, for art school, even for my wedding to Peter....'' Claudia thought back on the outrageous bills for her formal wedding and the elegant reception that followed, at the country club the Arnolds belonged to in Darien. "Did you pay for all that?''

Tina shrugged slightly.

"You could have kept me and acknowledged me, Tina. Women keep their babies all the time. There's nothing shameful about being a single mother,'' Claudia maintained stubbornly.

Tina sighed in exasperation. "Look, Claudia,'' she said patiently, "I know the fact that I'm actually your mother has been a big blow to you. I'm trying very hard to put myself in your shoes and feel how you feel right now. But you're being extremely selfish and hard on me, don't you think? You're not trying to see my side at all. I did what I thought was best at the time. I kept you, which is the most important thing. I didn't abandon you and, believe me, my life would have been a lot easier if I had. Most everyone who got pregnant in those days either married young—usually for the wrong reasons—or gave up the baby for adoption. I admit, looking back, that I made a mistake. I should have told you. But by then I was so deeply into the lie, I couldn't extricate myself. When would I have told you? When you were five? When you were fifteen? Yesterday? When? Can't I be forgiven for a mistake?"

"A mistake? Is that what you call it? A mistake?"

"Yes. But I loved you. I've always loved you. You were my baby and you still are. I'm grateful that Mother and I worked out a way to keep you no matter how you judge me."

Claudia signaled the waiter for the check. He nodded understanding from across the room. "Take care of one more bill for me, Tina, then just forget I even exist. Thanks for the drink," she added, intending to be as cruel as her sarcastic words sounded.

"Don't go—please, don't go! Claudia, promise me something, please."

"What? What do you want from me? Everybody wants a promise from me. Is it Willy you're worried about? I won't tell your precious Willy anything if that's what you want. What you do is none of my business. I'll never be seeing you or Willy again, so it doesn't matter, anyway."

"I don't care what you tell Willy—or anyone else for that matter," said Tina with resignation. "I didn't want him to find out about you at first, of course. But I was more worried about you making the discovery through him and Austin than about what they would think. I felt safe for so long. Mother would never have betrayed my confidence. She loves you and me too much to hurt either one of us. I knew your ALMA search was going nowhere. All your papers were sewn up tight—there was nothing for you to discover. Then suddenly the circle kept getting smaller and smaller, choking in on me, and I knew even before Austin called me that it was only a matter of time...." Tina's voice trailed off. She brushed away a tear on her cheek with the back of one hand. "Claudia, I love you. I've always loved you. Don't be so angry, so cruel. I had no idea you'd react like this—"

"Your fortune-teller didn't warn you? The one you paid to tell me that my mother was dead? Everything is so clear now, Tina. All of it."

"Yes, you're right, of course, I did ask her to say your mother was dead," Tina admitted. "She promised she would, too. She took my money, but then she refused to lie. She told me afterward that she couldn't betray her gift. I wonder who she meant was dead?"

"Well, at least someone has ethics. I feel betrayed all around. Every one of you was in this against me." Claudia pushed her chair back from the table.

"Willy wasn't," said Tina weakly.

"To hell with Willy!" Claudia stood stiffly, cradling the pain inside her as if it were a child growing there. "To hell with all of you!" She walked away from the table with her head held high, never once looking back at Tina. *I know who's dead,* she said silently as she crossed the gracious café, oblivious to the murals, unaware of the stragglers at the tables, unconscious of the admiring stare of the maître d'. *My mother is dead. Dead to me.* But if she was dead, why did it hurt so to think of her?

Claudia trembled with the cold. She retied the knot of the silk scarf covering her hair and huddled down into her mohair cape. Icy salt air blew unremittingly over the back of the Block Island Ferry and whipped the cape around her legs. The few cars on the chugging boat, including Austin Harwood's racing green MG, offered no protection from the biting autumn wind, but she stalwartly stood facing its strength and refused to take shelter inside. She knew she was an off-islander riding alone in the off-season. She had no desire to feel the curious stares of the handful of Block Islanders who were on the last Friday night ferry. She stared into the churning black waters of Block Island Sound and pretended that the tears on her cheeks were the effects of the piercing wind and not of the jolting revelations of that afternoon. She was grateful to Austin for the car, grateful that he had thoughtfully provided her with a haven to which she could escape to lick her fresh wounds. He had accurately surmised how drained and hurt the meeting with Tina would leave her. Tina! She shook her head again in bitter anger.

Driving toward Rhode Island on the New England Thruway there had been ample time to reflect on Austin's behavior of the previous Tuesday morning in his office. She understood why he had refused to reveal the name of her mother: What choice had he? Only Tina had the right to tell her such nerve-shattering news. She realized that Tina must have gone to Austin sometime after the dinner the two couples had shared in Montauk, gone to him and begged him to keep silent, and somehow she had woven Austin into the fabric of her lifetime of lies and deceit. Yet Austin had prevailed upon Tina to confess her true relationship to Claudia, even after Austin knew that Claudia's compassion for Glenda Shorter's children guaranteed her silence. He had urged Tina for Claudia's sake, she knew—and against Tina's will, too. The revelation might cause her to lose Willy. No wonder Tina had been acting as nervous as a cat. Right up until the last minute on the street outside the Café des Artistes, Tina had hesitated, not really sure she was going to admit to her motherhood.

Claudia told herself that Tina was worried that Willy would be judgmental, that he would turn his back on her, because long ago she had given birth to an illegitimate child. Why shouldn't Tina worry? Her girlhood had been shaped by morally fanatic people who had wasted no time telling Tina how bad she was. But Tina had never before worried what the Geraldines of her life had thought. Hadn't she dismissed Aunt Geraldine totally in their conversation at the café? Claudia longed to blame Tina's fear of others' opinions for her deceit, but she knew that Tina's real fear was the one that grew from the years of living with a lie too enormous to disclose—the fear that Claudia would reject her—a self-fulfilling fear....

Claudia leaned against the MG and asked herself what she actually felt for Tina, but the well of her emotions had run dry. She understood Cynthia Cleary's behavior better. Her adoptive mother had been raised in another era; she had married into a strict and fundamentalist family of judgmental bigots. Cynthia had done what she thought was right at the time. But Tina! How could Tina have lied to her all those years?

"Mrs. Harwood, y'best come inside. There's a big blow."

She turned around to face the deckhand, who had shouted at her over the wind.

He looked at her in surprise. "Excuse me, ma'am. I thought you were Mrs. Harwood. Looked like the Harwood car. Best come inside, young lady. We're going to have rain in a minute. Glad I was mistaken, ma'am," he said politely. "I would have been right surprised to see Mrs. Harwood here." He touched his hand to a black knit cap and disappeared.

"All right, I'll come in," she called after his yellow slicker. *No rain, please. I can't put up the top on the car and I don't have a raincoat. It's dark, and I don't know where I'm going.* Everything was a disaster. She felt betrayed by everyone she held dear—by Tina, by Austin, by Cynthia Cleary—and she was truly alone in the world. The entire rhythm of her life had exploded, leaving her disoriented, like a person stuck in a whirling cage in an amusement park, suspended upside down over the fairgrounds, looking down on all the normal people whose feet were on the ground. New rules and no scorecard. *No rain, please.*

But rain it did. It rained heavily while she searched the unlit Block Island roads for Austin's beach cottage, finally locating the weathered shingled bungalow after twenty additional and unnecessary minutes, because the rain had blurred some of the directions on the map he had provided. By the time she parked the MG under the roof of a shed next to the house, her mohair cape was sodden, smelly, and ruined. Rain poured down the chimney when she tried to build a fire in the hearth, snuffing out the feeble flames in the grate. She longed for a cup of tea but was unable to figure out how to turn on the water pump, despite the instructions handwritten by Austin. At least the gas and electricity were functioning, and an unseen person had recently been in to prepare the simple house for her arrival. She heated up a can of chicken noodle soup she located in the pantry. She found some soft crackers in a tin that had not protected them from the island's pervasive dampness and she crumbled them into the hot soup. She ate ravenously, surprised that she had any appetite at all after the traumatic revelations of the day. Rain beat on the roof of the small bedroom she chose to occupy, picked purposely because its tiny dimensions, among the three admittedly attractive bedrooms on the second floor, made her know that Austin and his wife did not sleep in the single cot, where the cold damp crept into the sheets, leaving them clammy and smelling of mildew. She knew that they slept under the splendid Amish quilt on the double bed of the large corner bedroom that overlooked the beach. She had heard the ocean pounding outside the windows when she peered into their room and she had closed the door softly and continued down the hall until she found the small room with a slanting roof and two dormer windows.

Claudia crawled into the narrow bed and sighed with fatigue. Despite the cold and the discomfort she fell asleep immediately, giving herself over to the roar of the surf and to the welcome oblivion of darkness, which was preferable, a hundred times preferable, to the thoughts of betrayal that beseiged her.

Saturday dawned clear and cool. When Claudia made her way down the narrow stairs to the kitchen in search of Austin's directions for opening up the house, all the rooms looked more inviting, smelled fresher, and, in fact, appealed to her very much, unlike the night before. Sunlight poured through tall windows in the simple living room, which was entirely decorated with white wicker chairs and couches, their cushions covered in white canvas duck. The wall facing the sea was comprised mostly of windows and French doors that opened onto a wide deck. She reread Austin's directions and went back to try again the myseriously uncooperative water pump. The pump started at once for her. "It's all in your attitude," she said aloud, a small smile on her face, and she felt a perceptible easing of tension of the muscles in the back of her neck. While water for coffee boiled she dressed in blue jeans and an Irish knit sweater, deciding to wear no makeup, and tied her hair in a long pony tail that hung down her back. She made a mug of instant coffee and took it out to the deck, where she sat with her legs dangling off the edge and drank the contents of the mug while she watched the endless breakers. The off-shore October wind was cold and fresh and salty from the sea. Although the sky was cloudless, a thin mist hung over the water.

After a while she went out to the shed and backed the green MG into the sunshine. With a towel she wiped the dampness from the leather seats and the wooden dashboard and left the car in the sun to dry totally. An hour later she drove to town in search of a grocery store. The main street was uncrowded, and she parked the car directly in front of a small market. She went in and took a canvas basket in which to put her purchases, but before long she exchanged the basket for a cart that she half-filled. She was third in line to check out and was leafing through the pages of a magazine when she became aware that she was the object of curiosity. She looked up to find the woman ahead in line staring openly at her. The woman sniffed and turned her back, and Claudia returned her eyes to the printed page, but the sensation that she was being watched persisted. She found the woman eyeing her openly while unloading her full cart for the cashier. At last the woman paid and left. When her turn came, the man checking out the groceries was curt and cold, just short of impolite. Claudia began to feel like an unwelcome interloper. Perhaps the islanders really hated tourists there, she mused, and only tolerated them during the season, jealously guarding their post-Labour

Day privacy. The cashier, a middle-aged man with a strong New England accent, fairly threw her groceries into two brown bags. She grabbed the half-dozen eggs just before he did, and she gently placed them on top of one of the bags.

"Will this be charge, Mrs. Harwood?" the clerk asked her after he had finished. He practically spat the name as he flipped open a loose-leaf book that contained the names and addresses of charge customers.

"Cash, and I'm not Mrs. Harwood," she said stiffly. She opened her handbag and counted out the bills.

"You're not? But the car—" He eyed the MG outside on the sunny street.

"I borrowed the car."

"Oh, I see. May I carry your bags out?" Suddenly he was polite and helpful, fairly tripping over himself to help her as if in apology for his previous rudeness.

"I can manage," said Claudia.

"I insist." He lifted the two bags and carried them to the car, depositing them on the passenger seat. Claudia tried to tip him, but he refused her offer.

"Are you staying long? Come back again, Miss—"

"Cleary. Claudia Cleary. A few days, a week, perhaps. I don't know. The Harwoods lent me their house."

He introduced himself as the owner of the small store. "Young Austin's the only one to use the house now. Nice fella—known him since he was a baby. Knew his parents, too. I've known 'em all since I was a little one myself. Enjoy your stay here. Block Island's at its best in autumn, not so crowded, good weather."

Claudia climbed into the low car and started the engine. A thought occurred to her. She said to him above the roar of the motor, "But you don't know Mrs. Harwood," she said. "You thought *I* was Mrs. Harwood."

"Hardly anyone ever met her, but everyone knew all about her—she saw to that! Must be ten years or more since she was here. Guess she knew she wasn't welcome hereabouts. So long, Miss Cleary. Nice to meet you."

"What do you mean, not welcome?" she called to his retreating back as he turned to enter the store, but he was already out of her sight and had not heard her.

Claudia made one more stop at a bookstore and purchased three paperback novels. She drove back to the shingled house on the narrow, twisting roads that sometimes curved around surprising corners to present quick views of gray ocean beneath steep cliffs. Block Island was a wonderful retreat, she mused. Its rolling meadows and steep bluffs made her think of Scotland, a Scotland of her imagination, since she had never been there. She pushed thoughts of Evangeline and Austin from her head. Although she ate and slept and read in their house, she made herself pretend she was elsewhere. The ruse was not as difficult as she imagined, as the house seemed anonymous. No personal trinkets adorned the rooms. The closets were empty. The one dresser drawer in the master bedroom she ventured to open contained three faded bathing suits— men's bathing suits—and a shirt. Next to the fireplace she found a faded copy of *The New York Times* dated an August Sunday more than a year before. As she made a fire to ward off the night chill she wondered if no one had used the beach house in all that time.

Reading, walking on the beach, riding a bicycle she found in a storeroom on the first floor, and exploring the winding roads took up her energy and her thoughts. Little by little she got used to the idea that Tina was her mother. The urgent, painful ache of the misery of abandonment by Tina—and Austin—abated somewhat. In no way did the pain disappear, but she grew used to the gnawing heartache, temporarily lulled into remission by the bracing air and the beautiful scenery. On Monday she decided to stay another week and called her agent in New York from a pay phone in town, charging the call to her home number, since there was no working telephone in the house. He agreed to send her a job by overnight Express Mail, and she found a small shop that carried art supplies adequate to do pencils, as preliminary sketches for approval were known to commercial artists.

Tuesday at noon she went to the small local post office and asked for her mail. The clerk handed her the oversize Express Mail envelope.

"Cleary, eh? I think I have another letter for you that just came in—care of the Harwood place, right? Wait here and let me take a look."

Claudia waited several minutes while the gray-haired woman went behind a partition. She returned at last and handed her a stiff, expensive-looking ecru envelope.

"Yep, I knew I'd seen it. Letter from Austin Harwood, it is. We haven't seen young Austin here for a long time. How's he doin'?"

"Fine, I guess. I haven't seen him in a while myself. He's busy on the Shorter trial in Montauk."

"I read about it. That Shorter woman sounds just like Mrs. Harwood to me. It's a wonder he'd defend her, but then, he was always the perfect gentleman about his missus, too, no matter what she did."

"What *did* she do? I don't know anything about her, as I've never met her," Claudia said.

"Little late for that, I guess. I suppose it's not my place to tell you anything you don't already know. Let sleeping dogs lie, eh?" She leaned across the counter, however, and said in a confidential tone, "But I'll tell you one thing: The Harwoods've been coming here for years and years. Austin's father gave that house to his mother when young Austin was born. They're almost like islanders to us, and we don't have truck with outsiders who carry on like she did. Good riddance, and may God forgive me for saying it. Enjoy your stay." The counter clerk looked past Claudia and greeted a woman in line behind her, effectively dismissing her and the topic.

Claudia left the post office and returned to where she had left the bicycle leaning against the brick building. Evangeline hadn't been much loved around Block Island, that much was obvious; even after ten years people remembered her with venom. Claudia burned with curiosity, but who was there to ask? She couldn't buttonhole a stranger on the street and say "Tell me everything." She would have to wait until she got home and could ask Willy, she thought, but then she remembered she wasn't going to be seeing Willy again — or Tina. Somehow, she wasn't so certain about her decision to cut Tina totally out of her life. Tina might truthfully be her birth mother, but Tina was still her sister in some vague, confusing way — and she had been her best friend for years and years, despite a litany of Tina's irritating defects that immediately sprang to mind. After having a few days to ingest the shocking news of Tina's parenthood, Claudia realized she missed her sister. *My mother*, she corrected mentally.

Claudia opened Austin's letter, which wasn't really a letter at all, but rather a quick note on a stiff card. He said that Tina was most anxious to talk to her, but that he hadn't divulged to anyone where Claudia had gone. And then he wrote, "You asked me to remind you. *Il n'importe qu'on vivre, mais comment.*"

She had forgotten her request, but the words he'd said in the nursing home—it seemed a year ago at least—came back to her as she stood in the Block Island autumn sunshine. *"It matters not how long we live, but how."*

She stared at his signature—"Austin." Not even a "yours truly." How that hurt!

He was right. She had a chance to make an entirely new life for herself if she chose to—a life free from all the past: family, husband, even beloved lover. She wasn't going to dwell on the wrongs of the past anymore. Maybe she'd move, meet new people, do new things. She could receive a fine price for her apartment in the booming cooperative market, certainly enough to start over in a smaller town. She had talent, she had her health, and she had a good name in the commercial art field already. With an aggressive and efficient agent there was no need for her to live in Manhattan. She was free to go anywhere, even stay on Block Island if she chose to—a thought she rejected immediately. She'd go crazy in such a claustrophobic environment, as lovely as the Island was. She needed people, not that ingrown existence where everyone knew everyone else's business as the past few days had taught her.

Claudia rode to the south side of the island and looked across the misty waters of the Sound. On a clearer day she imagined Montauk was visible from where she stood straddling the bicycle on top of a steep bluff. Just across the water Austin was in a stuffy courtroom. Was it only a few short weeks since Claudia had shared blissful happiness with him? All she could remember was the pain of their parting, the pain that gnawed at her heart, filling her with its heaviness. She knew it was only a matter of time until she gave in and went to him, accepting him on any terms he wanted.

She vowed she'd fight that desire for him with all she was worth—leave New York if she had to, cut herself off from everyone, but most especially from Austin.

"Liar," she said out loud, "You may sound noble, but all Austin has to do is beckon—and you'll go to him."

A week later on a Tuesday Claudia returned to New York, arriving in mid-afternoon. She decided she would go to her own apartment first and unload the MG. She'd return the car to Austin's house after the rush hour was over. She had stopped to buy fall apples, a pumpkin, and a gallon of cider on the way home and she knew she couldn't manage her purchases as well as her luggage in a taxi. First she took the MG to a car wash on the West Side and had it cleaned and waxed to remove all traces of salt air, then she stopped to fill the tank with gas. When she arrived at Gramercy Square, she tipped the doorman of The Players to let her park for two hours. She let herself into her apartment and immediately opened all the windows to get rid of the oppressive odor of its stale air.

Claudia pressed the play-back button on the answering machine and listened to the garbled, high-pitched sounds as the tape rewound.

Beep. Hang-up.

Beep. "Claudia—please call me!" The anguished voice of Tina. *Click.*

Beep. "Claudia, it's Tina again. I know you're there and not answering the telephone. Please pick up if you're there. Or call me right back—I'm at home." *Click.*

Beep. "Claudia, I'm really getting angry. Call me back as soon as possible. What the hell is Peter up to, by the way?" *Click.*

Beep. Hang-up.

Beep. "I've just spoken to Austin, and he told me you've gone away," said the slightly calmer voice of Tina. "I am so worried that you'll do something drastic like go back to Peter. Austin won't tell me where you are. I asked him if you'd gone to California, but he won't say a word. I beg you to stop this cruelty and call me—please! I'll be at the office until late." *Click.*

Beep. "Hello, my dear, I have wonderful news for you. I'll be in town next week. I have made firm hotel arrangements this time, but I'll miss our little snuggles. Glad to hear things are the same. *Click.*

"Peter, the wonderful news is that I'm changing my phone number tomorrow," she said to the tape while switching off the machine. Why Tina would even imagine that she would go to California to be with Peter was beyond her.

There had been no calls from Austin, but then he knew she was on Block Island. She riffled through the stack of mail that had filled her lobby mailbox. Bills, circulars, nothing from him.

She washed her hair, which was dusty and tangled from the wind in the open car. Afterward she made a cup of tea and switched on the six o'clock news, turning automatically to WNYZ. She came in on the middle of a story about the trial, just in time to see Alex Gómez flashing capped teeth and grinning seductively in front of the courthouse in Montauk.

"And so, the most sensational trial in the history of this sleepy Long Island village comes to an end with the unexpected acquittal of Glenda Shorter, accused of shooting her millionaire husband. The defendant is shown leaving the courthouse at mid-morning today in the company of her twin five-year-old sons and her attorney, Austin Harwood."

The camera swept the steps of the courthouse. Glenda Shorter was shown surrounded by jostling newspeople, all of them shoving microphones in her face. Austin stood behind her, holding one young boy in each arm. The children looked stunned and fearful of all the noise and attention. Claudia knew that hot, bright lights shone in their eyes, lights of which the television audience would be unaware.

"A statement, Mrs. Shorter, a statement!" A dozen microphones nearly obscured her face, but in the few seconds the camera was on her, Claudia noticed she seemed ten years younger and infinitely more beautiful. And she looked uncannily like the photographs of Evangeline Harwood.

"I owe everything to Austin, my lawyer, the best lawyer in the country and a dear, dear friend, as well," she said, beaming with happiness. "He saved my life!" She grabbed Austin awkwardly because of the two children in his arms and kissed him soundly on the lips while wolf whistles shrilled from the reporters. Austin looked as if he rather enjoyed the spectacle. He hugged the identically dressed boys tighter and whispered into one tiny ear, then the other. The twins looked at Austin and grinned.

One big happy family, Claudia thought, instantly amazed at the surge of jealousy that shot through her. And just as suddenly she knew that Evangeline was dead, and that there on the television screen, smiling adoringly at Austin, was her reincarnation in Glenda Shorter. *"The woman is dead. Not long ago."* The fortune-teller might have been in the room with Claudia, she heard her words so clearly, words she had, at the time, naturally assumed applied to her birth mother. But she didn't believe in fortune-tellers, she admonished herself. She tried to remember all the things she had heard about Evangeline Harwood: *"Evangeline doesn't have to come between you,"* and then *"Little late for that . . . Good riddance"* — weren't those the words of the woman in the post office?

She raced to the telephone and dialed Tina's number. Certainly Tina knew the truth. Willy might be as mum as a monk with a vow of silence, but surely he would have discussed Austin with Tina. The telephone rang six, seven, eight times. She broke the connection and called Harwood and Harwood, knowing almost all attorneys worked long hours. She identified herself, quickly asking the switchboard operator for William Lindhurst, hoping Willy had gone in to the office after returning from Montauk that morning.

"Did you say *Claudia* Cleary? Hold one minute." She came back on the line. "Mr. Lindhurst has left for the day. The office closed at five, ma'am. Can you call back in the morning?" Did she dare ask for Austin? What would she say?

"Is—is Mr. Harwood there?"

"He just walked out the door, Miss Cleary. I'm sorry."

She hung up and hastened to dry her hair, turning the dryer to the highest setting to hurry the process. Finally she gave up and rolled it into a thick French twist, inserting the heavy gold comb to hold her damp tresses. She stood at the open door of the bedroom closet, indecision delaying her choice. She wanted to look spectacular. What if Austin was already interested in Glenda Shorter? Stranger things had happened, she knew. Men often married replicas of their dead or divorced wives, no matter how painful the first relationship might have been. She had seen it happen over and over. And the look she had seen in the Shorter woman's eyes was a look any woman recognized. She was more than half in love with Austin, as a woman loves her doctor, perhaps, but what that feeling could lead to sent chills up Claudia's spine. To be that close, to know the truth about his wife—and know the truth she did in some instinctive way—and to lose him anyway...

Peter had left her one piece of fine furniture: a cherry highboy that was in the bedroom. She went to it and opened the eye-level drawer in which she kept her best lingerie. She stood staring at the stacks of colored silk teddies and camisoles and slips that lay there, wrapped in tissue among fragile net bags of lavender sachet she had tucked around them.

Tina had given her every sample size of embroidered silk and satin luxury underwear she and Jake had brought back from Hong Kong when he bought the lingerie factory. Most of the things she had never worn, had never even tried on. She chose a dusky rose silk teddy heavily embroidered with ecru flowers and leaves and trimmed with thick antique lace of the same color. From the back of the drawer she pulled a rose-colored garter belt that coordinated with the teddy. Somewhere she remembered, she had a pair of real silk stockings that she had bought long ago and had never worn. She found the stockings and sat on the bed to pull them on, running her palm down her calf and listening to the sing of her hand on the sheer silk. Why had nylon taken over the market? she wondered. The silk was unbelievably glowing and erotic on her long legs. She hooked the stockings to the garters and pulled the rose teddy over her head, gazing at her reflection in the closet mirror.

The silk and lace covered her breasts and hung more or less loosely on her body, ending in short trunks with bands of lace at her thighs. She snapped the teddy closed. Clothing certainly didn't have to be skin-tight to be undeniably alluring, she mused, thinking of Jean Harlow in "Dinner at Eight," a fifty-year-old film she had seen in revival at the Museum of Modern Art not too long before, as the champagne lace front of the teddy nearly reached her collarbone, covering her totally.

Claudia wanted to look spectacular, but not like a courtesan on the streets. She had to drive all the way uptown, after all. She stared into the closet and finally chose a hand-knit wool tweed sweater to keep her warm in the car and a softly pleated wool skirt of a burnt sienna color that picked up the dominating color of the thick sweater. She took a final look in the mirror. *Nothing is what it seems at first glance,* she thought, noting how the conservative clothes belied her seductive undergarments. *Nothing.* She tied an orange-and-brown-and-gold Hermès scarf around her head and raced down to the MG, gunning the car uptown in the direction of Seventy-fourth Street. She had been hateful to Austin, so involved in her own problems that she had refused to recognize simple truths about him—his past, his feelings for her, his need to do what he had to about Tina. She prayed he'd forgive her. She prayed he still loved her, although he had said he did not.

She prayed she wasn't too late.

Chapter Ten

By seven o'clock, when she pulled the car into the short driveway on East Seventy-fourth Street, Claudia knew enough time had elapsed so that Austin was probably home from the office, even if he had chosen to walk the twenty-odd blocks. She gazed up at the windows, noting that lights already burned behind drawn curtains on the two lower floors. She set the hand brake and left the car to climb the six steps to the front door, where she lifted the heavy brass knocker with a trembling hand.

A full minute elapsed before she heard footsteps approach the door. Unconsciously she touched the comb that held her upswept auburn hair. Another few seconds passed while eyes peered through a peephole in the door. Finally the heavy door swung open. She looked up shyly, still uncertain what she would say. She only knew she had to see him.

"Yes?"

An elegant gray-haired woman in a beautifully tailored black silk suit looked at Claudia with polite curiosity.

She found her voice and looked into familiar light blue eyes. "May I speak to Mr. Harwood? I'm Claudia Cleary."

"Oh, yes, Claudia! Come in, my dear. My son has told me about you. Come in, come in." The woman's quiet enthusiasm was an unexpected surprise. She stepped aside graciously and gestured for Claudia to enter the house. "Austin isn't home from the office yet, but I expect him any minute. Why don't you take off your coat and have a drink with me? We'll wait for him together. I am so pleased to meet you at last. I was afraid that I would miss you before I returned to Jamaica."

"I've brought Austin's car back. I'll pull it into the garage." Mrs. Harwood went to open the garage from inside while Claudia returned to the MG and pulled it into the narrow space. When she had locked the garage door, Mrs. Harwood led her upstairs to the library, where a warm fire crackled in the fireplace.

"I usually have a sherry about now. Would you care to join me?" She filled two delicate glasses with the pale amber liquid from a crystal decanter that rested atop a small writing desk and carried them to a camel-back sofa placed in front of the fireplace. Claudia saw that her long-fingered hands were nearly identical to those of her son and she realized how easily Austin had picked up the resemblance between Tina and her at dinner that night in Montauk. The bloodline was in the hands. He had been right. Claudia had been too obsessed to look in her own backyard, so to speak, for the truth. Instead of the anger she had felt when he accused her, she now saw that he had spoken out of compassion.

"Sit next to me, my dear. I'm terribly nearsighted, but I'm too lazy to go upstairs for my glasses."

"I'm nearsighted, too," said Claudia. "I know how awful it is when everyone is out of focus. I'd be happy to get your glasses for you."

"Would you, please? I'm afraid my room is all the way at the top of the house—first door to the left. I believe I left them on the table next to the bed."

Claudia knew immediately which room she meant: Evangeline's room, left as it was when she died—if indeed she was dead—left as a shrine, no doubt. She wondered why Mrs. Harwood would use that room during her visits when other bedrooms sat unoccupied in the house.

"I'll be right back." Claudia went up the stairs to the top floor, remembering another time she had ascended them. That night she had worn a red Viyella bathrobe and she had been fulfilled and happy, her future full of promise. Her legs were like lead and her body was filled with fear and apprehension at seeing Austin, and she began to worry that she had made a terrible mistake about him. Perhaps Evangeline lived in Connecticut, after all, and Claudia had created a fantasy scenario in which she longed to believe. But if that was true, then why was Austin's mother so welcoming? Nothing made sense except the feeling of love she nurtured inside. She went into the first door on the left and turned on the light switch.

The room was as she recalled, except that an elusive floral scent hung in the air and a leather suitcase stood in one corner. Another lay open and half-packed on a luggage holder at the foot of the canopy bed. She spotted a needlepoint glasses case on the bedside table and took it, switching off the light as she left the feminine room.

"Your room is lovely. The color is so restful," she told Mrs. Harwood when she returned to the library, hoping against hope to elicit a comment that would clarify her jumbled thoughts and possibly allay her fears and doubts.

"Yes, that blue always calms me totally. My bedroom in Jamaica is the exact same shade, although, of course, the furnishings are more suited to the tropics. You know, that room upstairs hasn't changed one iota since I was a young girl. Austin thinks I'm an old fuddy-duddy, but I've told him that I feel a greater sense of peace if I can count on certain things remaining the same."

"You mean that's always been your room?" Claudia was unable to hide the surprise in her voice.

"Why should that surprise you?"

Claudia flushed and looked down at the thin glass in her fingers. "I assumed that the room was Evangeline's," she answered at last, greatly embarrassed.

"Evangeline's," she said slowly. "I see. My dear, there's nothing of Evangeline's anywhere in this house. We don't even utter her name around here. What made you think such a thing?"

"I saw her photographs there," Claudia said.

"Not today you didn't," corrected Mrs. Harwood in a gentle voice, too gracious to mention the obvious implication that Claudia had been in the house—even in its bedrooms—previously. "Austin recently made me get rid of both of them. I didn't care too much about the wedding picture, but the one taken in Bermuda I loved. That was the nicest picture I had of my son as an adult. Before she gave him that horrid scar, that is."

"Evangeline gave him the scar? I thought it came from a childhood accident."

"Did Austin tell you that? I'm not surprised. It's just like him to say anything to avoid using her name! She gave him the scar. She cut his face with a broken glass, and the poor boy nearly lost an eye. Well, not really, but had the laceration been a bit closer to the eye, he might have." Mrs. Harwood looked away.

"Where *is* Evangeline? Is she dead?"

Mrs. Harwood turned back toward Claudia. "You mean you don't even know that she's dead? Hasn't Austin told you anything? I must say that is carrying silence a bit too far. No wonder you two have had your problems. You poor dear—he can be so stubborn. He was always that way, even as a boy."

Dead! Evangeline is dead, after all! A small glimmer of hope kindled in Claudia's breast at the realization that Austin had discussed her with his mother. Somehow that the obviously sympathetic Mrs. Harwood knew they were estranged was almost more significant than the news that his wife was dead. *Don't press,* she told herself. *Let her go on at her own pace.* "He merely told me he wasn't married. Nothing else."

"Of course, there's more to the story—much, much more. Since Austin won't talk about Evangeline, I'm going to tell you everything, but you'll have to make me a promise, Claudia. And please call me Elisabeth, my dear."

"Of course, Mrs. Harwood—I mean Elisabeth. And I'll promise whatever you ask," she said. The delay was maddening. Claudia bit her lower lip in apprehension.

"Promise me that you won't mention our chat to my son. He gets terribly angry, you see, and we've all had to promise him that we won't bring up *her* name. It's one of his foibles. If he should come in while we're talking, I'll have to change the subject. Sometimes we women have to do things our own way. Men can be so mule-headed, don't you think? Another sherry?"

"I do. That is, I agree and I promise." Claudia left the gold brocade sofa to fetch the crystal decanter and hand it to Elisabeth, who refilled their glasses.

"Evangeline was always what you people today call a

flake. She was given to running away ever since she was a young girl of ten or eleven. She ran away when she was in her third year at Miss Porter's School, and her family finally found her living in some unspeakable commune in Greenwich Village. They took her back at Miss Porter's, heaven knows why. Obviously their standards were slipping even then." She wrinkled her aristocratic nose in distaste. "And then she ran away from the hospital quite a few times. Apparently she was chronically unhappy, a condition that worsened as she grew older."

"Excuse me, but what hospital do you mean?"

"Why, Silver Hill in New Canaan. It's a private psychiatric hospital that incidentally specializes in the treatment of alcoholism, another one of poor Evangeline's problems. Personally, I never thought she was an alcoholic, but there's no doubt she used to drink too much—just another, painful variation of running away, in my opinion. She virtually lived at Silver Hill the last two years of her life."

Claudia said nothing, but she realized that her mouth was open and she was staring openly at Elisabeth. All the worry, all the suspicion, all the times she had thought Austin was lying to her... She hoped she wasn't too late. She prayed she could still fix things with him.

"You look stunned—as if you don't believe me. You must believe me, because it's all too true."

"You must believe them when they tell you." "Certainly I believe you. And I *am* stunned, you're right. The possibility never occurred to me until just this evening. So few young people die, except by accident."

"So few people lived like Evangeline. And, naturally, her death was an accident. She ran away to Puerto Rico just before Christmas a year ago. We don't know why she was going. Perhaps she wanted some excitement. Who knows? There was a boating accident. She was cruising the islands with three not very nice men. All the details were hushed up, because her family is quite influential. Nothing was ever in the papers." Elisabeth took a sip of her sherry.

"But why won't Austin talk about her? Or permit anyone else to? He hasn't done anything wrong."

"Even the best of families has its skeleton in the closet. And Austin is a gentleman through and through, a gentleman who would never air his dirty linen. But there's more to his silence: those years with Evangeline were very painful ones for him. He was always a good husband. He was faithful and kind—two qualities Evangeline did not cultivate in herself, believe me. My son paid her bills without complaint and he went to Connecticut to visit her nearly every weekend. He'd even leave the Rolls for her to use on Mondays and take that horrid train back to the city. We all urged him not to see her so often, because when she demanded to come home, which she often did, Austin allowed it graciously, although the visits ended in disaster more often than not. She would drink, matters would get out of hand, and she was occasionally violent. Sometimes she brought quite unsuitable people back to the house." Elisabeth shuddered at the memory. "I think that he simply cares to blot her out—blot out all the years he knew her."

"Did he—did he love her?" asked Claudia, somehow fearful of the answer.

"Yes, I think he loved her when they were young. I must admit she was a lot of fun when she wasn't in one of her sick spells, and I'm certain he was attracted to her devil-may-care attitude. We Harwoods tend to be a bit stuffy, as you may have noticed. Evangeline was not stuffy, not by any means. Later, when she began to get out of hand—"

Such as on Block Island, perhaps? Claudia thought.

"—later he simply accepted his lot as would anyone who had made a bad bargain. Austin is a very loyal man."

"Yes, I know he is," Claudia said, thinking of how he had protected Tina's secret. "And a very good man. I'm sorry for what happened."

"We all make mistakes."

"How true." She thought of Tina's decision to remain silent about her motherhood, of her own ill-advised marriage to Peter. Yes, there was no denying she had loved Peter when she was young, but love could turn on you. Love without nourishment died, faded away to nothing.

"Claudia, I'm going out to dinner with some old friends and I'll have to leave shortly. No, don't get up. You wait here for Austin. I can't imagine what's keeping him. He always calls me when—"

As if on cue a telephone on the desk tinkled melodiously. Mrs. Harwood crossed the Oriental rug and picked up the receiver, nodding in Claudia's direction to signal that indeed it was her son who was on the line.

"Austin, your friend Claudia has been here waiting to see you. What a pity you didn't bring her around sooner. She's delightful, but you had better hurry home before we decide to talk about you." *As if we haven't spent all this time doing just that,* her conspiratorial smile signaled to Claudia. Her blue eyes turned serious, however, as she listened to her son's next words on the telephone. "Yes, I have it. Young man, I believe I am capable of repeating a message! Are you certain that's what you want me to say?" A long pause. "I shan't wait up for you. Good-bye." Her voice was glacial at the final words, all pretense of banter and sociability gone in a few seconds. Claudia knew the news would be bad, very bad.

"What did he say? You can tell me, Mrs. Harwood. I'd rather hear it from you now than go on not knowing. Tell me, I can take it." Claudia's hands were clenched together in her lap. Lately she seemed to be telling everyone that she could take it, come whatever. She wasn't so certain she was capable of taking much more, however, but she would be gracious and serene, no matter what his mother had to tell her. She vowed she would not break down, sensing that hysterics were the wrong reaction in front of the aristocratic Mrs. Harwood. She dug her fingernails into the skin of her palms until all she concentrated on was the pain.

"My dear Claudia, I am so sorry. He said, 'Tell the former Mrs. Arnold to go home. Tell her that I plan to have dinner with a woman who knew how to get rid of her husband once and for all.' I had no idea my son could be so cutting. He certainly doesn't get it from *my* side of the family."

Claudia stood on the corner of Park Avenue and Seventy-second Street and fumbled for a coin in her change purse. She had accepted Mrs. Harwood's embarrassed apology and left the Harwood town house without shedding a single tear. Amazingly she was still dry-eyed as she stumbled down Park Avenue in a daze, buttoning her tweed sweater against the gusting wind of the October night, searching for a pay telephone that had not yet been vandalized. She couldn't go home just yet—not to the empty apartment, not to the late show on television, not to the hollow void, where she would have to confront the pain. She had been alone long enough on Block Island, and the forced solitude—self-enforced, true—echoed mournfully. Right then she needed company and life and a sympathetic ear. She needed her sister—her mother. She needed Tina, whoever Tina was to her. She needed someone who loved her and whom she loved. She had been unremittingly hard on Tina. Examining her behavior, she realized that she had practiced what Tina so deplored in the Cleary family—the self-righteousness, the judgmentalism that had driven Tina from Cincinnati. Yes, Tina had lied to her; yes, Tina had allowed her to persevere needlessly in her search, to worry uselessly about her heritage. What difference did any of it make? After all, the total picture was just as Tina had said: She had kept Claudia. Despite the hardships, despite the fears, she had not abandoned her daughter. Tina had always loved her and done what she thought was best, flawed as the best sometimes was. Tina had always cared for her as if she were her acknowledged mother—supported her, educated her, nurtured her. Tina had always been available to dole out her time and advice freely, to comfort Claudia in times when she hurt. She had even pressed those unnecessary expensive clothes on her in demonstration of her affection.

The pain in Tina's voice evident in the messages left on the answering machine came back to haunt Claudia as she heard the clunk the coin made as it dropped into the pay telephone. Claudia no longer wanted to be the source of Tina's pain. She had enough with the residue of her past. They had to deal with the present.

The telephone at Tina's rang and rang. Claudia was about to hang up when Tina finally picked up on the seventh ring.

"Claudia, thank God you're back. Thank God you've called at last. I've felt just terrible. Yes, come right over," she added in a rush. "We'd love to see you!"

"Who is we?"

"Willy and I. We're celebrating the outcome of the trial. You must have heard by now Glenda Shorter was acquitted. We're drinking champagne and eating pizza. Isn't it divine, Claudia? Willy loves junk food as much as I do."

"But only with champagne, the way you like it." In spite of the pain Claudia had to laugh at Tina's enthusiasm.

"But, of course. Why else would one put that poison in one's body?"

"Never mind, Tina. I don't want to intrude. Everything is fine with me now," she lied. That night was not the time to cast a shadow over Tina's happiness. They had the rest of their lives to be friends, to be sisters, to share heartaches and problems. "I'll talk to you tomorrow. Give me a call in the morning, all right?"

"Wait! Where have you been all this time?"

"I've been on Block Island. Austin lent me his house."

Tina whispered into the phone. "Claudia, I told him."

"Told who what?"

"I told Willy that you're my daughter." Claudia knew that imparting her secret to Willy must have cost Tina most of her considerable nerve.

"What did he say?"

"All he said was, 'No wonder Claudia is so lovely—look at her mother.' Oh, isn't he wonderful?"

"Yes, Tina, he's wonderful. And I'm very proud of you. That must have been hard for you."

"Not so hard. I thought a lot about some of the things you said to me about Willy and I decided I don't really care what he knows about me. If he loves me, he has to take me with all the wrinkles, my bad habits, my gray hair, even my fortune-teller. Not that I'm going to fill him in on *all* the details, you understand." Tina giggled. "That might be asking too much."

"That's none of his business."

"Right. But the important thing is not to live under a cloud of secrecy anymore. In any way."

"Tina—" Claudia swallowed painfully. "Tina, I'm sorry about the way I behaved. I was only thinking of myself, I guess. I didn't try to put myself in your shoes, not at all. I don't think I can ever call you mother. You know—it's too big a change. But you're the best, the most courageous sister a girl could have. And I love you very much."

There was a short silence before Tina said, "I understand. I never expected you to call me Mother. You already have a mother. It's not my right to demand a new position in your life. I gave up my right to be your mother many years ago."

"I didn't mean that."

"No, but I do. I've done a lot of thinking about us. About Mother, about you and me, about the whole situation. I'm very happy being your sister and your friend, if you'll still have me in those two roles. I don't want to change anything. It's too late to change our lives. But I'll go along with whatever you decide. However you want to handle things, handle us, is all right with me. I just want to be certain that you understand I never meant to hurt you. I love you, Claudia. I need you in my life."

"I am in your life, Tina. I'm not going anywhere."

Claudia let herself through the street door of her apartment building and, ignoring the elevator, she climbed the stairs slowly to the third floor. A dull weight pressed on her heart and made her legs feel as heavy as lead. Austin and Glenda Shorter! The image of their smiling faces on the six o'clock news kept returning to her mind. Those two adorable children...the way Austin had held them, one on each arm.

"What took you so long?"

"Austin, you're here!" He was sitting on the top stair. His tie was loosened, his jacket lay beside him, and the sleeves of his white shirt were rolled up to reveal his muscular forearms. Beside him on the carpet sat a brown grocery bag and a dark green bottle of champagne.

"Didn't we have a dinner date? I thought my mother would give you the message to come home." His blue eyes smiled mischievously into hers.

"You and I? Us? You meant me?" She ran up the few steps remaining and threw herself into his open arms, knocking him over. She lay half on top of him and stared, astonished, into his face. "I thought you meant Glenda Shorter. You said someone who got rid of her husband for good—"

"And haven't you?" He smiled.

"Yes! Yes! Ages ago—a lifetime ago! I couldn't find a taxi," she babbled. "I had to take a bus. I'm sorry I'm late. If I'd only known you were here."

"No, I'm late, my sweet. I almost missed the bus. I love you, you know that, don't you? I've been sitting her for ages just waiting to tell you how much I love you."

"I love you, darling. I have from the first time I saw you—"

"In the bathtub."

"No, I was in the bathtub." She giggled.

"Don't argue with the attorney. Outarguing is my business."

"I know, I know. I'll shut up only if you kiss me."

"You're on top of me. You'll have to kiss m—" But her lips were already on his, smothering his words. An apartment door down the hall opened, and the curler-studded head of Claudia's next-door neighbor popped out. The woman already wore a clear look of irritation on her face, but her eyes widened in shock when she saw Claudia lying on top of a man unfamiliar to her.

"Really, Mrs. Arnold, all this noise! And that man's not your husband! What's going on here? Heavens above, what's the place coming to?" She slammed shut the door.

"The name is Cleary—Miss Cleary, if you please!" Claudia shouted back. She looked down into Austin's blue eyes and giggled happily. He nuzzled his nose against hers.

"I have something for you," he said. "If you would roll your delectable body off mine, I'll give it to you. Unless you'd rather make love here in the hall first—"

"The lady may have a point about the public corridor," Claudia said, still giggling. "Come into the apartment." She stood up and smoothed her skirt. Austin got to his feet and retrieved the grocery bag and the bottle of champagne. They went into the apartment, and Claudia crossed automatically to the answering machine, checked the light that indicated that no calls had come in, and switched the machine off.

"When you play back the calls that come in, do you have to listen to your own message every time?" he called from the kitchen, where he'd taken his bundles.

"No, never. You record it once and forget it," she answered from the living room. "The only time you hear your own message is if you call yourself and use the remote retriever, but I broke the retriever the first week I had the machine. Mechanical things are mysterious to me."

"Why don't you listen to your message now?" He sat down on the new couch and smiled at her devilishly.

"Why?"

"Just listen. You'll understand."

She turned on the machine and pressed the button that played back the message she had recorded long before.

Instead of her own voice the unexpected tones of a man came out of the speaker. At first her eyes widened in surprise as she heard the familiar voice of her former husband, but surprise turned to overwhelming anger as the import of his words penetrated her understanding.

"Hello, this is Peter. Our friends will be pleased to know that Claudia and I have lovingly reconciled. We're either out or—heh, heh, heh—otherwise engaged right now, but if you leave your name and number after the tone, one of us will return your call when we come up for air. Cheerio." A beep followed.

"Oh, my God! How long has that been there?"

"At least since we went to Cincinnati. That's the message I heard when I called you after the misunderstanding we had that weekend."

"Oh, darling. No wonder you wouldn't talk to me! I'll kill that bastard! I'll—I'll— He must have changed the tape after I left for Montauk. He said he'd get even. I should have been more wary! Why didn't anyone tell me? Oh, God, all the people who've called—you, my agent, your secretary, Lord knows who else! What can I do? Can I sue him?"

"Slow down, it doesn't matter, Claudia. And as for suing him, you'll have to get in line, I'm afraid."

"What do you mean?"

"I'll tell you after I open the champagne. I won a big case, you know. We must celebrate the victory. You really do have some temper!'' He shook his head and laughed and began to unwind the wire that fastened the cork.

"I know you won. I love you for it. Those children won't have to wonder who their parents are.''

"Or know all the sordid details about the two of them, either.''

Claudia got two glasses and ran toward him when the cork popped and the champagne frothed out of the bottle. He filled the glasses and she sat next to him, snuggling into the crook of his arm.

"You're a wonderful attorney. Congratulations on the acquittal.'' They raised their glasses and looked into each other's eyes before tasting the champagne.

"It's already warm,'' he complained.

"Who cares?'' she said happily.

"So you think I'm a wonderful attorney? Well, I did something totally unethical today.''

"You? Mr. A. Remington Harwood the Fourth, late of Yale and Harvard Law School? I cannot believe my ears.''

"I'm serious. I've never been so unethical. Your ex-husband came to me and asked me to defend him.''

"Peter? Defend him from what?''

"He's being sued for plagiarism by one of his former students. It seems he lifted this person's thesis intact and based his second book on it.''

"The second book was his big seller; it made him famous.''

"That's right. He's ruined, you know. He's as guilty as sin. He told me so himself.''

"You're not supposed to tell me this, are you?''

"It's all right. He's not my client.''

"Then what have you done that's so unethical?''

"Well, the firm had already agreed to represent the

other party in the suit. I shouldn't have listened to Arnold's version, you see."

"But, sweetheart, you didn't know!"

"Yes, I knew. I let him talk, anyway. Actually, I didn't realize who he was until he walked into my office. I had only met him that one time and I didn't remember his last name. I'd never heard of *How to Swingle* or *How to Be a Lion in a Lamb's World.* What rot!" He set down his glass.

"You didn't know who Peter was?" She giggled. "Peter thinks his name's a household word."

"I know he does. He was shocked when I told him I wasn't familiar with his work. When he began to explain his case, I should have stopped him, but I was curious to see what kind of man he is. When I asked about you, he said he hadn't seen you in a month. Then he asked me if I still saw you, and I said of course not—not since I realized that you and he were back together again. He said, 'Oh, the tape!' and he began to laugh in the most malicious way. He's an evil man, you know, really evil."

"Yes, but I feel sorry for him. His career is ruined. He'll be like that Clifford Irving after his book on Howard Hughes—he was ruined, no one ever trusted him again. Could Peter go to jail?" she asked.

"That depends on what he's charged with and who actually ends up charging him—the government or a private party," Austin answered. "And how good his defense counsel is, of course," he added with a grin.

"I suppose he deserves the disaster, but it's such a waste. He didn't need to steal anyone's ideas; he's a very intelligent man. What's your firm going to do now?"

"We've withdrawn totally from the case. We didn't have a retainer yet. Anyway, I hate to defend a loser, you know that. I did enough misplaced defending in my personal life; I certainly don't need the hassle in my professional life."

"You mean your wife, don't you?" she asked, tracing her index finger down the scar on his face. He grasped her hand and looked into her eyes.

"That happened a long time ago. When she died, I promised myself that I'd never mention her name again, but the past doesn't matter anymore. I'll tell you about her—I'll tell you anything you want to know. Our misunderstanding was all my fault. I realized it immediately, but you got away before I could explain. I've been unforgivably stubborn."

"But, Austin darling, I was totally self-absorbed, just as you accused me of being. I couldn't see the nose on my face. And I don't need—or want—to know anything about your wife, anything at all." *Your mother told me all I need to know,* she said to herself. "I made a bad marriage, too, you know. We'll make a pact. We won't mention either of them again. All right?"

"Just one more word about Peter," he said. "It crossed my mind that I might work out a way to take the case—as his adversary, of course. I knew it would be so very gratifying to win the suit against him, but then I thought, what the hell? I already have his wife, why do I need to scalp him, too? Don't I—have his wife, that is?"

"You bet you do. Case closed."

Austin took the champagne glass from her fingers and laid it aside and he began to undo the buttons of her tweed sweater. "I'm impatient to make love to you. Just this morning I was in despair of ever seeing you again. I'd just won a big case and all I could think of was that I'd lost you forever. I've never stopped thinking about you. You're on my mind all the time."

"Oh, and you're on mine! But you never lost me, darling. I would have come back to you, wife or not. I was coming to you today. I had already decided that I couldn't go on without you, even if you had told me you didn't love me."

"I never meant that. I only said that because I though you and Pet—"

"Don't say his name!" She put two fingers on his lips.

"I promise." Suddenly she was in his arms, held so tightly that she could scarcely breathe. He kissed her and she opened her mouth to admit his tongue, which she could feel pushing against her lips, but he did not put it in her mouth. Rather he began to tease the sensitive skin of her lips by running his tongue lightly and gently around the opening. The end barely touched her skin, but the sensation was evocative, heady, impelling her to draw closer and closer to him, impelling her to push her lips against his gentle mouth until, finally, he allowed the tip to enter her mouth and meet the impatient waiting tip of her tongue.

As he kissed her, he raised an unseen hand and slowly pulled the heavy gold comb from her hair. She felt the hair's weight fall down the length of her back and the sharp coolness of the air as it hit her scalp, which was still imperceptibly damp from her shower in the late afternoon. He ran his left hand through her auburn hair, combing it with his fingers, and all the time he was kissing her, teasing her with his silver tongue, exhaling his sweet vapor into her mouth. Claudia drank in the liquor of his breath, the lemon-sweet odor of his body. His right hand continued to undo the buttons of her tweed sweater. When at last the sweater fell open, she smelled traces of her own perfume escape from the confining wool and float into the air. He slipped his hand inside, and she heard the silk lingerie rustle when he ran his palm around her waist and pulled her to him. Never abandoning the kiss, he took off her sweater in one easy movement. Then, and only then, did he move his lips away from hers. He took the sweater in both his hands and buried his face in the scratchy wool.

"I love the way you smell," he said, his voice muffled by the wool. "The way you smell intoxicates me. The feel of your skin under my hand is like no one else's. You're like a drug to my senses." His voice trembled with passion and he set the sweater aside and took her hand, pulling her to her feet.

Without another word Austin unzipped her skirt and let it fall silently to the floor at her feet. She stood before him and she heard the quick intake of his breath as he stared at her body, stared at the dusky rose teddy and the champagne lace and the glowing silk stockings suspended from rose satin garters. He lifted her hand, and she stepped away from the crumpled skirt at her feet. He never took his eyes off her. Claudia stood in the center of the living room and watched him as he raised his long fingers and slipped a lace strap off her shoulder, exposing the curve of one breast, which he bent to kiss. Gently he pushed down the silk until a nipple peeked above the antique lace. The tip of the breast was already hard, but at the sudden graze of cool air it hardened even more. He lowered his mouth to the darkened skin, and she felt his tongue flick at her breast, felt the soft inner skin of his mouth cover her with moistness and heat.

With his mouth still warming one breast, Austin's hand moved to lower the second strap. He turned his lips to the other nipple, running the tip of his tongue around the areola in a line of moist fire until its hardness equaled that of the other. She heard her own breathing getting faster and watched the top of his head when his lips moved to the space between her breasts and began a path through her cleavage and down to the sensitive skin of her midriff. He gently lowered the teddy as he trailed his kisses down her feverish skin.

"Oh, my God. Do you always wear clothes like this?" he whispered between small bites and kisses. "*Always* wear clothes like this!" He dropped to his knees on the floor before her. His fingertips were on the skin covering her ribs and he was lowering the silk inch by inch as his lips blazed a path over the skin that had been covered by the teddy. His tongue entered her navel, probing its tender recesses for a quick moment. Then his lips were on the slight swell of her abdomen and his mouth nibbled at the sensitive skin of her stomach, sending waves of pleasure radiating through her torso and down to her thighs. She pressed her body closer to him as her knees weakened and she leaned her legs against his shoulders and the hard muscles of his chest. He ran his fingers behind her hips and she felt him slip the gossamer teddy off her body. The nearly weightless silk whispered as it fell to the floor around her ankles. He buried his face in her.

"The way you smell," Austin repeated, "I *love* the way you smell." He sounded drunk with the aroma of her.

His strong arms went around the back of her knees and he lifted her as if she too weighed nothing and got to his feet with her in his arms, his face buried intimately against her. The starched collar of his pima cotton shirt and the roughness of a day's growth of beard on his cheek scraped against the patch of exposed, tender skin of her bare thigh above her stockings. Her knees grasped his body and her fingers twined in his hair as he carried her into the bedroom and to the edge of the bed, but he did not place her on its surface immediately. Instead he held her tightly in his arms and slowly, very slowly began to lower her body down the length of his. Her knees, through the silk stockings, and then her naked thighs felt the smooth cotton of his shirt, the unyielding leather of his belt, and the pleasant irritation of his wool trousers. Her knees touched the quilted surface of the bed and she then knelt in front of Austin. She began to open the tiny white buttons of his shirt, exposing his tanned chest, which she kissed as he had kissed her—slowly, patiently, and gently. Her fingertips manipulated the buttons, working down to the buckle of his leather belt, which opened easily for her. She undid his zipper.

"Lie down. I want to look at you," Austin said. Claudia lay back on the blue quilt at his command, her head resting on one arm crooked behind her while he gazed at her by the light of a bedside lamp that cast a muted yellow glow over the room. He removed the rest of his clothes and stood at the foot of the bed, obviously as desirous of her as she was of him. His lips were half parted and his breath was ragged. Then he knelt on the bed at her feet. She raised a knee and unhooked one garter to free a stocking. He leaned across and put a hand on her thigh, over the tab that held the thin silk.

"No, leave your stockings on." Austin redid the tab she had loosened. His fingers, where they touched her thigh, burned her skin. He put one leg on either side of her thighs and his hands on the bed next to her head and covered her body with his, as if to create a tent, not touching her. He kissed one eye and then the other. She smelled his citrus scent mixed with the dry grapes of the champagne they had drunk, melting tantalizingly on his breath with the musk scent of his desire, which then she readily recognized. Until Austin, she had never known the subtle variations of human scent, had never known the permutations that took place at arousal. She inhaled deeply of the scent she had loved on him from the very beginning as his lips moved from her eyelid across one cheek and to an earlobe and as his tongue entered her ear. She felt his warm breath, smelled the spicy, musky flowers of his love. The his tongue was on her neck, drawing a moist line around to her collarbone and across one breast to the nipple, which was as hard as if fashioned of marble, but as warm as the flesh and blood that palpitated beneath his lips.

Claudia pressed his head to her with her free hand and closed her eyes when his mouth went on to the other breast. Austin's tongue delineated a path down her midriff—slowly, tantalizingly, maddeningly—only hesitating at the garter belt, then beginning once again, but on the silky, sensitive skin of her inner thigh. She lay as if in a trance, vibrating with certain anticipation of his tongue's path. Her legs parted for its insistent stroking and soon both her hands were on the back of his head, her fingers twined in his hair, pressing his mouth eagerly to the center of her ardor, telling him, as mere words could not, of the fires he had ignited within her, of the aching demand in her body. She clutched at him, moaning, begging him for release from the flames coursing through her limbs. She felt she could not tolerate without losing consciousness the waves of ecstasy washing through her and she pulled at his hair until he slid his muscular body upward once more so she could wrap her trembling arms around his back and pull him into her. She moaned when he entered her as he said her name twice—"Claudia, Claudia"—and lowered his mouth to hers and kissed her. When she felt his mouth on hers, she barely knew where she ended and he began. Their skin, their tongues, their scents, were as one. She tasted herself, the sweet, salty musk of her own perfume on his skin when he kissed her.

Austin wound his fingers in her hair, and she pulled her lips away from his to bury her face in the hairs on his chest. They abandoned themselves to the rhythm of two lovers responding to the natural instinct to become as one being, murmuring their need and passion to one another, smiling and whispering and melting together in joy.

Claudia pushed him over on his back and sat atop him, her knees on the bed, her feet behind her, and she lowered her head until she covered his face and chest with heavy auburn curls. He stroked her hair, entwining its lengths around his hands as she moved above him. She felt his breath quicken and his own responsive movements increase beneath her, and at last she felt him pour his fires of love into her and heard his groan of release in the still air of the room. She fell forward on him and wrapped her arms behind his neck, covering him with her long hair and unconsciously holding him tightly—unconsciously because she was already passing into her own exquisite delirium, a continuous series of ecstatic surges that shook her limbs to the tip of each finger and to the bottom of each silk-clad toe, surges that raised her to dizzying heights of pleasure she, until that moment, had not known existed.

As the waves of ecstasy slowly subsided to be replaced by a languid sense of peace and belonging, Claudia rolled off Austin and lay at his side, holding his body closely in her arms, as if to bind him to her forever.

Austin gazed into her eyes and ran one hand over her head and down the length of her hair. "I love you, Claudia. You're everything to me. You are my entire life."

"Darling, I've never felt anything like that. Never..." She closed her eyes and sighed, letting his strength and warmth flow into her from his hand. "And I love you—more than I ever thought anyone could love." She remembered the last time they had made love, how he had drawn his message of love on her, how she had never responded to his words. She knew she had gone against her own beliefs about love, against all the advice she had espoused so righteously to Tina. She was ashamed at how blindly self-absorbed her search had made her. "When I found your drawing, I was so happy to know you loved me, too, and yet I never told you. If only I'd said something, we could have avoided such pain."

"I'd go through the pain again to have you at my side—all of the pain, a hundred times over," he said seriously. Then he laughed. "Do you still have my drawing? Turn over." He looked at the silky skin of her hip. "No, the ink is gone, but the love I felt when I drew it is still there, except that my love is more intense than ever. So much for indelible ink. Maybe you could get a tattoo back there."

"A tattoo! Nice people don't have tattoos."

"Of course they do. And who but your husband would ever know? You're a nice person and you're going to get one." His eyes twinkled. "Would you do that for me?"

"I'd do anything for you, you know that. But a tattoo... Austin, you constantly amaze me. You're so unlike my original impression of you."

"I know, you think I'm a stuffed shirt, an old bore—

Ivy League, men's clubs, croquet on the back lawn before tea. Admit it, that's what you think, isn't it?" He pushed her onto her back and pinned her arms to the bed.

"I do not think you're stuffy! Well, I did kind of expect you might be, just a little," she admitted. "After all, those fancy credentials of yours—"

"I even have a design in mind for the tattoo."

"You do? What's your idea?"

"I'll tell you after we're married. I know of a place in San Francisco where they do fabulous tattoos. We'll go there on our honeymoon. And you haven't told me that you'll marry me, either."

"Well, you haven't asked me. Anyway, you know I will. Don't actions speak louder than words?" she asked him.

"Words are important to me. I'm a lawyer, after all."

"I'll do it on one condition." She giggled.

"Another promise for a promise, eh? What's your condition?"

"That you get a tattoo, too—one that I design myself," she answered, laughing, certain that he was joking with her. "Here, turn over. I'll show you." She took a pen from the table at the side of the bed and began to draw on his hip. She bit her lower lip in concentration as she sketched rapidly.

"What are you drawing?" he asked her.

"A picture of me—a self portrait, you might say." She outlined an old-fashioned claw-footed bathtub with just a topknot of hair peeking above mounds of bubbles in the water. She began to make tiny circles of various sizes to depict soap bubbles filling the tub, spilling over the side, floating up across his skin.

"What are they going to say at the racquet club when they see your face on my rear end?"

"Oh, you can't see my face," she said.

"What's the doctor going to say when I go for my physical?"

"You are a stuffed shirt, Austin! You want me to have a tattoo, but you won't do it. Want to plea bargain, Counselor? More tit for tat?"

"What's your proposition?" he asked warily.

"There's really no proposition. I'll do whatever you want," she answered. "And, of course, I'll marry you. I don't care about anything else. I love you, that's all."

"I *am* a stuffed shirt," he admitted. "You have a deal. I'll get the tattoo—sight unseen!" He jumped up from the bed. "I almost forgot: I have something for you." He went to the living room and returned with the jacket of his suit, reaching a hand into a pocket and bringing out a folded sheet of paper. He got back into the bed, pulling the quilt, which had fallen half to the floor, up on the bed to cover first Claudia, tucking the corners around her and smoothing the fabric over her breasts, and then himself. He wrapped his feet around her ankles underneath the periwinkle-blue cover. At last he handed her the paper.

"What's this?" she asked, taking it from him.

"Your birth certificate." he answered. "Look—look at your original name."

Claudia unfolded the paper and looked at the copy of her true birth certificate, the document that had been sealed by the Ohio courts more than a quarter of a century before. It was all there—name, date, and place of birth—legal and official.

"My real name was Claudia Nicole Cleary all along. What do you know," she whispered. She stared at the paper for a long minute.

At last she looked up at him and her green eyes swam with tears. He looked at her lovingly, and she knew from his eyes that he understood perfectly the fullness of emotion in her heart. He was waiting for her response.

"What a shame," she said finally.

"What a shame? I thought you'd be happy. I thought you wanted the information on that sheet of paper more than anything in the world."

"Oh, I am happy. But this brings up all sorts of legal problems. I'm going to need a good attorney, the finest in the city. He's probably going to have to devote all his time to my case. I'm about to change my name again, you know—change it to Harwood." She threw her arms around him and whooped for joy. "And I promise: that's the last change—ever!"

Yours FREE, with a home subscription to SUPERROMANCE ™·

Now you never have to miss reading the newest SUPERROMANCES... because they'll be delivered right to your door.

Start with your **FREE** LOVE BEYOND DESIRE. You'll be enthralled by this powerful love story...from the moment Robin meets the dark, handsome Carlos and finds herself involved in the jealousies, bitterness and secret passions of the Lopez family. Where her own forbidden love threatens to shatter her life.

Your **FREE** LOVE BEYOND DESIRE is only the beginning. A subscription to **SUPERROMANCE** lets you look forward to a long love affair. Month after month, you'll receive four love stories of heroic dimension. Novels that will involve you in spellbinding intrigue, forbidden love and fiery passions.

You'll begin this series of sensuous, exciting contemporary novels...written by some of the top romance novelists of the day...with four every month.

And this big value...each novel, almost 400 pages of compelling reading...is yours for only $2.50 a book. Hours of entertainment every month for so little. Far less than a first-run movie or pay-TV. Newly published novels, with beautifully illustrated covers, filled with page after page of delicious escape into a world of romantic love...delivered right to your home.

Begin a long love affair with

SUPERROMANCE.

Accept LOVE BEYOND DESIRE **FREE.**

Complete and mail the coupon below today!

- -

FREE!

Mail to: SUPERROMANCE

In the U.S.
2504 West Southern Avenue
Tempe, AZ 85282

In Canada
649 Ontario St.
Stratford, Ontario N5A 6W2

YES, please send me FREE and without any obligation, my **SUPERROMANCE** novel, LOVE BEYOND DESIRE. If you do not hear from me after I have examined my FREE book, please send me the 4 new **SUPERROMANCE** books every month as soon as they come off the press. I understand that I will be billed only $2.50 for each book (total $10.00). There are no shipping and handling or any other hidden charges. There is no minimum number of books that I have to purchase. In fact, I may cancel this arrangement at any time. LOVE BEYOND DESIRE is mine to keep as a FREE gift, even if I do not buy any additional books.

NAME _____ (Please Print) _____

ADDRESS _____ APT. NO. _____

CITY _____

STATE/PROV. _____ ZIP/POSTAL CODE _____

SIGNATURE (If under 18, parent or guardian must sign.)

134-BPS-KAJ9
SUP-SUB-2

This offer is limited to one order per household and not valid to present subscribers. Prices subject to change without notice.   Offer expires June 30, 1984

Enter a uniquely exciting new world with

Harlequin American Romance™

Harlequin American Romances are the first romances to explore today's love relationships. These compelling novels reach into the hearts and minds of women across America... probing the most intimate moments of romance, love and desire.

You'll follow romantic heroines and irresistible men as they boldly face confusing choices. Career first, love later? Love without marriage? Long-distance relationships? All the experiences that make love real are captured in the tender, loving pages of **Harlequin American Romances.**

What makes American women so different when it comes to love? Find out with **Harlequin American Romance!**

Send for your introductory FREE book now!

Get this book FREE!

Mail to:

Harlequin Reader Service

In the U.S.
2504 West Southern Avenue
Tempe, AZ 85282

In Canada
649 Ontario Street
Stratford, Ontario N5A 6W2

YES! I want to be one of the first to discover **Harlequin American Romance.** Send me FREE and without obligation *Twice in a Lifetime.* If you do not hear from me after I have examined my FREE book, please send me the 4 new **Harlequin American Romances** each month as soon as they come off the presses. I understand that I will be billed only $2.25 for each book (total $9.00). There are no shipping or handling charges. There is no minimum number of books that I have to purchase. In fact, I may cancel this arrangement at any time. *Twice in a Lifetime* is mine to keep as a FREE gift, even if I do not buy any additional books.

Name _____
(please print)

Address _____ Apt. no. _____

City _____ State/Prov. _____ Zip/Postal Code _____

Signature (If under 18, parent or guardian must sign.)